before I knew you

Beth Steury

DEDICATION

To the family, friends, and fellow writers who must have grown weary
waiting for this series to become a reality.
Thank you for your patience and encouragement.

ACKNOWLEDGMENTS

Heaping mountains of gratitude to my writing partners and dear friends the *Scriblerians*, who labored faithfully labored alongside me in the creation of this series: Tim Akers, Cynthia Toney, Vanessa Morton, Gretchen Engel, Lisa Gefrides, Linda Samaritoni, Karen DeBlieck, and Loraine Kemp; and to editors, Linda Yezak and Kathrese McKee (now a *Scriblerian*), for believing in this story and in me.

Memorial Day weekend

Preston

I won't do anything illegal or immoral. Just hanging out. No big deal." Muttering to an empty room, I grabbed an Indianapolis Colts sweatshirt and opened my bedroom door to scope out the hall. Right toward Mom's and Dad's room, left toward my brother Patrick's.

The hall was empty. Good.

I found Mom in the kitchen rinsing the supper dishes. "Hangin' with the guys tonight, Mom. Won't be too late." Not that an almost seventeen-year-old should have to report his every move to his mom, but considering what I'd put my parents through last year, it wouldn't kill me.

"Okay, Preston." She tapped my arm with wet fingers. "Have fun."

I zipped toward the front door, hoping to avoid Patrick's older brother advice.

"No big deal." More muttering, to convince myself there was nothing wrong with a night of hanging out with the guys. As I jabbed the key into the ignition, I scanned the front of the Jacoby family, ranch-style house.

Patrick filled the doorway, his arms crossed, a menacing glare shooting from his narrowed eyes.

I jerked away from his obvious disapproval and backed onto the street in my hand-me-down Honda Accord that would scream *middle class* in Jake Nelson's east side neighborhood.

Zach Tate's description of the latest hangout did nothing to ease my conscience. "A huge house, lots of booze, and practically non-existent parents. The best setup ever."

My plan was simple—keep a Mountain Dew drink in my hand at all times, maintain a low profile, leave before the pairing off began. Simple and harmless.

I parked behind a brown Dodge Durango at the end of the block so I could take off without a hassle then yanked a couple of cans from the six-pack I'd stashed in the car.

The front door opened as I strode up the wide, stone walk.

"Jacoby!" Zach's booming voice must have echoed through every room of the huge house. His fist slammed against mine as he jerked his head toward the preppy looking guy behind him. "You know Jake."

"Glad you could make it." Jake bumped his fist with mine.

Zach slapped my back. "You've been missed, buddy."

Not three feet inside the door, half of Madison High's in-crowd saluted me with their drinks of choice, welcoming me to the weekly bash.

So much for that low profile.

"Here." Zach thrust a beer in my face.

"I'm good." I waved the can of soda in my sweaty palm, popped the top, and chugged it.

"Dude." Dark, shaggy hair grazed Zach's shoulders as he shook his head. More disapproval. But of a totally different kind.

I pushed past him and maneuvered to a corner of the dining room.

"Hey, help yourself." As he passed by, Jake jerked a thumb toward the kitchen.

"I'm good, thanks." I guzzled more of my drink.

"Your loss." He scooped up two cans and three bottles from a countertop lined with Coors and Budweiser and the rest of the boys—Jack Daniel, Jim Beam, and Jose Cuervo. The smell of alcohol hung in the air, a scent that still appealed to me in a huge way. But that part of my life was done.

With a death grip on my soft drink, I mingled and ordered myself to relax. A study of the crowd revealed a few new faces, but mostly regulars.

"'Bout time you showed up." My best buddy, Connor Johnson, socked my shoulder. "We're up the next round of euchre."

I shook my head.

"Uh, yeah, we are." His normal, cocky grin challenged me. "Dude, it's euchre. Didn't ask you to chug shots. Besides, I'm done with losing. Haven't been on a winning team since you stopped showing up a couple of months ago."

"Sure, whatever." Our long history of partnering gave us an edge, and we almost never lost.

I sank into the fancy dining room chair across from him. After our second win, he thrust his fist across the table to knock with mine. "That's what I'm talkin' about. Good to have you back."

I'd missed hanging out. And some of the other stuff, too.

When we hopped up for the next round of players, I pulled the other can of Dew from my pocket and tried to fade into the background.

Rob Finney pulled me aside. "So, you came alone, right?"

"Yeah, but—"

"Several possibilities in there." He nodded toward the other room. "Heard your name come up a couple of times already."

"I'm gonna take off before—"

The lights dimmed, and the noise leveled off immediately.

"Too late, dude." He chuckled as he hustled off toward a smiling blonde.

Time to make my escape. I was almost to the front door when Connor blocked my way. A petite strawberry blonde followed several steps behind him.

"Bree came alone tonight, too."

Bree Masterson's light blue eyes met mine. Her thin, shiny lips pressed together, then eased into a shy smile. "Hi . . ."

Connor fiddled with his backward IU hat, darting glances between me and Bree. He motioned her closer, then disappeared.

I scanned the room. Hushed whispers had replaced loud conversations, and a slow, romantic song pulsed from the whole-house sound system. Couples snuggled on couches and chairs, wedged into corners, or stretched out on the floor.

My attention returned to Bree. Pale, smooth skin peeked from her low-cut t-shirt. Another section of exposed skin between the short shirt and her jeans sped my mind to places I didn't want to go. My pulse hammered. Forcing my eyes up, I shook my head to clear the images.

She inched closer, and I caught a whiff of vanilla.

Her nearness, that scent, the soft skin of her exposed belly— it was all too much. I grabbed her hand and led her to the corner of the living room and an empty chair-and-a-half lounge thing.

Her body brushed against my arm as we settled into the comfy chair. As she pressed close in the small space, reality jolted through me.

I sucked in a ragged breath. "Bree . . ."

"Even you get nervous, huh?" Her breathy whisper turned to a soft giggle.

I leaned forward to put space between us. "So, you're a freshman, right?"

She frowned, and her eyes narrowed. "Yeah, but I'm older than almost everyone in my class."

I gave her a vague nod. "We can just talk. We don't have to do anything."

She inched closer, stretched out her legs, and kicked off her shoes. "I don't want to talk."

I was about five seconds from caving. I glanced away from her obvious eagerness. Not helpful. Some pretty intense making out was going on around us already.

Bree's fingernail traced a path down my arm, and my resolve crumbled. What was the harm in a little kissing? I slipped my arm around her shoulders.

She turned toward me and leaned her soft, warm body into my chest. Her sweet scent surrounded me.

My gaze strayed from her bright eyes to her lips, then back to her eyes which were practically begging. I brushed my lips across her silky cheek, then found her mouth.

She kissed me back without hesitation. Her lips tasted like strawberries instead of alcohol.

Desire pulsed through me, and I pressed her closer. My hands roamed across her back. *She's a good kisser.*

I flattened my palms against her lower back—on bare skin. Her short shirt had shifted up. Heat surged through me. The making out intensified past a little kissing.

Light blazed across the room. "Parents' ETA thirty minutes!"

I eased my mouth away from Bree's neck. "What?"

Groans, complaints, and lots of swearing echoed around us.

"Wrap it up, guys. Mom's not feeling well so they're coming home early. Sorry." Jake hurried to the next room where he shouted his apologetic instructions.

Bree stroked my chest. Her eyes sparkled with what I recognized as an "I really, really like you" expression. She smiled and touched my right cheek where a dimple would have been if anything about this situation brought a smile to my face.

What had I done? I gently pushed her away and swung my legs over the edge of the lounger.

Voices rose in panic as the seconds ticked by.

"Get the people upstairs!" Jake yelled.

Connor sprinted up the stairway, trash bag gripped in his hand.

As if in slow motion, I pulled out my phone and tried to focus on the blue numbers. Nine fifty-seven.

Bree leaned toward me, but I pulled away from her.

"Bree, where are you?" A panicked female voice called out.

"I'm in here." A dreamy smile covered Bree's face as she pulled the phone from my hand, tapped in something, then closed my fingers around it. "Call me, okay?"

My head nodded without my consent.

"There you are! Let's get out of here." A tall brunette tugged on Bree's arm.

She leaned against me and kissed my cheek.

The brunette tugged again. "Come on!"

With a last look of longing, she was gone. A string of partiers followed her out.

"Preston, we could use some help here." Zach strode by, a trash bag in each hand.

"Yeah, sure." My mind still in a fog, I carried bottles of alcohol to the liquor cabinet.

Rob and Connor stashed the garbage while Jake ushered out the last of the crowd. His footsteps pounded through the house as he surveyed each room for evidence of a party.

"I think we're good," Zach announced. "Five minutes to spare."

Jake returned and headed for the liquor cabinet. "Thanks, guys." He locked the cabinet door and stuffed the key in his pocket. "My parents will be gone again in a couple of weeks. How 'bout a rain check?"

Zach clapped Jake on the back. "Sure thing."

"Later, guys," Connor called on his way to the door. He waved his hand in front of my face. "You comin'?"

"Yeah."

The cool night air smacked me like a slap to the face.

"Next time—"

"No next time, Connor." I stared straight ahead. "I'm not coming back."

"We'll find you someone better—"

"I said I'm not coming back."

Connor stopped at his Jeep.

I kept walking. So much for thinking I could just have a good time hanging out with the guys and skip all the other stuff.

I was not about to go down that road again. So why had I even risked it?

Maggie

Mom peered from the kitchen doorway, a mix of hopeful concern stretching a strained smile across her lips.

I shook my head and continued to pace the length of the living room or the "company" room as Dad called it, or the "small TV room" as my younger brother Michael would say. I peered out the picture window for the tenth time, willing Logan Wallace's car to appear. He was already five minutes late.

"Please don't stand me up," I murmured.

Just then a gray, sporty-looking car jerked to a stop, and Logan hopped out, unleashing a wave of relief that promptly crashed into a wall of anxiety.

I pulled in a long, steadying breath. My first real date. Because going to a youth group banquet or concert or fundraiser with a guy I'd been friends with since childhood didn't count as a real date. I gripped the doorknob, tugging on the hem of my a-little-shorter-than-usual shirt. Too late to change now. I opened the door.

"Maggie, hey. You ready to go?"

"Hi, Logan. Can you come in a minute?"

His hands stuffed in his pockets, he rocked on the threshold, half in and half out. "What's up?"

I stepped back, hoping he'd actually clear the doorway. "My parents want to meet you."

His eyebrows scrunched together as an exasperated sigh blew through his lips. "Really?"

"Won't take a second. Mom, Dad," I called over my shoulder.

With Dad leading the way, they strode from the kitchen through the dining room but stopped more than ten feet from us. *Thanks, Dad.*

I inched toward them, hoping Logan would take the hint.

He trudged slowly behind me.

"Mom, Dad, this is Logan Wallace."

"Logan." Dad took a big step, hand outstretched, toward my wary date. "It's good to meet you."

Logan jerked his hand out of his pocket and accepted Dad's handshake. "Uh . . . you, too . . . sir." His gaze slid from Dad to Mom. "Ma'am."

"Nice to meet you, Logan." Mom grasped his hand lightly before he plunged it back into his pocket and darted glances between me and my insistent parents.

"So . . . we'll see you later." I backed toward escape.

Logan surged toward the door.

Dad glanced at Mom, who looped her arm through his and murmured something I couldn't make out.

Her eyes locked with mine, and she nodded once, her way of saying, *See, everything worked out fine.* "Bye, guys."

Outside, Logan sprinted to his side of the car, smirking. "That was fun."

"Sorry. My dad's big on introductions." I sank into the passenger seat beside him. With the formalities taken care of, it was time to concentrate on calming the storm brewing in my stomach.

He winked. "No problem. So, everyone's hanging out at Jake Nelson's tonight, like I said. Should be a good time." His hand grazed my knee, hovered by the radio controls for a couple of seconds, and then rested on the steering wheel.

I'd been wondering exactly what *hang with friends* meant, but had squashed the urge to bother him with a bunch of questions. I had no idea who Jake was, where he lived, or who *everyone* included, but I pushed aside all lingering concern as I sneaked a glance at Logan's profile and put on a happy-to-be-out-with-you smile.

Because I was. Happy to be on a real date with a real guy—someone I hadn't played alongside since toddlerhood in the church nursery.

Logan and I had finished our sophomore year at Madison High School yesterday. And I hoped like crazy this date would end my *new girl* status in Pine Crossing, the Indiana town five hundred miles from my old life and friends in Little Springs, Minnesota.

Logan's shaggy blond hair and cute smile matched his witty, flirty personality and made accepting his offer of a date a no-brainer. Well, almost. I'd ignored the maybe-you-should-actually-get-to-know-him-first doubts, deciding that being too cautious about guys would only slow my becoming an accepted part of Madison High's Junior class.

We pulled up in front of this gorgeous, mansion-like place with a yard that could have graced the cover of any magazine. Logan cut the engine. "Cool house, huh?"

As we made our way up a wide sidewalk surrounded by beautiful beds of red and white flowers, his fingers brushed along the hem of my shirt. I tensed as a shiver danced up my back.

Without knocking, he opened the door, and the exact meaning of *everyone* became clear. The huge, high-ceilinged room was packed with people, many that I recognized from Madison. As we weaved our way through the crowd, Logan made a couple of quick introductions but didn't stop for conversation. Soon we stood in an elaborate kitchen where the center island was lined with lots of beer cans and dozens of amber bottles. More alcohol than I'd ever seen or wanted to see. I swallowed a gasp as my pulse quickened.

Logan grabbed a can of beer. "You want anything?"

I shook my head, the array of containers blurring in front of me.

"A soft drink maybe?"

The familiar logo of a Diet Coke came into focus. I pointed with a shaky hand.

"Here ya go." He handed me the can, then grabbed a second beer for himself. "Let's walk around."

I followed him around like a puppy, trying to control the panic raging inside me. *This is a drinking party.* No one acted like I didn't belong. Not one person seemed the least bit surprised to see me, yet every cell in my body silently screamed, *"I don't belong here!"* While most of the partiers clutched some type of alcohol, no one commented about the Diet Coke in my hand. Every warning I'd ever heard about the hazards of drinking and driving blared simultaneously in my brain.

Logan reached back and wrapped his hand around mine. He pumped my fingers in a tight squeeze a couple of times. He wanted to be here with me. A warm, tingly sensation flooded through me, silencing the mental warnings for half a second.

But this is a drinking party!

He stopped, turned his head toward me, and pulled me against his side. His eyes swept across my face as a grin hiked up the corners of his mouth. "Great party, huh?"

"Uh . . . yeah." Really, no. Not great at all.

"Do you play euchre?"

"Euchre? No, sorry." He led me to a plush dining room where four guys, each pondering a handful of cards, sat in burgundy- and blue-striped upholstered chairs around a highly polished wooden table. A lone Mountain Dew stood out among ten or so cans and bottles of alcohol.

"I don't mind if you want to play." *Then maybe I can just go home.*

"Nah, I'm not that good anyway."

Cheers erupted and a fist thrust across the table to connect with the knuckles of the guy with the Mountain Dew. Apparently, his team won.

Logan tugged on my arm, leading me away from the game, through rooms packed with strangers. How would I ever get to know everyone at this huge school? A couple of people called me by name. They smiled. I smiled. At least after tonight I might be able to match a few more names with faces. Madison was twice as big as my itty-bitty school in Minnesota where I'd still be going if two months ago my parents hadn't ripped me out of my sophomore year so they could launch their dream ministry—The Least of These Clinic. *Their* dream—not mine.

We strolled again through the kitchen where Logan left his empty beer bottle and helped himself to a third. "Sure you don't want something?" His hand panned across the vast assortment.

"I'm good. Still have half my Diet Coke."

About an hour into the party, the music abruptly shifted from a hundred decibels to something soft and romantic. The lights in every room dimmed. Couples gravitated like magnets to each other and quickly found a place—couch, chair, floor—to cuddle up.

Logan pulled me to a dark corner of the living room as several whispering, giggling couples made their way upstairs, some stumbling, others tiptoeing.

"Perfect," he murmured, sinking into a puffy recliner. He set his two beers—one maybe half gone, and the other still unopened—on an end table and tugged me down beside him.

"I'm pretty sure this chair is meant for *one* person, not two."

He lifted and angled his lean body to the side. "Nah." His arm snaked around my shoulders. "This is just right."

I squirmed and twisted, pressing my backside against the chair's poofy armrest.

His shaggy hair fell across his forehead not more than six inches from my face.

I craned my neck to confirm what I already suspected—we were surrounded by couples making out. Great. A drinking party *and* a make out party.

Logan cradled my chin, turning my attention back to him. Only three inches separated us now.

I swallowed and bit into my bottom lip.

His nose grazed my cheek. He slid his hand up my jaw. His fingers inched into my hair.

And my heart pounded in a fast, erratic pattern. This was completely insane. I was about to be kissed for the very first time by a guy I barely knew.

His warm lips lingered on my cheek.

Was this what it took to fit in? Did I really want to do this?

Logan's mouth brushed across mine once, then twice.

I jerked back.

"It's okay," he whispered, planting tiny kisses on my temple and along my hair. His beer breath fanned across my face before his lips slipped over my jaw to nuzzle my neck.

So, *so* not good. I tipped my head back, breaking the suction of his lips on my skin.

"Aw, come on," he murmured, capturing my mouth in a hungry kiss.

I kissed him back, sort of, which he must have considered encouragement because his hand slipped from my hair to my shoulder, and stroked down my arm. Then his fingers slid up under my shirt. "Logan—stop." I pushed against his shoulders.

More beer breath puffed from between his lips. "Sorry."

I shook my hair and straightened my shirt. "So, this is what *hanging with friends* means?"

He smirked. "You're getting this upset about a little making out?"

I studied his soft lips, his bright blue eyes, the fringe of blond hair he swiped off his forehead. I wouldn't make out with strangers just to fit in.

"I guess I am. Take me home, please, or if that's too much trouble, I can call my parents." Uh . . . he'd been drinking. But when I insisted I call my parents, he shot from the chair and yanked me to my feet. "I'll take you home," he growled.

The ride home was silent except for Logan's loud, anger-punctuated, huffy breathing. And the endless commentary from my raging conscience. *Why didn't you listen to those you-know-nothing-about-him doubts?*

If I made it home alive, I would never, *ever* make that mistake again.

September

Preston

Welcome to fourth period Psychology. Please raise your hand when I call your name." Mr. Martin, proving his Madison High coolest teacher status, wore khaki shorts, flip flops, and a Madison High t-shirt. His shaggy haircut and thick, dark stubble further set him apart from most of the other teachers. Perched on the edge of his desk, he waited for the chatter to die down. Then he read the class roster in random order, catching about half the students off guard. Especially the guys whose attention fixated on more exposed female flesh than I'd seen since last school year. Could the shorts and skirts get any shorter?

I rubbed a hand across my own measly stubble and pressed the other one against my growling stomach. Half listening for my name, I scanned the posters lining the walls in an attempt to keep my eyes above shoulder level. Bold in color and message like the one that announced in huge block letters, "EXCUSES STOP HERE." And "Time to GROW UP and take RESPONSIBILTY for your attitude and actions."

"Margaret Kathryn Jennison."

Up in the front row, a small hand belonging to a brunette went up. Her name didn't sound familiar.

"Preston Andrew Jacoby."

A muttered chant rose from the guys in the back row. "Ja-co-by. Ja-co-by."

I jerked tall in my seat, smiling and waving in all directions.

Mr. Martin smirked and rolled his eyes at the burst of giggles from girls all over the room. He called the remaining four names before tossing the attendance book on his desk.

He stood, cleared his throat, and crossed his arms. His dark eyes traveled across the first row, then the second. He scanned the third and fourth rows.

"Some of you already aced your first assignment. Congratulations. Some of you, however, failed miserably." He raised his hand to stifle the murmured protests. "Yes, listening is considered an assignment in this class. And stop the whining. I *hate* whining." A hush fell over the room. "Assignment number two offers another opportunity. You will observe fellow classmates whose last names fall within the same section of the alphabet."

Muffled groans echoed through the room.

Mr. Martin's glare brought instant silence. "Wallace, Xavier, Yancey, Zimmer—back here." His thumb jerked over his shoulder. "Grab paper and pencil."

"Jacoby, Jennison, Johnson, Jones—left rear corner, please."

We shoved the desks together to form a lopsided square. Folding my six-foot frame into the uncomfortable chair-desk combo, I glanced at Connor beside me. Across from him sat Cindy Jones who lived about three blocks from me. Beside her and across from me was the brunette from the front row. I was sure I didn't know her at all.

Cindy and Margaret leaned over their open notebooks and began scurrying their pencils across the paper.

Connor shrugged. He looked odd without a backward hat on top his blond mop. His tanned face held the typical look of disinterest in anything school related.

I drummed my finger against the desk top. "What to write, what to write."

Cindy rolled her eyes.

Margaret looked up, her dark eyes connecting with mine for a couple of seconds.

I stroked my pencil across the paper. "Connor—non-participant who hates that he can't wear a hat at school. Cindy—facially expressive blonde female. Margaret . . . "
Amazing eyes.

A shy yet appealing smile tugged at her full lips. "Everyone calls me Maggie."

"Okay, Maggie." I squinted at my paper. "Prefers shortened version of her first name."

She grinned, and dark brown waves swayed across her shoulders as she shook her head. She met my gaze again for just a moment, then looked away.

"Brilliant, Preston. You always were at the top of the class." Cindy scoffed with another dramatic roll of her eyes.

"How could you, Cindy?" I placed my hand over my heart.

"Preston—overly dramatic, always good for a laugh." Connor recorded his lame observation on the blank page in front of him.

Ha, ha, I mouthed.

"You got that right." Cindy scribbled again in her notebook.

I arched an eyebrow and shrugged, not caring what either of them thought.

Maggie glanced at Cindy, then Connor. Then those brown eyes found mine. Her teeth pressed into her lower lip.

"One more minute, everyone," Mr. Martin said.

Maggie continued to add to her list of observations. I doodled and tried to snatch glances at what she was writing. But her hair distracted me.

Several strands the color of dark chocolate fell across her face. She twirled it around her finger, then tucked it behind her ear before propping her hand under her chin. My gaze strayed to her white button-up shirt and Capri jeans that covered more of her slim body than most of the other girls' outfits. I peeked down at her fancy flip flops that matched the purple polish on her toenails.

"Time's up. Stay where you are," Mr. Martin instructed. "Anyone want to share?"

Hands shot up, probably those hoping to make up for that first "listening" assignment. Four or five students read their observations, and then it was Cindy's turn. She boldly questioned, "Does Preston still think every girl in our class is dying to go out with him? Oh wait, half the girls already have."

Thanks a lot, Cindy. I shook my head as Mr. Martin's narrowed gaze pierced through me.

Martin crossed his arms and stroked his stubbly chin, his eyes still trained on me. "I'm afraid that doesn't qualify as an observation, Cindy. Despite how intriguing that particular premise is to ponder." His arms dropped to his side as he turned toward Cindy. "Sorry."

She shrugged and launched into a list of observations about Connor.

Maggie looked my way, her eyes wide as they connected with mine for several seconds.

"She has no idea what she's talking about," I murmured, maintaining a calm exterior despite the irritation building inside.

Laughter rippled across the classroom, pulling her attention and mine to Connor, standing beside the desk, bowing to the now applauding class.

I was relieved his comedy act had directed the spotlight away from me and my questionable reputation. As Cindy's commentary shifted to Maggie, I couldn't peel my eyes away from the brown-eyed brunette whose cheeks were now a warm pink. She sank lower in her chair. At least Cindy's description of her was a lot more complimentary than her jabs at me and Connor had been.

The bell rang, and Maggie disappeared into the hall.

Connor and I headed to lunch. "Do you know Maggie?" I asked.

"Not really. She moved here last year from somewhere. Her parents are big into that new clinic, I guess."

"Clinic?"

"That place for people with no insurance. Has a Bible name of some kind."

"I don't remember her at all. She's pretty."

He shrugged. "Yeah, I guess." His eyes narrowed, meaning he was calculating how long it'd been since I'd commented on an attractive girl.

All through lunch I scanned the cafeteria for those brown eyes. Spent the rest of the day looking for her too. It was like I couldn't help myself.

After the final bell, I finally spotted her in the crowded hall. My heartbeat shifted up a notch. Or two. "Hey, Maggie."

"Hi." Gold flecks sparkled in her dark eyes.

The mass of students came to a halt, leaving us side by side.

"First day of school." I angled my head toward her. "No one really knows where they're going." I cranked up the dazzle on my smile and winked.

She gave me a hint of a smile and shrugged.

The crowd inched forward.

I dipped my head to her as we passed. I peeked over my shoulder and checked her out head to toe. *Oh, yeah.* But then I jerked my gaze away. Old habits died hard.

Suddenly, Bree Masterson loomed beside me. She stretched on tiptoe to see what was causing the holdup. And then she saw me. Her blue eyes grew huge. "Preston," she whispered.

"Bree." I cleared my throat and craned my neck to see above the crowd, then shifted my focus behind me. Anything to not look at her.

"You never called me."

A whiff of her perfume floated my way, unleashing a flashback of her soft, bare midriff.

I forced myself to look at her. She wore the same expression of longing I remembered from the party. "Uh, yeah, listen, about that night—"

"Maybe we could hang out sometime. Just the two of us."

"I . . . we . . . can't."

Her shoulders sagged, and she closed her eyes.

"I'm really sorry."

The crowd moved forward, but she didn't budge. A tear slipped out from between her eyelashes. Man, I hated it when girls cried.

"I'm not the right guy for you, Bree."

A couple of students pushed by us. She swiped at another stray tear. "But how do you know?"

"Trust me, it's a bad idea. I'm really sorry."

The hurt, the rejection that poured from her eyes hit me like a kick in the stomach.

I'd managed to avoid her all summer, but if our paths crossed every day now, *man.*

The crowd lurched forward, and so did I, leaving a dejected Bree in the middle of the hall.

~ ~ ~

The next morning when Maggie reached into a locker just two down from mine, my throat went dry. How had I missed this?

I sucked in a breath, then swung my locker shut when hers closed. "Maggie, hey."

She nodded vaguely as she pressed her hand against her locker door and closed it. "This better be fixed. Keeping all my stuff in the office yesterday while the janitor replaced this lock was a huge pain."

"Well, if it gives you any trouble, just let me know." We started down the hall together.

"Between the locker situation and a mistake with my schedule, I missed my first class, but Mrs. Morrison said I didn't miss much."

My feet dug into the carpet in the middle of the hall. "Mrs. Morrison? Your first class is Advanced English?"

"Yes."

"Mine too!" My voice boomed way too loud.

She looked up at me with a small but shaky smile.

I cleared my throat. "She's right though. You didn't miss much." I stepped aside for her to go ahead of me into the classroom and checked her out again before I could stop myself.

"Ah, Maggie," Mrs. Morrison called. "There's an empty seat right there in the third row." She pointed toward *my* row. "The fourth seat back, I think."

Maggie put her books on the fourth desk and slipped into the seat.

I stopped at the third desk and grinned down at her. "I'm not sure this is gonna work." I sat and straightened my back.

"You may be right."

"I'll take care of it." I strode to Mrs. Morrison's desk and explained the situation, suggesting that Maggie and I switch seats. She agreed and thanked me for solving her first problem of the day.

I returned to Maggie. "Mrs. Morrison and I agree you should take the third seat, and I'll take the fourth. Unless you have some objection."

"No objection."

I picked up her books and put them on the third desk, then stepped aside for her to move past me.

"This will work better, thanks." But she didn't look at me, at all, as she messed with her notebook.

"Hey, no problem." I frowned and sank into my new seat. So much for getting in good with the pretty new girl.

Maggie

Chelsea Carter openly ogled the guys at the lunch tables around us. Now I knew why she'd wound us through the entire cafeteria to the very center table before plopping her tray down. It was all about the view, and who could blame her? I'd been scoping out the guys myself, despite the forever-etched-in-my-brain memory of the worst first date ever.

No longer *boys*, the guys of Madison's junior class were now *men* who had changed over the summer in amazing ways. They were taller, with a lot of very hot stubble, rippling muscles, and the swagger that went with being upper classmen.

I'd already thanked Dad like a hundred times for hiring Chelsea's mom, Sarah, to be the clinic's social worker. Meeting her had been the only decent thing to come out of the whole clinic-relocation situation so far. Chelsea and I were opposites, yet somehow, we'd hit it off. While I was the definition of shy, backward, and awkward, she was tons of fun, outgoing, and crazy. And she knew *everything* about *everyone* and had promised to help me fit in at Madison.

My forkful of salad halted in mid-air, and I held my breath as Logan sauntered by. He'd ignored me completely—practically looked right through me—each time we'd passed in the hall. Which was fine by me. Thank goodness we only had one class together and our lockers weren't close, so I was counting on minimal contact.

I managed to get the fork to my mouth as Chelsea's gaze flitted from me to Logan.

"You can't let that one night with the handsy Logan Wallace scare you away from guys. You know that, right?"

"It's not that I'm scared, but in the future, I'll pay a lot more attention to the who and the where. It was stupid of me to go out with someone I knew nothing about." I winced at the memory of all that alcohol and Logan's roaming hands.

"So, he wanted to make out. It's not that big a deal."

"I barely knew him." And my first kiss had been wasted on someone I never wanted to go out with again. Which Chelsea didn't seem to understand.

"Whatever." She tossed long golden-blonde hair over her shoulder and squirmed until she found a position that let her eat and keep a close eye on the table of hot guys closest to us. "Lighten up. You don't want to be alone forever, do you? High school is so much better with a boyfriend."

I stabbed at my salad. I didn't doubt that. At all. But how many of the guys were like Logan?

"Too bad you spent the summer in Minnesota instead of here, checking out the guys."

I'd been a mess after the move to Pine Crossing—even worse after the disastrous date with Logan. Mom and Dad worked night and day to get the clinic going, and my brother Michael made a bunch of friends in our new neighborhood. Me? I made everyone's life miserable with my wallowing-in-self-pity act—according to my parents—so they shipped me back to Minnesota three weeks into the summer to take care of Grandma after her hip surgery. She didn't need me that much, but it turned out, I needed her big time. She sent me back to Pine Crossing two weeks before school started, a new and improved Maggie.

Chelsea popped open her Hostess cupcakes. "I know who I plan to get to know a lot better—"

"Let me guess. Connor Johnson. The guy you've talked about non-stop. You two would look cute together, all blonde and tan."

"Don't I know it." She shifted to the right and fixed a smoldering gaze on the back of Connor. If stares could turn heads, his eyes would be locked with hers any second. "You better get going so you can make up for lost time."

"Checking them out is one thing, but going after guys is so not me."

"Yeah, well you need to get over it. If you want to get to know them first, fine. Get to know them. Chat, hang out, whatever."

I shook my juice bottle. "I'm not like you. I'm not good at any of that stuff." But I wanted to be. I was tired of being shy and awkward . . . and alone.

Chelsea's green eyes widened. "Lucky for you, getting to know guys is my specialty. Watch and learn." Her thin eyebrows bounced.

Just then Connor glanced over his shoulder and offered her a slow, seductive wink. And Preston slid into the seat across from him amid a chorus of grunts and a round of fist bumps that went totally unnoticed by both Chelsea and Connor.

~ ~ ~

In just three days, Chelsea had perfected eating while simultaneously flirting with Connor at the next table. "So, who have you talked to today? Guys I mean." She licked a stripe of yogurt from her spoon.

"Just Preston Jacoby."

Chelsea pulled her piercing gaze from Connor to squint at me. "Preston?"

"He sits behind me in AP English, and there's just one locker between mine and his."

Lips pursed, Chelsea nodded.

"And we have Psychology together too."

"Talk about hot . . ." Her mouth creased in a grin, and a thoughtful look narrowed her eyes again.

"I'm sure he has a gorgeous girlfriend."

"Actually, he doesn't. He's not with anyone. And he could have *anyone* he wanted."

That, I believed. I studied the contours of his back outlined by his black t-shirt. Cindy's less than complimentary comments about him circled through my mind like they had every time I couldn't help but notice him. Which was every time we shared the same breathing space. Had he really dated half the girls in the class?

"He's helped me with my stupid locker a couple of times. He's nice, all gentlemanlike, too."

"A gentleman, huh? Well, all I know is he's totally hot. I had a thing for him last year, but he was dating this girl, Alyssa."

"You liked Preston?"

She nodded. "His smile with that hot little dimple and those amazing blue eyes, not to mention all the other good stuff." Those expressive eyebrows of hers danced again across her forehead.

I was well aware of all the "good stuff." How could I not be? But I busied myself scraping the last traces of raspberry cheesecake yogurt from the carton and said nothing.

"Oh, come on. Like you haven't noticed." She grabbed my wrist. "You have a pulse, don't you?"

I eeked out a squeaky giggle. "Of course, I noticed."

"I was *thrilled* when Alyssa moved away, but he had no interest in dating me or anyone else apparently." She bit into her sandwich and chewed for a few seconds. "I ran into Connor—another fine, male specimen—several times over the summer, and let's just say we hit it off." A seductive grin slid across her glossed lips that never smudged even when she ate.

"Did you two go out?"

"Not exactly." Her attention zeroed in on him again, and I allowed my gaze to rest on Preston.

Unlike Connor's unruly blond waves, Preston's very light brown hair was cropped close on the sides and in the back with longer, kind of spiky hair on top. His smile dazzled, and even the slightest grin made the adorable dimple on his right cheek dance. Most days, stubble a shade or two darker than his hair peppered his chin and the line of his jaw. His ocean blue eyes swam with these cool, shimmering flecks of silvery gray. He was tall with broad shoulders and what appeared to be very strong arms, all tanned a golden brown.

Okay, yeah, I'd noticed.

" . . . are you even listening to me? Earth to Maggie." Chels snapped her fingers in front of my face. "Oh, I see. You're taking my advice about guys."

I rolled my eyes and quickly scraped the last pieces of my salad into a pile in the bowl.

"Tell me who you're interested in, and I'll tell you if he's seeing anyone or if he's a loser."

"Or only interested in one thing."

She wadded her napkin into a ball and shrugged. "You'll have to figure that out on your own."

Preston

The next morning Maggie rounded the corner at the end of the hall—all pretty and sweet and innocent.

My pulse raced as I pretended to sort through papers in my notebook. I pawed the top shelf of my locker for my stash of spearmint Tic Tac candies. Ah, man, I hadn't bought any yet this year. Stuffing the papers back into my notebook, I glanced her way. "Hey."

"Hi." She spun the dial on her locker, then tugged on the handle. Her smile vanished.

"I take it your locker still isn't cooperating."

She shook her head and sighed. "Okay, one more time."

When the handle didn't respond to a second try, a pouty frown tugged at her mouth.

I slid across the space separating us, psyched for any chance to be close to her. "I can try again, if you like."

"Please." She stepped aside. "You know the combination by now."

The locker swung open with an easy pull.

"I guess you have the magic touch. Thanks."

"Happy to help." She had no idea *how* happy. "It's just a little glitchy. I wouldn't worry about it."

I motioned for her to go ahead as we merged into the hall traffic toward English. I sucked in a breath as the crowd pressed us closer than I ever would have tried on my own.

We found our seats as the bell rang, and Mrs. Morrison clapped her hands to silence the class. "First thing I need you to do is pick a partner, someone who will have the privilege of grading and critiquing the paper you wrote last night. Or this morning, whichever the case may be." She wagged her bony finger at us. "Move so the two of you are sitting next to each other."

Connor waved from two rows over. He pointed to himself, then to me.

I nodded toward Maggie.

A grin broke across his face, and his thumb jerked up.

I tapped her on the shoulder. "You want to be my partner?"

She turned around. "Sure."

Mrs. Morrison had warned against including deep, dark secrets as we wrote about a significant event in our lives during the last three months. Maggie would discover in like five seconds that I hadn't put much time into the assignment.

"I don't think it's very good." She wrinkled her nose and handed me her paper.

"I guarantee it's better than mine. Keep askin' myself why I took this class."

Mrs. Morrison strolled across the front of the classroom. "If you see spelling, grammar, or punctuation errors, please underline them and make a correction. If something is unclear or just, well, *bad*, circle it and make a suggestion. Then, give a general critique of the paper as well as a letter grade."

Silence fell over the room. Maggie's brown eyes focused on my opening statement:

> "I guess you could say the last three months of
> my life have been about getting my priorities in
> line."

My essay went downhill from there—as far as a decent English paper went—as I circled around the issues I'd dealt with all summer, just trying to fill the page.

I exhaled and raked a hand through my hair. Too late to give the assignment more effort at this point. I forced my attention from Maggie to her paper. She had written:

"I once read that the summer between a person's sophomore and junior years of high school is a pivotal time, often setting the course for the rest of his or her life. Considering the summer I had, I have to wonder if that very statement was penned with me in mind."

I forgot to watch for errors as I quickly read on. "This is good."

Maggie peeked over the edge of my paper, meeting my gaze before looking again to my essay. Which she had probably decided by now was nothing more than a bunch of random words sharing space on a piece of paper.

"It's awful, right?"

She shook her head. "No, not at all."

The silent reading continued. Not until I finished did I realize I hadn't corrected anything. Her paper was so well-written and easy to follow, I wouldn't have changed a thing. I grabbed my pencil and scrawled in large letters exactly what I thought. "Awesome!"

She pressed her pen against my paper. I leaned closer to see what she was marking.

"Hey, there." She pulled the paper against her chest. "Not finished yet."

"Your pen will probably run out of ink before you're done."

She pursed her lips and shook her cute head, then covered the paper with her hand as she wrote comments at the bottom.

"Do we have to give it a letter grade?" someone from the back row asked.

"Yeah, do we?" from a guy up front.

Mrs. Morrison shrugged. "If you prefer not to, you may skip that part. But you must give a thorough critique of the work. And be sure to sign your name."

While giving Maggie's paper an *A+* would have been easy, I didn't want her to feel she had to give me a good grade. I signed my name and added, "I found nothing to correct. Ms. Jennison is an amazing writer with great insights."

"Now hand the papers back and take a few minutes to review your partner's critique."

Loud protests echoed across the room. "Harsh!"

"Oh, like yours was any better."

"I thought you were my friend."

I smirked at the dramatic responses.

Maggie giggled behind her hand.

She had noticed my inability to use punctuation correctly, but somehow, she actually liked what I wrote. "I appreciate Mr. Jacoby's description of a pivotal time in his life. Wish he had written more about himself." She'd used the same word—*pivotal*—to tell her own story. Her name appeared in a cool, small mix of cursive and printing at the bottom of the page.

"Ah, you were easy on me."

She tilted her head and smiled. "It was good. Well, maybe not the spelling and the lack of commas, but I liked it. I just wished you'd added a few more details."

My pulse accelerated at her compliment. Or was it her smile? "Well, like I said, English isn't my thing, especially writing. Yours was great, really. I couldn't find a thing wrong with it."

"Please pass your papers to the front. Now it's my turn." Mrs. Morrison rubbed her crooked fingers together.

The bell rang, and a couple of minutes later, we parted ways at our lockers. Bummer we only had two classes together. Well, maybe not. As much as I might want her to be in all my classes, I'd be way too distracted. I wasn't that great a student the way it was.

I'd missed half the psychology lecture yesterday, watching her. Maybe I could ask to borrow her notes. Or have her look over my English assignment. Maybe both.

I bolted to my locker at the end of the day, psyched about the best locker setup ever and hopefully another Maggie encounter.

"Preston, give me a quick ride home before work, will ya?" Connor with a request that would probably wreck my chances for seeing her again.

"Where's your car?"

"In the driveway. No gas till I get paid tomorrow." He took off for the door.

I scanned the hall for Maggie but reached the exit before I found her. Bummer.

Connor had climbed into my car and angled himself against the passenger side door before I got there. "So, you're going this weekend, right?"

I shook my head as we pulled from the parking lot.

"Dude, you can't miss it. It will be *epic*." Excitement rolled off him in waves. "Three days at the lake cottage—just you, me, Rob, and Zach, and more hot girls than—"

"Your parents are actually letting you take the guys along without them being there?"

"I begged, made a huge deal about the end-of-summer festival being the highlight of my summer. I promised there'd be no drinking at the cottage and played the whole trust-me card. Mom was holding out, but Dad finally said okay."

"No drinking? You promised that?"

"*At* the cottage." His eyebrows spiked, and a grin tugged at his mouth. "Whataya say?"

"I've got two shifts at Guido's and the Labor Day tournament to ump."

"Preston. Come on. Blow off work, just this once."

I shook my head. "Can't do that. I'm barely a month past that ninety-day probation I got for skipping shifts. Besides I'm not—"

"Call in sick. You haven't missed a year at the festival since we were ten. Don't bail on me now. It will be amazing."

By Connor's standards, yeah, it would be amazing. By the flimsy guidelines I used to live by? Totally sweet. But since I'd worked so hard to get my life straightened out, it would be a

31

ridiculous situation to put myself in. Worse even than hangin' out at Jake's a couple of months ago, which I hadn't handled well at all.

"I can't. Sorry."

"Dude, don't make me beg. Get someone to work for you. And Coach can get another ump." He sighed and rolled his eyes. "If you don't wanna drink, fine. And if you bypass the women, great, more for the rest of us. Just come. It won't be the same without you."

I chuckled at his determination and intensity. "Honestly, I can't ditch work or bail on Coach."

His grin faded into a hard, thin-lipped scowl. "I don't get you. You've always gone to church, but you were never any different than the rest of us. But now you're all religious and this—" He thrust his hand through the air. "This new Preston is annoying, boring, and *so* not cool."

My chest tightened. "So, because I don't wanna lie to my boss to spend the weekend pukin' my guts out and makin' out with girls I'll never see again, I'm boring and annoying? Good to know."

I whipped around the corner into his subdivision faster than I should have and sailed over the speed bump. Slowing to a crawl to avoid being reported by the neighborhood watch, I sucked in a couple of deep breaths to cool my anger.

He slouched against the passenger door, his head knocking on the window. A loud sigh hissed from his mouth. "What's it been? Like six months since you broke it off with Alyssa and basically swore off girls and dating and fun?"

Alyssa. Guilt surged through me at the mention of her name.

At the time, I thought I was cool, a stud and all. The first of my friends to have sex. But it had complicated our relationship big time. When her parents announced they were moving two hours north, she assumed we'd do the whole long-distance thing. But by then I wanted out in the worst way. "How can you do this to me?" she'd cried and screamed and pleaded when I insisted we end it.

So, I treated her really bad—so she'd *want* to break up with me. Things got incredibly ugly, and then she was gone.

I gripped the steering wheel, grinding out my oft-repeated explanation through clenched teeth. "I've been focusing on more important things, that's all. There's more to life than girls, being cool, and partying. You know that, right?"

"I go to church, too, but it's not my whole life."

"Yeah, well, it's my life we're talkin' about. And what I used to base my life on, that's all changed."

"Yeah, yeah. I know. You and God are tight now." He rubbed his jaw and stretched his mouth wide a couple of times. "Not gonna change your mind about this weekend, are you?"

I pried my hand from the steering wheel and shook it to get the blood flowing through my tingling fingers. "Nope."

We drove on in silence as my mind continued to replay the past. What had been minor use of alcohol here and there turned into major abuse after the breakup. But no amount of numbing the guilt helped. Only messed with me more. My parents were on my case like crazy, all worried and suspicious. Came within a half inch of losing my job because of ditching shifts. Drove home drunk so many times, it's a miracle I hadn't killed myself or someone else. It was like being caught in a never-ending nightmare.

"Fine." A dramatic groan-growl-sigh rumbled from Connor's chest. "Least you're showing interest in girls again. You're hittin' it off with Maggie pretty good."

I stopped in front of his house. "You just worry about yourself."

"Nothin' to worry about when it comes to me and hot babes." A big, cocky Connor-smile took over his face. "Later, dude, and thanks."

We knocked knuckles, and he hopped out. He got over stuff fast. He'd bust my chops about something, but then he'd drop it, and we'd be cool again.

While I'd been worried that getting my life in order would mean I'd have to give up my best friend, God had thrown it back at me as a question: Can you be his friend and live the way I want you to? I was giving it my best shot, and so far, it was working.

But the issue consuming my thoughts the last couple of days had nothing to do with Connor and everything to do with my self-imposed break from girls. Was I ready to end the dating hiatus? Wrong question. I was way past ready to end it. But was I up for the challenge of a complete one-eighty in my approach to girls in general, especially the physical stuff?

And with who?

A particular brunette whose chocolate brown eyes I couldn't stop thinking about filled my mind. Did I have a shot with Maggie Jennison?

Maggie

By the end of the week, Preston had basically taken over opening my locker, and I was perfectly content to let him work his magic. But today he was late. I sorted through random papers in my binder as another minute ticked by with no sign of him. So, I reached for the stubborn lock, determined to finally get it on the first try.

"Hey, I thought that was my job." He appeared beside me, like really close, and his hand brushed across my fingers as I pulled back.

I caught the scent of his masculine soap or shampoo, maybe cologne, and breathed it in.

"Sorry I'm late. I had to ask Benton something about the history assignment." My locker door swung open, and he stepped back. "I'll do my best to be more punctual in the future." That dazzling smile tugged at the corners of his mouth.

He shuffled to his own locker, which swung open with ease. His glance flitted my way as he shoved in books. In no time, he was back at my side. "Say, about that psychology project. Have you picked a partner?"

"I haven't. What about you?"

He shook his head and motioned for me to go ahead of him as we squeezed into the flow of students heading toward the exit. "We could be partners, if you want." His mouth eased into a gorgeous whole-face smile that crinkled the corners of his eyes.

Wow. My heartbeat stuttered. "Yeah, we could."

He stepped up to open the door. "Well, okay then, partner. When can we get started?"

"Whenever it works for you."

"I work until eight tonight. If that's not too late, maybe we can meet at your house?"

"Sure." I stopped in front of my car and propped myself against the front fender because for some reason, my legs felt like rubber.

"Your address?"

"Oh. 8697 Rosewood Lane."

"Got it. Might be eight-twenty till I get there."

"That's fine."

He opened my car door, offered a goofy grin and a bow, then swept his hand toward the driver's seat like a chauffeur. "Until then, Miss Jennison."

I pinched my lips together against a giggle and settled in. "See ya tonight."

He winked, closed the door, and strode across the parking lot, all confidence and hotness, to a taupe car.

~ ~ ~

The doorbell rang at eight-nineteen, interrupting my fifth last-minute, face-hair-outfit check in the downstairs bathroom. I pressed a hand to the dancing butterflies in my stomach. What was wrong with me? Gasping in a couple of deep, calming breaths, I gripped the doorknob and opened the door.

In a navy t-shirt and khaki shorts, wearing *that* smile and gazing at me with amazing blue eyes, Preston filled the entire doorway. "Hope I'm not late." The warmth oozing from his voice sent goosebumps racing down my arms.

"Right on time. Is it okay if we work at the dining room table?"

"Lead the way."

He pulled out the one chair that didn't match the others and leaned his crossed arms on the lace tablecloth that covered up fifty years of scratches. "Any ideas for the theme of our project?"

I shook my head and sat down across from him. When would I have had time to come up with ideas? With straightening the house and trying on half a dozen outfits, and—

His finger tapped his chin. "Let's see . . . "

I suppressed a giggle. Almost. He was so cute.

"What?" His eyebrows scrunched together.

I bit my lip. "Nothing. Ideas, hmm."

We tossed around several premises before going with a survey about students' communication preferences—phone, email, text, Facebook, Twitter, Instagram, or Snapchat.

"Your writing is much neater than mine." He pushed his notebook toward me. In no time, we came up with ten questions to explore our theme.

"That was easy." He directed a flirty smile my way.

"How about something to drink?" I forced myself to glance away. Why was it suddenly easier to put sentences together—and breathe—when *not* looking at him?

"Yeah, sure."

He followed me into the kitchen and peered around the refrigerator door when I opened it. "I'll have a Mountain Dew."

I handed it to him and grabbed a Diet Coke for myself. He eased the can from my hand, his fingertips stroking across mine in the process, and carried both back to the table.

I followed with a plate of cookies to find he'd opened both cans of pop and slid mine into the perfect spot in front of me.

He grabbed a cookie and took a big bite. "These are good."

I nibbled on the smallest cookie from the plate. "They're my favorite, Ultimate Peanut Butter Chocolate Chip."

"I can see why." He grabbed two more, then slowly trailed his index finger down the page. "S'pose we should type up these questions?"

The cutest little muscle bulged in his jaw every time he chewed, and the way his dimple blinked on and off almost hypnotically—

"Maggie?"

"Oh—the questions. I'll get my laptop." My cheeks warmed as I scurried to the kitchen. I fanned my face and tried to get a grip.

When I returned, his whole face shifted into that irresistible smile—again. "Thanks for being my partner, by the way," he said.

"No problem." Really? That was all I could think of to say?

"I'll read the questions. You type, 'kay?" He brushed crumbs from his hands.

"Ready in a sec. This laptop is slow."

As my dad's hand-me-down laptop booted up, he ripped the page from the notebook and snapped the paper in the air dramatically,

I completely failed at hiding my amusement. The screen finally blinked on, and I nodded. "Ready."

"Very well, Ms. Jennison. Question number one."

His voice was smooth and so masculine—serious and proper one minute, cracking jokes the next. I laughed so much that my fingers stumbled over the keyboard, spelling half the words wrong.

"Wait." I squeaked between giggles, backspacing furiously.

He hopped up and stood behind me, reading over my shoulder. "Do you preefarr to amail, text or twit? Where'd you learn to type?"

"It's your fault. Stop making me laugh."

"My fault? I think not." He leaned so close, his cheek ruffled my hair.

My fingers stilled on the keyboard.

He straightened up fast, and the paper scrunched in his hands. Bell tones from the living room chimed out ten o'clock, filling the awkward silence.

I held my breath and smoothed invisible wrinkles in the tablecloth.

"I should go, school night and all. You can probably fix all those typos without me." He smirked, sending that dimple into action again.

"I'll do my best."

In one swift motion, he dropped the questions beside me and gathered his books.

I hopped up and followed him to the front door.

He shuffled from one foot to the other and plunged his hand into his pocket. "Thanks for the cookies."

I just stared and nodded because words refused to make an appearance.

"Guess I'll see ya tomorrow." He reached for the doorknob.

"Yeah. See ya."

With a nod and a grin, he was gone—before my brain resumed normal function.

Preston

The old me would have tried to kiss Maggie last night. No question. The chemistry was so intense. But the new me didn't want to mess up the chance for a relationship. Talk about a change in M.O. When had I *ever* worried about the relationship part?

As I trudged to U.S. History, mind racing with the possibilities of there being an "us," Caroline Branson slithered to my side.

"Hey, you. You been hidin' or what?" She slipped her arm through mine, brushing her hip against me. "I looked for you all last week."

I edged away from her and shrugged. "I was here."

"Obviously we don't have any classes together." She pushed her shiny lips into a pout.

"Guess not." I shifted farther from her and stared straight ahead, hoping my expression clearly showed indifference.

She snuggled closer and stroked my arm. "I was hoping we could hang out sometime."

I dared myself to look at her. Her huge, blue-green eyes that had always been almost impossible to resist pleaded with me. I unwound her arm from mine. "I'm not interested in getting back together."

Her pout hardened. "We were a great couple, Preston. Don't you remember?"

Oh, I remembered all right. But now it didn't seem all that great. I sucked in a deep breath. "I'm sorry, Caroline." *For so many things.*

Her expression softened. "You'll come around. I just hope it won't be too late." She surveyed the length of my body.

I focused on the floor.

Her fingertips traced a slow pattern down my arm, then she gripped my index finger. With a final tug, she released my hand and strutted away.

I raked a hand through my hair. *Wow.*

I glanced back toward the clock over the office doorway, and there was Maggie.

Our eyes connected for just a second before she lunged into the crowd, going the opposite direction.

"Maggie!" I didn't care that I yelled or that heads turned my way a good fifteen feet in either direction. The one person whose attention I cared about at all was Maggie's, and she didn't turn around.

Maggie

I stumbled to Algebra, blinded by repeating flashes of Preston and that girl, Caroline something, walking down the hall all snuggled together arm in arm. How did Chelsea not know Preston had a girlfriend?

Maybe they were just good friends. Could be a cousin. Did he have a sister?

Why do I even care?

Mr. Clausen's explanation of the equations in chapter two floated around me as I tried to answer that question and a million others. Like why did I feel like throwing up, and why, oh why was I about to cry?

Did I want us to be more than friends? Had I fallen for Preston?

He was so totally out of my league. Even if by some unbelievable miracle he showed real interest in me, what then? Did I know him well enough to guarantee there wouldn't be a repeat of the Logan fiasco? Nope. I really knew nothing about him except that he was incredibly easy on the eyes, his grammar skills needed a lot of work, and oh, yeah, he was good at opening stubborn lockers.

The bell rang, ending the class discussion I knew I would regret zoning out on. My stomach continued to churn, and the dryness in my throat made swallowing as painful as my last bout with tonsillitis.

A strange mixture of hope and irritation engulfed me when I spotted him ready and waiting beside my already opened locker door. What was he doing?

And then he cranked up the dazzle on his smile and anger shot through me. How *dare* he flirt with me after sauntering down the hall with *her?* I brushed past, ignoring him as I rummaged for the right combination of books.

His smile vanished as he moved to his own locker.

I sucked in a calming breath then closed my locker with a harder-than-necessary shove. And found myself gazing directly into his slightly bluer than normal eyes and super serious expression. My heart skipped a couple of beats.

He released a heavy sigh.

But before he could say anything, I spun around and stalked down the hall, my pulse throbbing so loud in my ears that all other sound was blocked out.

He wasn't waiting at my locker the rest of the day. Which was fine by me. If he and Caroline were together, this flirtiness between us needed to end immediately. And if they weren't, did it really matter? There was no reason for me to care this much if he was or was not with some girl.

Preston

For hours I kicked myself about overreacting to Maggie's cold shoulder after the Caroline incident. I'd been so incredibly irritated at Caroline for getting in the way of what I hoped was a shot with Maggie. Then I couldn't think straight and had made the idiot choice to keep my distance from Maggie the rest of the day. A really bad move on my part. Or maybe it wasn't.

Flashbacks of me and Caroline as a couple had assaulted my mind through my entire shift at Guido's last night. We'd been a big deal freshman year. I lived for the status of being with the hottest girl in our grade, but I got tired of her manipulation and finally ended it. She'd been trying to get us back together ever since.

Another piece of the mountain of baggage from my past that I couldn't seem to shake.

There was no denying I wanted a chance with Maggie. My instincts told me she had little experience with guys and probably none with the physical stuff. So being with her would be a win-win for me because I wanted and *needed* someone who knew nothing of my dating past and did not have a sexual agenda of her own. She fit the bill on both counts—I was sure.

But how fair would that be to her? Even though I was all about charting a new course as far from the old me as possible, next to her innocence, I looked like Jack the Ripper.

~ ~ ~

After wrestling all night with the dilemma, I made the decision to walk away from the possibility of being with Maggie. Yeah, I wanted a chance with her, but it would just be too unfair to her. The locker situation—not to mention AP English and Psychology—would make it tough to put distance between us, but I had to try.

I skipped the locker scene totally and slipped into English without book, paper, or pencil a half second before the bell. Nothing I hadn't done dozens of times the last two years. I bummed a pencil from Connor and tried to focus on the six-page test that was supposed to gauge how much we'd forgotten of all the English stuff we'd been taught since kindergarten.

Being that close to Maggie, attempting to ignore her over-the-shoulder glances, and making a huge effort not to breathe in her amazing scent was torture. I doodled on the test pages, giving almost no effort toward getting the right answers. Didn't count for a grade anyway.

I handed my papers in three minutes before class ended and begged Mrs. Morrison to let me go to the restroom. I feigned a sick, pathetic look that must have passed as genuine because she didn't hassle me at all. To be honest, I felt lousy after barely sleeping last night.

And then I remembered the psychology project. Being in the same class was one thing, but how could I stay away from Maggie *and* partner with her on the project? It would be even more unfair to her if I bailed on our presentation now.

Anyway, who was I kidding? One class period of pretending she didn't exist had practically killed me. I could not consciously walk away. Because fair or not, I couldn't pretend there wasn't something between us. All through third period, every second of being close to her rewound through my mind. Followed by a repeating chant of more than a dozen reasons why I didn't want to ignore whatever was building between us.

Just let whatever happens, happen.

That made sense. I wouldn't push. Would try not to pursue—if I could help it. And just to set the record straight, I'd very casually mention that Caroline meant nothing to me. If Maggie and I ended up as more than friends at some point, well, okay then. Awesome.

I raced from class to beat her to our lockers and had already dialed her combination when I remembered the whole not pursuing thing. I gripped the handle, every fiber of my body screaming to yank it open.

I caught sight of her down the hall, alone and shuffling along slowly. No smile. No spark in her amazing eyes. Nothing.

I jerked the handle, and the locker sprang open. I kicked mine closed and slammed the door on the doubts pinging my conscience. Standing a little off to the side, I amped up my smile, and waited through her painfully slow approach.

She noticed the open door, then her eyes flitted to me.

I took a step closer. "Maggie. Hi."

As she glanced from me to her open locker then back to me, I launched in. "Hey, in case you're wondering—Caroline is an ex-girlfriend. Her interest has continued. Mine hasn't. In case you're . . . uh, wonderin'." I shoved the toe of my shoe against the lockers and held my breath.

"Oh." Emotions I couldn't quite put my finger on flickered across her face. She bit into her bottom lip.

"And I'm sorry I wasn't around to help with your locker yesterday. Or this morning."

A hint of a smile. "I managed."

"Won't happen again, I promise."

She said nothing more but got real busy, digging through her locker.

Had I done the right thing, bringing up Caroline? Searing stabs that I'd been an idiot, again, mixed with the slow burn that insisted I was being selfish. Only concerned with what I wanted. Not about what was best for Maggie.

I shoved the whole mess of doubts aside. I *could* be good for her. I *would* be good for her.

Preston's rather interesting explanation circled through my brain all through Psychology. He wanted me to know he and Caroline were not together. But *why*? Was he interested in me as more than a psychology project partner and grammar checker? And why did that idea make my heart pound?

No time now to consider all that because I had to psych myself up for the first National Honor Society meeting during homeroom. Joining NHS at the end of last year had seemed like a good idea—to my parents. For reasons that escaped me now, I went along, knowing it would look good on college apps, forgetting that I freak out in new situations where a). I didn't know anyone, b). had no idea what to expect, and c). couldn't blend into the crowd.

Would anyone know if I didn't show? Surely, they didn't take attendance or anything. But Mom knew about the meeting and would expect a detailed report. At least I sort of knew Mr. Martin, the sponsor, and how to find his classroom. I'd slip in the back and leave ASAP.

Mr. Martin closed his classroom door with a loud thud, quieting the group of students far too small for me to get lost in.

"Welcome to National Honor Society." He waved his index finger across the group. "Seems half of your fellow comrades couldn't drag themselves away from homeroom. Spread the word—from now on we'll meet at lunch at least once every other week, beginning next Tuesday. Attendance is mandatory.

No participation, no NHS accolades on those college applications."

"Lunch?" A pretty blonde, maybe a senior, raised her perfectly plucked eyebrows.

"Yes, Lindsey, lunch."

The brunette beside her frowned. "But last year—

"I know, Erin, last year NHS met occasionally for five minutes during homeroom. Let's just say my approach for this year is different. Now let's get started." He shoved his hands into the pockets of his baggy jeans. "While I appreciate the spirit of last year's efforts to raise money for a small trophy case at the main entrance, I'm counting on this year's efforts to be more—" his head see-sawed from side to side "—*others-minded*. As a group, you'll choose a cause or an organization to present to the student body as a focus project."

Too bad Chelsea wasn't an NHS member. Or better yet, Preston. Actually, neither of them seemed like the NHS type. No Caroline whatever-her-name-was either. I could have sworn she shot daggers right through me when we passed in the hall this morning. What was *that* about?

"Maggie."

I jumped at Mr. Martin's raised voice.

"Yes?" How long had I zoned out?

"Your parents work at The Least of These Clinic?"

I gulped and cleared my throat. "My dad's the business manager, and my mom's a physician's assistant."

"Could they use our help?"

"Maybe." I slouched lower in my seat.

He nodded. "We'll add them to the list. Okay, guys and gals, come next week ready to cast your vote for our focus project."

Vote? List? Project?

"What about eating?" A tall guy—I think he played football—called out as everyone stood to leave.

"What about eating." Mr. Martin shrugged. "Bring your lunch, Tyler, or buy it. Skip if you want, doesn't matter to me. Be here with or without food by 12:05 next Tuesday."

~ ~ ~

Despite Cindy's "observations" that labeled Preston as a player—the kind of guy I'd never want to go out with—I thought about him all weekend. The you-know-nothing-about-him argument did nothing to stop the invasion of what-ifs and possibilities.

And on Monday morning, when I saw him looking totally hot in faded blue jeans and a striped button-up shirt, leaning against #7725, the lone locker between mine and his, I forgot how little I really knew about Preston Jacoby.

"And how are you this fine Monday morning?" He gripped the top of my opened locker door which kept him super close.

The breath caught in my throat. "I'm good and you?"

"Couldn't be better." His smile seemed especially dazzling today.

I closed my locker and faced him.

"So . . ." He stepped closer.

I swallowed and barely dared to peer up at him.

"We need to finish our presentation." His dimple danced. "I'm free tomorrow if you are."

A fluttery nod from me.

"My house okay?"

"Yeah, sure," I croaked, my mouth so dry I could barely form words.

His face lit up with a big, eye-crinkling smile. "Seven o'clock?"

I sucked in a shaky breath and tried to clear the squeak from my voice, but then I gave up and just nodded again.

As we headed to English, he nudged the purse dangling from my shoulder. "Man, I'm starving. Don't happen to have any of those awesome chocolate chip cookies in there, do you?"

"No, sorry."

"Bummer." His lips twitched in an ornery, momentary pout.

When we slipped into our seats, my shaky legs welcomed the chance to sit down. Had we just leaped into an entirely new realm of flirting?

As Mrs. Morrison launched into a lecture on prepositional phrases, I gave up trying to silence my mental debate that had nothing to do with grammar. Was I ready for *this*? Whatever *this* was?

Something rustled against my hair then Preston's hushed, very close voice whispered, "Remember, Martin said we can bring food to class tomorrow. What would it take to get you to bake some of those cookies?"

I glanced up, expecting to catch the teacher's glare.

"Morrison went to the library for a second." He couldn't have been more than two inches from my hair. "I'll beg if that's what it takes."

"That won't be necessary."

Maybe I was more ready than I thought.

Preston

As I followed Maggie up the walk to my house, I memorized the outline of her petite body.

She paused on the bottom step. "I appreciate the ride. Mom and I share a car, but with Dad's in the shop, I'm without transportation."

I jerked my gaze up. Not that her face was hard to look at. She seemed prettier every day. "No problem."

Just inside the front door, my brother rummaged through the closet. His eyebrows shot up, then settled back down. He was trying to pretend it hadn't been months since I brought a girl home. At least Mom and Dad weren't around to make a big deal about it. "This is my brother Patrick. This is Maggie."

"Hey." He glanced away from his search long enough to give her a casual nod.

"Hi, Patrick."

He issued me a sly thumbs-up after Maggie passed.

I sniffed the warm, covered pan I'd taken from her when I picked her up. "Something smells awesome."

"Chocolate chunk marshmallow brownies."

"Wow, that sounds amazing." I pulled the cover open to take a peek.

"Hey, work first, then we eat."

"Yes, ma'am. Something to drink? Diet Coke, right?" I put the brownies on the dining room table.

She nodded.

I returned from the kitchen with a Mountain Dew, a Diet Coke, and a bag of Doritos. "Drinks now. Doritos later." I popped the top on her can of pop and slid it to where her fingers tapped the table next to her laptop.

She glanced up and sighed. "Thanks. Sorry it's so slow."

I sat across from her. "It's fine." I tipped my head and pulled out the stops on my smile.

Her eyes flitted toward me, and she grinned. But then her teeth pressed into her bottom lip like she was trying not to smile. Her attention returned to the computer just as our presentation flashed on the screen.

"May I?" I ran my hand along the edge of the laptop.

"Sure."

I scrolled through the slides we'd put together in class. "This is really good—not that I'm surprised. You're a pro at this kind of thing."

Another half-smile. "It wasn't all me."

"I guess we're just good together."

Her gorgeous eyes met mine and stayed. I held my breath. One unreadable expression after another flickered across her face. I hated having no clue what she was thinking.

She relaxed back in her seat. "Maybe so."

At least she wasn't disgusted by the idea. I'd take that. "Let's get this thing done. Those brownies are calling my name."

In no time, I had her laughing just like the last time we worked on the project. She had such an amazing smile. We finished up the presentation, and I tore open the Doritos while she scooped two large brownies onto paper plates.

"Mmm . . . mmm. These taste even better than they smell." I took another bite and closed my eyes. "Man, I could get used to this."

She stared at me, all wide-eyed and speechless. How could she not be getting the same vibes as me? I'd had about as much "backing off" as I could stand. I popped another piece of brownie into my mouth.

She pressed her fork into her brownie over and over, cutting it into tiny pieces.

"Would you go to the football game with me on Friday?"

More flickering emotions that I still couldn't read swept across her face. "Okay . . . "

Not the most enthusiastic response, by a long shot, but I refused to back down now. "Maybe after the game we could get a pizza or something."

A little smile tugged at her mouth. "Sure."

My confidence spiked. "Pick you up at six-thirty?"

A bigger smile formed, and she nodded.

"Well, okay then." I pulled the pan of brownies closer. "These are awesome. Can I have another one?"

"Have as many as you want." She scooped another brownie onto my plate.

Our eyes connected in a long, intense look. What *was* she thinking? I'd banked on a lot more enthusiasm, but she'd said yes without too much hesitation so . . .

She dropped her gaze to her brownie and resumed dissecting it.

"So, we're all set for the presentation tomorrow, right?"

"As long as you do the talking and let me run the laptop, I think we'll be good." Creases lined her forehead as she bit into her bottom lip again.

"Oh, come on. We can't do that."

She frowned, her eyes clearly pleading with me. "I hate talking in front of groups."

"You have to say somethin'." I leaned toward her. "How about you read the text on the first few slides. I'll take it from where the graphs start."

"I can probably handle that."

I cocked my head to the side. "I'll be right there beside you."

An obvious wave of relief washed over her face. "Then I should be fine."

~ ~ ~

The razzing from the guys kicked in at lunch the next day. Connor announced that he'd "called it" the second day of school and patted himself on the back to no end.

I boasted about asking Maggie out before he asked Chelsea. "Dude, what's up with you? This isn't how you usually operate."

"My sources tell me I have nothing to worry about."

"Sources?" I snorted a laugh.

He grunted. "Trust me. By the time I ask her out, she'll be so into me—"

"You better treat her right."

"Oh, it'll be the best night of her life. I guarantee you that."

"Hey, Jacoby." Logan Wallace strode up to us. He knocked his knuckles against the top of the table. "So, you and Maggie Jennison, huh?"

"What about it?"

"Thought I'd let you know, she's not your type."

"What's that supposed to mean?"

"I took her out last summer and, trust me, she's not *your* type."

Heat crept up the back of my neck as I glared at him.

He stared back.

"Like you know anything about me." My voice was hard but controlled.

"Just don't expect to have a good time." His raunchy laugh faded as he sauntered across the cafeteria.

I slammed my fist on the table causing Connor and Zach to grab their rocking bottles of Gatorade. Way too many people knew stuff about me that I never wanted Maggie to find out.

All the questions about a relationship between us being fair to Maggie screamed at a hundred decibels in my head.

Please . . . I can't stand the thought of losing her before we get a chance to be together.

Maggie

So, what can you tell me about Preston?" I hadn't mentioned the growing connection between Preston and I because I knew Chelsea would push and prod and badger. I didn't want to be pushed, prodded, or badgered. But she knew him, and I didn't. And now that we were going out—

"He and Connor are best friends. They're together like all the time. They—"

"I didn't ask about Connor."

She popped a chip in her mouth and tipped her head to the left. Her green eyes studied me as she chewed. "He's hot."

"I already know that. Can't you tell me anything else?"

She shrugged and popped another chip in her mouth.

"Cindy said he thinks every girl wants to go out with him or already has and that's not exactly a glowing endorsement. Of course, *he* said she had no idea what she was talking about, even though everyone laughed, probably in agreement. And this thing with Caroline, all clinging to his side. Who knows what that was about. She's glared at me every day since, and I swear it's *not* my imagination." I heaved a frustrated sigh. "Plenty of reasons to keep my distance, huh?" Except I didn't want to.

Chelsea's hand shot up in front of my face. "First off, Cindy who?"

"Johnson."

She shrugged. "Why does it matter what she or anyone else thinks? And as far as Caroline goes, they were a couple a long time ago. He couldn't care less about her anymore. She just can't accept it."

Her green eyes bored into mine. "If you're interested in him—and you obviously are—then do something about it. He and Connor *are* together a lot, and once me and him are together, the four of us could hang out. It'd be fun." She rubbed her hands together to brush off the chip crumbs. "And he *is* hot."

Like I needed to be reminded of that every five seconds. "I already did something about it, I guess. I have no idea if it's an actual date or not, but he asked me to the game tonight, and I said yes."

A huge smile burst across her face, and she offered me a high five. "Mag-gie li-ikes Pres-ton, Mag-gie li-ikes Pressss-ttton."

"Shh." I closed my eyes and dropped my head into my palm. "Keep it down, will you?"

She pushed her tray toward the center of the table and plunked down her crossed arms. "That *is* a date, duh. Listen, stop worrying so much and just give him a chance. He's a fun guy. An amazingly tall, strong, *handsome,* fun guy." Her eyebrows wiggled across her forehead.

I swatted her arm. "You're no help at all, you know that, right?"

The stem of the red rose stuck to my sweaty hand in spite of repeated swipes across my thigh. I sucked in a deep breath, blew a couple of puffs of air into my right palm, then pushed the doorbell. What if it was dumb, giving Maggie a rose on the first date?

Too late now.

Before the chime ended, the door opened, and there she stood. In a red sweater—that exactly matched the rose. She greeted me with a shy smile. "Hi."

"This is for you."

Her smile deepened, and those gold flecks in her eyes literally sparkled. She lifted the flower to her nose. "Ah, thank you."

I wanted to say *it's beautiful like you* or anything that would show her I was serious about her, about this date. But I settled for, "Glad you like it."

"Let me put this in some water." She held the rose carefully, pressed close to her shoulder, like it was something special.

I followed her to the kitchen, soaking up the confidence that came from being familiar with her house. When had I ever been this nervous on a date? Probably all the trying to convince myself that us being together was right. Not selfish on my part or unfair to her. But *right.*

A lanky guy bounded into the kitchen. He looked from me to Maggie. "Do ya wanna give me a ride to the game?"

"I'm sure they don't." A balding man a couple of inches shorter than me leaned through the doorway. "I'm taking you to the game, Michael. After Maggie introduces me and your mother to her date." His gaze pulled from me to Maggie then slid back to me.

A woman with the same dark brown hair as Maggie peeked around him.

Maggie bit into her bottom lip, her gaze shifting from me to her parents. I wasn't the only one nervous. "Dad, this is Preston. Preston, this is my dad, Tom."

Tom stepped forward and gripped my hand with force. "Preston."

I looked him in the eye and gave his hand one firm shake.

"And this is my mom, Cheryl."

Cheryl's light squeeze of my hand lasted half as long as Tom's iron-man grasp.

"Nice to meet you both." I usually hated meeting the parents, but this didn't seem all that bad.

"It's very nice to meet you, Preston." Cheryl glanced at me, then smiled at Maggie.

A grin tugged at Tom's lips. "Let's go, Michael." He grabbed a jacket from the back of a chair. "Enjoy the game you two." They headed out through the side door.

"What about me, huh?" Michael's loud whining seeped in through the slowly closing door.

Tom chuckled. "You too, Michael."

Maggie shot a desperate look toward her mom who only shrugged and waved. "In case you're wondering, Michael's thirteen. And yes, his manners are usually that bad." She picked up her coat from a chair.

I eased it from her hand and held it up for her to slip on.

She glanced at me, wide-eyed, over her shoulder. "Uh, thanks."

I dipped my head. "You're welcome."

As I backed from the lane, conversation starters bounced through my mind. "Guess what I finished already? Monday's English assignment."

"Wow, I'm impressed."

"Thought I'd get it out of the way. I wouldn't mind if you look it over, you know, in case I missed something."

"Yeah, sure. I haven't given any of my homework even a thought yet."

I'd probably missed more than a couple of the grammar errors, considering my mind was much more focused on tonight than on the assignment. Still my effort had paid off. Score one for me.

Soon we were climbing the bleachers at the game. Maggie shivered and scrunched her shoulders as we settled on a blanket at the top of the cheer block.

"Are you cold?"

"Not too bad." She reached in her pockets, then dug through each pocket again. "Great, only one glove."

"Did you drop the other one somewhere?"

"Who knows? Warm coat, shallow pockets. I go through gloves like you wouldn't believe."

She slipped the lone purple glove onto her right hand and tucked her left hand into a pocket as the teams lined up to kick off.

I pulled in a deep breath and ordered myself to stop worrying. About everything. That I was bad for her. That she didn't want to be here with me. That it would be all awkward and weird. It wasn't at all. It didn't feel much different than being with her at school.

She cheered as much as I did throughout the close game. Madison was up by six at halftime. And by then, she couldn't hide that she was cold.

"How 'bout some hot chocolate?" I offered.

"Mmm, I'd love that."

"Popcorn?"

"Yes, please." Her relaxed smile, the way she met my gaze, was like a shot of adrenaline, spiking my confidence.

As we waited in line at the concession stand, she bounced on her toes.

"You're really cold, aren't you?"

"I'm cold practically all the time, but this is helping, really." She crossed her arms and tucked her hands close to her body.

I stepped close behind her—careful not to actually touch her—to block the cool breeze ruffling her hair. An awesome scent swirled around me—sort of sweet like flowers yet sexy, too. I leaned in until the stubble on my chin caught in her hair. *Nice.*

Her bouncing slowed to barely moving.

We inched forward in the line and soon headed back to our seats armed with two hot chocolates and a huge tub of popcorn. I sat down at the very edge of our blanket, and she sat down beside me.

"I have an idea." I hopped up, grabbed the blanket on the other side of her, and held it above her lap.

With her gloved hand, she laid it across her legs.

"Better?" I sat back down.

"Yeah, but do you have enough blanket? Here, scoot over a little."

"I have enough."

Her eyes narrowed, and her lips pressed together. "Are you afraid of me or what?"

I couldn't suppress the grin tugging at my mouth. "I'm not afraid of you." I scooted until only a fraction of an inch separated our thighs.

She sipped her drink. "This is really good hot chocolate."

"How cold is your hand?"

She touched her fingertips to the back of my hand.

"You're freezing!"

"This hot cup feels great." Switching the cup to her gloved hand, she grabbed a handful of popcorn. "The warm popcorn helps, too."

Despite how much I liked football, my focus strayed at least every thirty seconds from the action on the field to the brunette beside me. And the issue of her cold hand. Since I'd already decided there'd be no physical contact without her permission, my options were limited.

When she finished her hot chocolate, her left hand disappeared into her pocket.

I turned toward her. "I'd be happy to keep your hand warm—if you want me to."

Her brown eyes, wide and gorgeous and swirling with emotions I couldn't read, stared at me for a full two-three-four seconds before she pulled her curled-up hand from her pocket.

I cupped her small, frozen fist between both my hands and rested them on my leg. "This okay?"

She nodded, that speechless look I was kind of getting used to, fixed on her face.

The crowd's loud cheering pulled our attention back to the game as the third quarter ended in a tie.

Before long, her hand no longer felt like ice against my skin. "Are you warmer now?"

She scrunched her nose in a cute way. "Much better, thanks."

The lead changed twice early in the fourth quarter. We jumped up, clapping and hollering, with nearly every play. And each time, settled back into the same arrangement, my hands cradling her hand on my leg.

The crowd erupted as the last seconds ticked off the clock. *Five . . . four . . . three . . . two . . . one . . .* Madison 24 – Washington 17.

We walked down the bleachers, pressed together by the crowd. Her fingers brushed across mine. By accident or on purpose? Before I could make a conscious decision, my hand wrapped around hers.

Maggie

Preston fiddled with the car's temperature controls as we waited to get out of the parking lot. "How's your hand?"

"Warm, thanks to you." I'd never considered it good luck to lose a glove, but the last couple of hours had changed my perspective.

The dimple on his cheek danced as a grin hiked up the corners of his mouth. "Happy to help."

"That's twice today you saved me," I murmured.

"Oh yeah?"

Did I say that out loud? "Umm . . . my knees, you know, were shaking like crazy before our psych presentation . . . " My voice trailed off to a whisper.

He'd stood so close, his eyes boring into mine, his big, warm hands hovering as close as possible over my freezing clenched fists, without actually touching them, and whispered, "You can do this, Maggie. You'll be great." It was the sweetest thing ever.

"Well, you did awesome, and I bet we aced it." A long sweep of his fingertips drew momentary swirls across my hand.

I nodded, as a stream of words piled up in my throat. Then my hand flipped over—all on its own—and our fingers kind of fell together as if we'd held hands dozens of times before.

A horn beeped behind us.

Preston cleared his throat, squeezed my hand, and accelerated to catch up to the car in front of us.

A loud sort of wow-this-is-really-happening silence filled the car on the drive to Pizza Hut. *Yep, this is a date.*

He parked and sprinted around the car to help me out. As we strolled across the parking lot, his strong, warm hand wrapped around mine. He stopped and pulled our hands in front of him. "This isn't too weird, is it?"

I shook my head, struggling again with actual words. "No," I finally managed to mutter.

"Not for me either."

Inside he waved to Connor at a table full of guys as we settled in a booth. "So, what's your favorite pizza?"

"I like just about anything."

"But your absolute favorite is?"

"Sausage, pepperoni, double mushrooms on stuffed crust."

"No way." That eye-crinkling smile again. "That's mine, too."

"Are you kidding?"

"Nope. I swear." He leaned into the aisle. "Johnson—over here."

Connor hopped up and sauntered over to us.

"What's my favorite pizza?" Preston quizzed.

Connor rolled his eyes. "Dude, you're supposed to let *her* choose the pizza. Maybe she doesn't like sausage, pepperoni, extra mushrooms on stuffed crust."

My hand flew to my mouth.

Connor's forehead creased. "What?"

"That's Maggie's favorite too."

"Yeah?" He shrugged. "I knew from the second day—"

Preston swatted his arm then grabbed for my hand. "You can leave now, thanks."

Connor smirked. He strode back to his friends who welcomed him with loud whoops.

When our pizza came, he let go of my hand gradually, like he really didn't want to. I didn't want him to either. I already liked the feel of his warm skin against mine. Except that eating and talking were enough to focus on at one time. Even though my nerves had calmed down a lot by the second quarter of the game, the realization that this was indeed a date had stirred them up again.

When he was sure I didn't want anymore, he finished the last two slices. As he tossed aside his crumpled napkin, he pulled his phone from his pocket. "It's ten-thirty. When do you have to be home?"

"Midnight."

"Well . . ." His smile dazzled, the dimple on his cheek danced, and I held my breath. "I can take you home now, *or* I could take you to one of my favorite places."

~ ~ ~

"Montgomery Park." Preston pulled into the parking area and turned off the car. "Have you been here?"

"No, only driven by."

"Then I'll give you the grand tour." He laced our fingers together and led me through the ball diamonds, the picnic area, the gardens, and finally to the playground. "The teeter-totter was Connor's favorite. Me, I rocked the swings." He lifted our linked hands between us. "Wanna swing?"

"I'd love to." I sat and began moving gently back and forth.

He grabbed the swing beside me, backed up as far as he could and pushed off the ground. "Why do you think Connor liked the teeter-totter? Because I always dominated on the swings."

Soon he was swinging as high as the chain would go. He made a goofy face each time he swooshed by. Finally, he let his feet touch and slowed downed.

With a big step, he closed the gap between us and leaned his head against the chain. "Had a great time tonight. Hope you did too."

My head bobbed. "I did."

He moved in a bit closer. "Can I ask you out again?"

"You may. *You'd better.*" Where did *that* come from? But who was I kidding? I wanted him to. Really, *really* wanted him to.

"Well, okay." His gaze swept over my face for a long moment. As his eyes found mine again, he murmured, "You have the most amazing eyes." And then he was on his feet, hand outstretched to me. "Time to get you home."

He tucked me into the car, settled in himself, and then pulled my hand over to rest on his leg. And while he drove, he told cute little stories about him and Connor playing at the park as little guys.

I giggled as I walked up the sidewalk, envisioning him and Connor duking it out over the sandbox toys. And then we were at the front door. I bit down on my lip as a major case of jitters swooped in. The date had been perfect but what now? Would he expect me to kiss him?

He held my hands in his, stroking tiny circles on the back of each with his thumbs. He took a step closer. "Can I call you tomorrow?"

I blinked and hoarsely whispered, "Yes."

The dimple on his cheek danced with a flirty smile. "Good."

Did I want him to kiss me?

He brought our hands together with a long, lingering squeeze. "I'd better be goin'." Ever so slowly, he released my hands and shuffled back, his eyes never leaving my face.

"Bye . . ."

He winked above a dazzling smile and then he was gone.

Why couldn't this *have been my first real date?*

Preston

Immediately, thoughts about our next date consumed me. When? Where? How long did I have to wait to ask her out again?

I must have driven home on autopilot because I pulled into the driveway without remembering how I got there. My gaze swept over the space where Maggie had sat. Something purple was stuck in the crease of the seat. Her missing glove. A trace of her perfume lingered on the soft, fuzzy material.

Pumped to have a reason to text her, I grabbed my phone. "guess what? found your missing glove"

Within a minute my phone vibrated. "You found it? Great!! ☺"

"I could drop it by tomorrow if U want" I held my breath.

"That would be very nice. I work at the clinic until noon."

"I'll text before I come over"

~ ~ ~

The next afternoon, I strutted up her walk like a hero and held out the glove to my . . . What? Girlfriend? Man, I liked the sound of that.

Maggie rubbed the purple material between her fingers and peeked up at me through long, dark lashes. "If you're not in a hurry, maybe we can sit out here and talk?" The question in her eyes echoed in her voice as she pointed to the porch swing.

"Not in a hurry at all."

The conversation flowed easily about Psychology, English, football—you name it. When I laid my hand across hers, she lifted her fingers and mine fell into place. A perfect fit.

The living room curtains moved in the window. My cheek brushed against her hair when I whispered in her ear, "I think we're being watched." The curtains moved again.

She groaned. "Probably Michael."

"Wanting a ride somewhere?"

She rolled those big brown eyes. "I could *not* believe that even from him."

"If I'm keeping you from something—"

"I could be folding laundry or loading the dishwasher, but I'd much rather be here with you."

Exactly what I wanted to hear. The urge to kiss her grew stronger by the second. *Can this be considered our second date?* This slow approach was new territory for me.

A shiver rippled through her. Then another.

I pulled my hoodie off and offered it to her.

She said she didn't need it, but when I insisted, she pulled it over her head and adjusted her hair around the hood. The x-large sweatshirt swam on her small body. Her eyes and nose scrunched in that adorable expression that was fast becoming a favorite of mine.

I brushed a strand of hair from her cheek. "Looks good on you." That wasn't half of what I wanted to say to her. But it was too soon to say more, right?

I fished my vibrating phone from my pocket. Connor. "can we push it back to 7?"

I was supposed to hang out with him and Rob later. "absolutely" I answered with one hand. I slipped the phone back in my pocket. "Hanging out with some guys later."

"If you need to go . . . "

"Nah, not 'til seven."

Somehow, I ended up staying for dinner. In the past, I would have made any excuse to get out of such an arrangement, but not tonight. Maggie's mom was very welcoming. Her dad, a man of few words, was nice enough. Michael's basic concern seemed to be that I didn't eat too much.

As Michael chowed down on seconds, Maggie glanced at the clock. "Preston has to be going soon."

I nodded and stood. "Thanks for dinner."

She led me to the front door where I grasped both of her hands and moved in close. "I'm glad you dropped your glove in my car."

"Me too," she whispered, eyes wide, teeth pressed to her lower lip.

"Dinner was great, thanks." How long could I stall?

"You're welcome."

I stepped forward. "I'll call you later."

"Yes . . ."

"I'd better go."

"Have fun with the guys."

"I'll try." I released her hands.

"Thanks for bringing my glove back."

"You're welcome. See ya."

I hustled to meet the guys even though I really wanted to stay with Maggie.

"You're late," Rob growled. "Where've ya been?"

"With Maggie. Had dinner with her and the family."

He offered me a smug grin. "Knew it wouldn't take you long to get back in the game."

"Nothing about me dating Maggie is a *game*."

He shrugged. "Whatever."

I shifted the attention away from my resumed dating status. "What about you, Connor? You ever gonna ask Chelsea out?"

"Just did. Going to a movie tomorrow."

"'Bout time."

He grunted. "She was thrilled—like I knew she'd be. If it goes well, which it will, maybe we can double sometime."

"I think Maggie would like that. If it *goes well*."

He finally asked me out!" Chelsea's shriek pierced my ear.

"Connor?" I held the phone away in anticipation of more screeching.

"Who else? Going to a movie tomorrow afternoon."

"I'm so excited for you! What are you seeing?"

"Who cares? I'll be with Connor—the movie is the least of my concerns. I hope it won't be too cold to wear shorts."

"Showing off those long, tan legs, huh?" I shivered just thinking about wearing shorts in this weather.

"My legs are my best asset, so, yeah, I'll be wearing shorts unless it's below fifty degrees. So, did Preston do an awesome job of keeping you warm at the game last night?"

"I lost a glove, so he held my hand."

"I've always heard, uh . . . is he a good kisser?"

"He didn't kiss me."

"*Really.*"

"He found my missing glove in his car and brought it back today, and we sat for a couple of hours on the porch swing—"

"So, he kissed you today then?"

"No." I prepared for more screeching.

"That's basically two dates in two days, and *the* Preston Jacoby didn't kiss you?" Her voice approached that shrieking volume again—this time with surprise. "He didn't even *try* to kiss you?"

"Nope."

"Wow, I guess he has—" Pause. Pause. "Well, I mean . . ." A long sigh puffed through the phone.

"It's fine, really. We had a great time. And now I know for sure he's nothing like Logan who got all handsy and puffed beer breath in my face when I clearly did not want to be squished in a recliner with him. Oh, and he gave me this gorgeous red rose. Preston, I mean. He gave me a rose."

"I still can't believe he didn't kiss you." I could imagine her green eyes, crossed and rolling toward the ceiling, and her wobbling head, flinging blonde hair against her shoulders.

"Give it a rest, will you? There's more to being with guys than kissing."

"How would you know?" She mumbled. "Well, if Connor doesn't kiss me tomorrow . . ."

I tuned out her detailed date-with-Connor expectations.

If he had tried to kiss me today, I would have let him. Not that I was ready to admit it to Chelsea, but yeah.

I zoned back in as her voice notched up again. ". . . and stop that ridiculous chewing on your lip thing. When he finally does kiss you, the last thing you want is ragged lips."

Preston

onday morning Connor immediately pronounced his date with Chelsea a success. "She's one hot babe, an awesome kisser, and—"

I held up my hand. "More than I need to know."

"What about you and Maggie?"

"Had a great time." He'd never believe I hadn't kissed her.

"Bet it's great to be hangin' out with girls again. You know what they say about the shy ones." He shot me a suggestive look.

"It's not like that."

He cocked his head to the side. "Not yet, maybe, but who can resist you?"

I raked a hand through my hair. "That's not what I want anymore." Why did he not get that?

"Chelsea said Maggie likes you a lot. Man, I gotta go. Chels is waiting on me." He sprinted through the door.

~ ~ ~

"Is it me, or are we getting an extraordinary amount of attention?" Maggie's gaze scanned the cafeteria. "You'd think it was the Maggie and Preston Show."

Heads had turned all morning as I'd walked her to each class. And now, while eating lunch together for the first time, the gossipy whispering was both obvious and annoying. The doubts I'd managed to sideline over the weekend had come back in full force to haunt me.

Now to keep the worry from seeping into my voice. "Did someone say something?"

"No, but I can't figure out what the fascination is."

My heart thrashed against my ribs. What should I say? I chugged half my Gatorade.

She turned around to find another group of girls gawking at us. "What in the world . . ."

I had to say something. "Well, I haven't dated in a while."

"Not since Caroline?" Maggie's eyes peered into mine, all innocent like.

My mouth went dry. "Actually, Caroline and I went out a long time ago."

"By the scathing looks she sends my way—"

"Really?" I shook my head, anger surging through me. Why couldn't Caroline just drop it? "Sorry about that, but hey, don't let her bother you, 'k?"

She shrugged. "Oh, yeah, Chelsea said you dated her freshman year. You were seeing someone named Alyssa last year."

The cheeseburger in my mouth refused to be swallowed. I snatched up my Gatorade and tried to wash down the stubborn hunk of sandwich. Whatever Chelsea knew, she hadn't told Maggie much—definitely not the whole story. Because Maggie was far too calm.

I stretched my hand across the table and brushed my fingers across the back of her hand. "I've been waiting for just the right person."

Her head tipped to the side. "Ah, you're sweet."

I gripped her hand, willing my racing heart to slow. Sporting my most irresistible smile, I leaned close. "We're a *remarkably* good-looking couple. I'm sure that's what all the attention is about."

She smiled and scrunched her nose in that cute way. Obviously, she knew nothing more than Alyssa's name.

Relief trickled through me, slowing my pulse. Time to change the subject for sure.

"So, I wondered what you want to do this weekend." I'd have made plans for us every evening if I wasn't scheduled for extra shifts this week.

"My family has plans Saturday night, but I'm free on Friday."

My pulse hiked up for a totally different reason. Not that I thought she's said say no. But still. "Me too. You have to meet my parents or they may disown me, but otherwise, what do ya think?"

She leaned toward me across the table. "Surprise me. I *love* surprises."

Maggie

I groaned at the morning announcements' strong reminder about the Tuesday NHS lunch meeting. "Member participation *is* required," noted Mr. Parker, the principal, rubbing in the fact that I would not be enjoying a second-day-in-a-row lunch with Preston. I'd never been so tempted to skip anything school related in my life.

Loud students, stuffing their faces with a variety of foods, packed into Mr. Martin's normally roomy classroom. I squeezed into a corner where I hoped to sulk unnoticed, clutching my brown-bag lunch and scanning the room for Caroline. I'd panicked all morning, wondering if she was part of the half that hadn't showed up for the first meeting. It didn't appear so. Thank goodness.

Mr. Martin whistled and waved his arm. "Much better showing today. Tyler," he pointed at Tyler Collins and thrust a clipboard toward him. "Take attendance, please."

"If you're here, say 'present'." Tyler cupped his hand to his ear and was rewarded with a loud chorus of responses. "I'd say everyone's here."

Mr. Martin shook his head. "Not how it works, Mr. Collins. Participation is required so attendance will be taken at each meeting. The clipboard will be passed around so many of you will have the privilege."

Chatter resumed as Tyler scanned the room.

"Our time is short," Mr. Martin's voice rose above the chaos. "So zip it, and let's get to voting. By a show of hands, vote for one of the following: our own school library, the student-to-student tutoring program, or The Least of These Clinic—all worthy causes, I might add."

After a quick tallying of the raised hands, Mr. Martin slashed his hand across his throat. "You're a chatty bunch, aren't you?" He tapped his foot until the talking ceased. "I'm more than pleased to announce The Least of These Clinic will be the NHS focus project this year."

As if on cue, heads turned my way. So much for hiding in the corner. I wanted to crawl under the carpet as heat crept up my cheeks.

"So, what will it be?" Mr. Martin folded his arms. "A fundraiser, an awareness campaign, volunteering our time?"

"Fundraiser," declared at least a dozen members.

"Yeah, fundraiser. What else?" Tyler piped up.

Heads nodded around the room, and a plan quickly fell into place. Donation canisters would be placed at the registers in each lunch line, at the sports concession stands and ticket booths, and in the office. A couple of artsy types volunteered to design labels, and groups were assigned to place the canisters by Monday and monitor them until the next meeting.

"Come back in two weeks with feedback." The bell rang, and Mr. Martin waved in dismissal.

Preston

Things were going so well between me and Maggie. But the constant threat of someone sharing with her the rather sordid details about my past never let up. Would she understand that regrettable things sometimes just happened? If she was as innocent as I suspected, that seemed a long shot.

And then there was Caroline who appeared out of nowhere multiple times every day. Dodging her had become a major chore. So far, she'd only shot death glares at Maggie, but what if she tried to talk to her?

Seemed my options were simple. I could let the whole past thing eat at me night and day. Or I could stop obsessing and just enjoy being with Maggie. I didn't have to give those two options more than a second's thought.

After school, Maggie's arm pressed against mine, all familiar like, on the way to the parking lot. "So, about tomorrow night. I need some information."

"Surprise, remember?"

"Yes, but how about a time? And what do I wear?"

"Oh, sorry. How about six? And wear whatever you like."

She frowned. "Casual, dressy, sporty, going to get really dirty—"

I snickered. "I'd say casual will be fine. We won't be getting *really dirty*."

She jabbed me with her elbow.

"Ow . . . *man.*" I rubbed my ribs.

Her eyes became round as saucers, and her teeth pressed into her lip.

I pulled our linked hands behind my back which pressed her body against mine. Our eyes locked in a smoldering gaze. I couldn't move, talk, or breathe.

"Are you okay?" Her breath tickled my jaw.

In a second, my other arm wound around her waist. "You have a wicked jab, but I'll live."

A sweet grin replaced the worried frown. "Remember that, buddy."

Maggie

"This fettuccine alfredo is amazing. If I worked at Guido's—
I'd weigh a ton." I twirled a long noodle around my fork as
Preston cut into his lasagna.

"I doubt that."

"No, seriously, it would be a problem." The soft glow of
candlelight cast shadows across the deep red walls. "This place
is so warm and cozy. Do you like working here?"

"It's a decent job. And I love the food, especially the lasagna.
The sausage-veal meatballs are the best." He cut a meatball in
half, grabbed my fork, speared one half, and handed the fork
back to me.

"Mmm, that is good."

He put two meatballs on my plate. "I got a double order so
we could share."

"Ah, there you go again, being all sweet."

Preston rolled his eyes, but his dimple danced at the
compliment.

The smiling waitress, her gray-streaked hair pulled into a
loose bun, sauntered toward us, then leaned casually against
our table. "So, Preston, did you two save room for dessert?"

"Maggie?"

"Oh, no. I'm too full, but thank you."

"Me, too." He patted his stomach.

"Okay, then here you go, honey." She slid the bill across the
table to him.

"Thanks, Becky."

"So, what's the next surprise?"

"What? I'm taking you home now. The date's over." His lips twitched with the effort not to smile.

"Oh, good. I was hoping to go to bed early tonight."

His head jerked back, and his eyes narrowed.

"'The date's over.'" I did a bad job of mimicking his deep voice.

His dimple dancing again, he hopped up and grabbed my coat. "I thought we might enjoy a stroll through the park."

~ ~ ~

"Here, so you won't get cold." Preston handed me a sweatshirt from the back seat.

I snuggled into the soft fabric of his Madison High black hoodie that smelled exactly like he did—a hard to describe, completely masculine, totally amazing scent.

His hand skimmed along my back until his arm slipped loosely around my waist. "You warm enough?"

"Mm hmm."

"Let me know if you get cold, 'k?"

I nodded as he tucked me a smidge closer to his side.

Crickets chirped as we strolled through the empty park, slower this time, not so much a tour as a romantic walk. "Wanna sit?" He pointed to a cute little bench under a huge tree surrounded by beautiful fall flowers.

"Sure. These flowers are gorgeous."

Fingertips brushed along my back as we settled on the bench. "You're still warm enough?"

"I'm good." I'd never been better.

"Hey, I was serious about my parents disowning me if I don't introduce you tonight." He tipped his head to the side. "I need to warn you—my mom's kind a gushy."

"Oh?"

"She gets excited about the littlest things and goes on and on. Not that meeting you is a little thing. It's just that she goes overboard about stuff—" He sighed and grinned. "I can't explain it. Just expect lots of excitement, multiple hugs, and general gushing."

"Consider me warned."

His gorgeous blue eyes swept over my face as he lifted his arm to circle my shoulders. The warmth from his hand on my upper arm seeped through every layer of fabric to my skin.

Now would be the perfect time to kiss me. I'd thought about little else all day. *Would* he kiss me? What would it be like? Would I do it right?

His gaze flitted between my eyes and my mouth. His warm fingers brushed a path across my cheek, along my jaw, and then slipped under my chin. "I've been dying to kiss you." His hushed voice sent tingles racing through me. "May I kiss you?"

Maggie

Confident no sound would come out if I tried to answer, I simply nodded.

Our lips came together softly once . . . then again. His arm drew me closer. Our lips met a third time with less hesitation in a much longer kiss. Then another.

A hundred times better than I ever dreamed. A thousand times better than being kissed by Logan.

He eased his mouth from mine, then grazed my temple with a soft kiss. He pressed his cheek to my forehead.

I relaxed into his chest, soaking up his warmth, breathing in his scent. The thumping of his heart near mine, his breath whispering in my hair, his warmth and strength surrounding me. Was it finally my turn? To be in an amazing relationship with an amazing guy?

He leaned back enough to peer into my eyes with such intensity I couldn't have looked away if I'd wanted to. He caught my chin, and his gaze flitted to my mouth. "May I . . ."

"Yes—kiss me."

A huge smile broke across his face for just a second before his lips found mine for a long, deep kiss that I felt all the way to my toes.

He trailed kisses across my cheek then whispered in my ear, "Better get you home to meet Mom and Dad before my phone starts blowin' up. You ready to go?"

Absolutely not, but . . . "Sure."

Preston

"Mom, Dad, this is Maggie. Maggie, these are my parents, Drew and Jacki."

Mom sprang from her spot on the family room couch like a cat after a mouse. "Oh, Maggie, it's so good to finally meet you!" She grabbed the hand I wasn't holding and pulled Maggie close for a hug. I loosened my grasp but didn't let go so I could rescue her if necessary. "We missed you the night you two worked on that project. And I told Preston he had better not come home tonight unless he brought you to meet us."

"Nice to meet you, Maggie." Dad nudged Mom's side. "Let her go, Jacki." He shook his head and tugged on Mom's arm. "We're watching a movie. You're welcome to join us."

I pulled a pink-cheeked Maggie toward me and away from Mom. "Thanks, but I have a surprise for Maggie. I'll be right back." Dropping her hand, I motioned Mom to the kitchen.

We returned a minute later, Mom tiptoeing and giggling like a five-year-old, me hiding a box of chocolates behind my back. I cupped Maggie's elbow and guided her to the formal living room and the best couch in the house. I placed the gold foil box on her lap.

"Hmm, chocolates. Expensive, fancy chocolates. Yum."

"I can't take all the credit. Grandma brought it over, and Mom put it aside for a special occasion."

Maggie flicked off the lid revealing rows of varying shapes, sizes, and shades of chocolate. "These look so good." She flipped the lid over. "Where's the guide showing what each chocolate is?"

"I guess it doesn't have one."

"One time, Michael cut each chocolate in half so he could find the ones he liked, and more importantly, to make sure he didn't bite into a coconut one. We all hate coconut." She wrinkled up her nose. "Mom had a cow, told him to take his chances and leave the chocolates *whole* the next time."

"We hate coconut, too. Yuck. What are your favorites?"

"I like truffles the most. Then it's pretty close between raspberry cream and chocolate butter cream. Of course, maple nut cream is really good, too, and so is chocolate whip. Actually, I like everything except coconut. What about you?"

"Wow, you know your chocolates. My favorite is strawberry, then probably caramel, I guess." I nodded toward the box. "Ladies first."

She chose a dark chocolate oval and took a tiny bite. "Pretty sure it's strawberry." A cute smirk pulled at her full lips. "If you're not afraid of my germs . . ."

"I'm not afraid."

She held the chocolate about two inches from my face.

I opened my mouth, and she popped it in. "Yep, strawberry."

She insisted I go next, so I grabbed at random and also took a tiny bite. "Truffle if I'm not mistaken." I waved the chocolate in front of her. "If *you're* not afraid of *my* germs."

She offered me an especially flirty smile and opened her mouth.

I pushed the chocolate between her parted lips.

"These are awesome."

My gaze locked on her mouth as she slowly chewed the truffle.

". . . said caramel, right?" She flipped a section of hair behind her ear and leaned over the box of chocolates.

"What? Oh, yeah, caramel." I couldn't take my eyes off her.

Her lips pressed together as she tried to determine the flavor of the square chocolate she'd chosen.

"Here you go, Mr. Jacoby. Caramel."

I grasped her hand and guided the candy to my mouth. Electricity zinged through me when her fingertips brushed my lips.

Still gripping her hand, I cleared my throat. "Raspberry cream, right?" Tearing my gaze from her, I studied the chocolates. A medium sized chocolate textured like a berry with a stem on top sat in the corner of the box. I snatched it up.

"That was too obvious."

"Says who?" A quick nibble confirmed the flavor. I touched the chocolate to her mouth.

Her lips parted, and the chocolate eased in.

A jolt of desire raced through me. *Easy there . . .* I slid the lid on the box. "Why don't you take the rest home."

"Grandma will be happy her chocolates proved to be so entertaining." Mom stood in the doorway, barely holding in all that gush from earlier. "It's so nice to finally meet you, Maggie. I do hope we'll be seeing a lot more of you."

Dad's hands on her shoulders directed her from the doorway. 'Night, you two." Their murmured conversation floated down the hall.

I pressed my palm to my forehead and shook my head. "Sorry about that."

"You don't want them to see a lot more of me?"

My head snapped up. "That's fine. As long as *I* get to see a lot more of you."

~ ~ ~

Maggie hunched inside her coat as we strolled up her sidewalk. We stepped into the warm house where a single lamp barely illuminated the living room. The porch light streaming through the big picture window added to the romantic vibe. As good a setup as if I'd planned it.

She peeked up at me through long, dark lashes. "You didn't have to ask. You could have kissed me anytime."

"Anytime, huh?" I pulled her close, slipping my arm snug around her waist. "Like maybe now?"

"Now would be perfect."

I cupped the curve of her face.

She wrapped her arms around my neck.

We kissed until she whispered against my cheek, "What time is it?" She stretched and leaned around me to switch off the porch light. "That lets my parents know I'm home."

I nodded, losing myself in being so close to her, breathing in her familiar scent.

She snuggled against my chest. "I love how warm you always are."

She'd never be cold again if I had anything to say about it. I tightened my other arm around her. "My parents loved you, in case you couldn't tell."

"And now you won't get disowned." She tipped her head back to look at me. "They're very sweet. You look a lot like your dad."

"Least I still have more hair than him." Heat rippled through me as her fingertips stroked the back of my head. I pressed a kiss to her forehead. "I should probably go." Even though it was the last thing I wanted to do. As if in protest, my arms hugged her a little closer.

She dipped her head against my shoulder. Guess she didn't want me to leave.

And I thought it was hard to say good-bye before I kissed her. Finally, I lifted her chin for one last kiss. "Call ya later. Maybe when I get home?"

"You better."

"Yes, ma'am." I separated myself from her but gripped her hand until I inched out the door.

I took the long way home, reviewing every minute of our time together.

Am I reading this right, God? We're supposed to be together?

I could swear I heard an answer.

As long as you do it my way.

Maggie

Chelsea knew what she was talking about all right. High school was so-o-o much better with a boyfriend. After the "Logan incident," when I worried that all the guys at Madison were like him, I thought I'd never find a decent guy. But they weren't all like Logan, and Preston was far more than just decent. As different from Logan as humanly possible and amazing in every way.

I couldn't imagine a more perfect guy or a more awesome relationship.

That had to be why I hadn't initiated the *virgin speech*, as Chelsea so bluntly referred to my plan, to go on record about saving sex for marriage. Or maybe it was her eyes-rolling-wildly every time I mentioned it. Was I making too big of a deal about it? Was it necessary to actually bring it up at all?

Preston had been nothing but extremely gentlemanlike. Sometimes he still asked before kissing me. Which was totally unnecessary. I loved being kissed by him.

The talk could wait awhile. If it needed to happen at all.

~ ~ ~

As I walked alone to Accounting on Monday morning, a tall blonde fell into step beside me.

I glanced her way and smiled. Her cool, ice-blue eyes narrowed. "FYI, Maggie. Preston's a player. He seems pretty into you now, but it won't last. Trust me." She squared her shoulders, tossed her shoulder-length curls, and marched down the hall.

Heat prickled up the back of my neck. What was she talking about? And who was *she* to *him*?

Chelsea could fill me in on Preston's past, if I wanted to know. So far, I'd ignored the urge to ask her, even though a couple of times her comments had sparked some concern. A sort of uneasiness. Things that reminded me of Cindy's comments the first day of school, about him having dated half the girls in the class. A gross exaggeration, surely.

But I wasn't an idiot. Of course, he'd dated before me. Caroline and Alyssa. This blonde, whoever she was, and maybe others. But so what? Nothing he'd ever done or said around me could even remotely be considered player-like.

This girl probably wanted him back, like Caroline wanted him back. Did I really want to know how many *other* girls wanted him back? Nope. There was no way a few unhappy ex-girlfriends were going to get in the way of this amazing relationship.

~ ~ ~

Apparently, *America's Got Talent* had become a family affair at Preston's house, and I was thrilled when he invited me to watch with them.

He squeezed my hand as he led me to the family room. "I need to warn you. This couch gives new meaning to the words *settle in*." We sat and sank in pretty far. "See what I mean? A spring or somethin' broke a while back, and Mom's been hinting like crazy for a new one."

The further we sank into the huge dent, the more I leaned into him. "Am I squishing you?" I tried to adjust myself out of the bottomless hole.

"I'm good, really." His hand slid down my arm until his fingers fell between mine. The silvery shimmers in his blue eyes pulled me in.

I reminded myself to breathe.

Jacki scurried in from the kitchen, balancing three huge bowls of popcorn. One for us, one for Patrick and his girlfriend Emily, and one for her and Drew.

"I'm so excited!" Her shoulders bounced as she settled beside Drew.

Preston and Patrick exchanged wide-eyed, heading-shaking looks with their dad. "She really gets into this," Preston murmured into my hair.

"I can see that," I whispered back.

"You haven't seen anything yet." His mouth moved against my hair which caught on the stubble along his jaw.

"Oh, Maggie's brownies. How could I forget?" Jacki hurried back to the kitchen, returned with the brownies and napkins, and put them on the coffee table. "These look absolutely scrumptious."

"They are." Preston winked and helped himself to two large pieces while I took a small corner piece.

"Dude, save some for the rest of us." Patrick grabbed the pan, and Emily scooped out two pieces. "One more," he murmured, thrusting the pan toward her.

She swatted his arm, then handed the pan to Drew who muttered, "About time."

A hush fell over the room as the first contestant's performance began. But not for long.

Jacki's enthusiasm jeopardized their bowl of popcorn more than once before Drew grabbed it and placed it on the floor. But she wasn't the only enthusiast. Nor was she the loudest. Preston and Patrick hooted and cheered like they were at a football game.

Jacki detailed exactly what she did and didn't like about each performance. Emily contributed to the discussion but in a quieter, less rowdy way than either the guys or Jacki. Drew did a lot of nodding, rolled his eyes a few times, and helped himself to the last brownie.

"Get the recipe for these," he said to Jacki, then pointed to me. "These are great, Maggie."

Preston's lips touched my hair again as he whispered, "Brownies are his favorite."

"I'll remember that," I whispered back.

Snuggled warmly against him, watching TV with his family, should have kept the blonde's ridiculous accusation from circling through my mind. But the *player* comment nagged at me even though spending time at home with his parents was the opposite of player behavior. I'd asked around—her name was Nikki—but that's all I'd discovered.

When the show was over, Patrick hopped up and pulled Emily to her feet. "Until tomorrow night, guys." They grabbed their coats and headed out.

"Bye, Emily." Jacki waved, then pressed her hand over a yawn. "That show exhausts me."

"It's not the show. It's your extreme level of excitement, my dear," Drew replied dryly.

She patted his leg then stood and moved toward us. "So nice to have you join us, Maggie. Hope you'll be back tomorrow night. We usually DVR it on Wednesday and watch after church."

"Good night, guys." With a hand on her lower back, Drew nudged Jacki into the kitchen before she could hug me again. A few minutes later they headed to bed.

"Tomorrow, I'll swing by church and pick you up after I get off work, if you can stand two nights in a row of the Jacobys."

"I think I'll manage." I wouldn't have missed it for the world. "So, how long have Patrick and Emily been dating?"

Preston shrugged. "A while, like six months, maybe more."

"She's nice."

"Yeah, she's great." He slipped his arm around my shoulders, easing me closer as his fingers inched into my hair.

"You don't need to ask."

That hot little dimple danced across his cheek. "Oh yeah?"

I relaxed against him, anxious for the feel of his lips on mine. Each kiss longer than the one before until I could barely catch my breath. He pulled away a little and expelled a long sigh. With a final squeeze of my shoulders, he loosened his embrace. "Time to take you home, Miss."

My lips tingled, and my insides trembled. He stood, then pulled me to my feet.

"Stupid couch." He pointed to the huge, very slowly-recovering dent and shook his head. "We get the loveseat tomorrow night. Let Pat and Em sit on this old thing."

"I didn't mind . . ."

He pulled me close for one last kiss. "Me either."

Maggie

"At this rate, we'll raise enough money by Christmas to buy the clinic a snow shovel. A cheap, flimsy one." Mr. Martin held the past two week's donations for The Least of These Clinic in his open palms. Ten quarters, three dimes, six nickels, and one penny. Three dollars and eleven cents.

"No one knows anything about this place, so why would they donate money?" Tyler asked.

Mr. Martin fisted the money and raised his arms in the touchdown motion. "Score. Mr. Collins is right. This project suffers from a lack of awareness. The canisters are great but not very effective if the clinic itself is an unknown. So, how do we generate awareness?"

All forty NHS members stared at me. Attendance had improved. Enthusiasm not so much, as evidenced by several zoned-out or half-asleep students and a couple in the back immersed in their homework.

Mr. Martin extended his hand to me in a waving motion. "Maggie? What can you tell us about The Least of These Clinic?"

Would I ever feel comfortable with this group? I swallowed and focused only on him. "Well, the clinic provides medical care to people with little or no insurance. Grants supply most of the money to operate the clinic, but I guess they run short a lot. The client load is huge. The staff is small and overworked." I shrugged. "That's about it."

Soon ideas buzzed around the room, pulling in even those buried in their homework.

"We need posters. Lots of them."

"Let's use spotlights in the morning announcements."

"And more canisters!"

An awareness campaign that included those ideas as well as the use of the bulletin boards near the cafeteria and gym along with the school's Facebook page came together in the next twenty minutes. Each canister group would be in charge of one campaign aspect.

"Now that's what I'm talking about. Keep monitoring the canisters and get with your group on your own time. Let's have an extra meeting next week to get this thing launched." Mr. Martin bumped fists with those closest to him. He caught my eye and gave me two thumbs-up.

I forced a smile. He obviously loved the idea of the clinic as the NHS focus project, but I'd voted for the student-to-student tutoring program. My parents talked of little else at home. Our church had adopted a couple of the clinic's regular families and made a huge show of support for my parents and the other staff. School was my only escape from all things clinic-related. At least it used to be.

Preston

"Mmm . . . you smell good." I leaned into Maggie's hair and closed my eyes. *America's Got Talent* wasn't holding my interest tonight. I buried my face in the soft waves of her hair. Applause erupted from the TV.

"Ooh, that was a great performance. I hope she wins."

I peered at the screen, only vaguely interested. "Me, too," I murmured with a wink.

"So where is everyone?" A very soft, warm Maggie relaxed against me with a sigh.

Oh, man. "Uh . . . no idea." Strands of her hair snagged in the stubble along my jaw. Pulling the soft waves back, I kissed her neck.

She rested her head against mine.

I heard little of the next song. Curving my hand around her chin, I turned her face toward me and wove my fingers through her hair. And then I pulled her mouth to mine.

She practically melted into me.

My breathing hitched up as one kiss led to another.

"Hey," Maggie whispered against my cheek, "I thought we were watching *America's Got Talent.*"

"We'll find out the results later." I claimed her mouth again.

She didn't resist.

I stroked the length of her back.

Her fingertips ran through my hair and caressed my neck.

The door from the kitchen to the garage slammed hard and loud.

Maggie jumped.

"'Prob'ly just Patrick," I mumbled. *Lousy timing, bro.*

She rested her hand on my chest. "Your heart's beating really fast."

"I know." I covered her hand with mine.

Patrick rushed through the doorway. He pointed to the credits rolling across the TV screen. "Who got voted off?"

"No clue." I brushed the side of Maggie's face with my nose. *Move along, Patrick.*

"Weren't you watching?" His eyebrows pulled together as his eyes darted between us. He pushed out a breathy sigh. "Guess not. Well, don't delete the recording." He tossed his wadded-up McDonald's sack at us, then stalked down the hall, muttering.

I pressed my mouth against her hair and closed my eyes.

She stroked my stubbly cheek. Her finger lingered near my dimple.

I grabbed her fingers and pressed them against my mouth. Was almost time to take her home, but neither of us moved to get up.

"Is it about time to go?" She murmured.

"Unfortunately, yeah." I forced myself to put some space between us.

She widened the gap and hopped up. But then she wobbled back toward the couch.

"Whoa." I grabbed her arm. "You okay?"

"Being with you makes me dizzy, Mr. Jacoby."

I pulled her close for one last kiss. *You have no idea.*

~ ~ ~

I tossed my keys on the kitchen counter and grabbed a Mountain Dew. "So, who got voted off?"

Patrick glared at me from the recliner. "Get online. You'll know in like two seconds."

I tossed a pillow at him.

He batted it back at me. "You and Maggie were awfully cozy."

"Just a little kissing. So, where are Mom and Dad anyway?"

"No idea." He cleared his throat, and I glanced at him. "I see the way you look at her. Dude, I see the way you kiss her. Be careful."

"I am being careful."

His smirk expressed heavy doubt. "Does she know about Alyssa or—"

"She doesn't need to know any of that." My defensive tone snapped like a broken rubber band.

"If this is getting serious, she deserves—"

"Would you just drop it?"

"*People talk,* Preston. Just sayin'. It would be better if she heard it from you."

~ ~ ~

I jammed a pillow under my head and stared at the lamp's eerie shadow on my bedroom ceiling. Maggie knew I'd dated before I met her. So what? No need to drag her though the muddy waters of my past. Things were good between us, and we *were* being careful.

I grazed my bottom lip with my knuckle. It still tingled from all the amazing kissing.

A knot formed in my stomach. Maybe a discussion about my past wasn't necessary, but what about making sure we were on the same page about *not* having sex. Did that need to happen?

Nah. There was no way her agenda included sex.

Maggie

"H"ey, Chels, wait up." I caught up with her at the end of the lunch line.

While Preston and Connor finished the guys' only part of the latest psychology project, us girls had to lunch on our own

"You busy Friday night?"

"I might have plans with Connor, why?"

"I need someone to keep me company while my parents and Michael are out of town overnight."

"And when Preston comes over, I'll disappear. You won't even know I'm there."

"Nothing like that—"

"Parents will be out of town." Chelsea quirked her perfectly shaped eyebrows. "And you're not planning a romantic night with your hot boyfriend?"

"He's going to a movie with the guys."

She dropped a cup of butterscotch pudding on her tray and frowned. "Oh, yeah, Connor's going, too." She shrugged, and the frown disappeared. "Preston can come over *after* the movie. Connor too."

"No guys. Come on. We'll watch a couple of chic flicks—you know how the guys hate those. And we won't get left with scraps after they wolf down all the snacks."

We paid for our lunches and slid into seats at the table closest to the line.

Chelsea shook her juice, then popped it open. "Didn't you even consider having Preston over? Being alone all night together . . . " A long moan-like sigh passed through her lips. "I'd love to spend the night with Connor."

"You guys aren't—"

She rolled her eyes. "We're not having sex—if it's any of your business. But sleeping pressed against Connor's warm, hard body . . . now *that* would be amazing." By the far-away look in her eyes, she'd already gone to places I didn't want to think about.

"Chelsea." I snapped my fingers.

Her lips pushed into a pout. "Sure you won't reconsider?"

I shook my head to chase away the sudden picture of Preston lounging in my bed. "I considered for like a second having Preston come over—not spend the night, of course—but just to hang out. Would you really spend the night with Connor?"

All wide-eyed and serious, she nodded very convincingly. "It would be amazingly romantic and—"

"A terrible idea for someone who's serious about waiting."

She shrugged and tore into her Hostess cupcake. "I'm keeping my options open."

"What?" The hand clenching my juice froze in mid-air. "That's the most ridiculous thing I've ever heard."

She stared at me with a blank expression.

"Well?" The five-minute bell rang.

She blinked and her happy, carefree expression returned. "No guys, fine. Romantic chic flicks and lots of chocolate."

~ ~ ~

I dumped the money from the office's collection canister for The Least of These into an envelope and dashed to the NHS lunch meeting. I was less than thrilled to miss lunch with

Preston for a second day in a row, but I knew I'd be in deep trouble with Mr. Martin if I ditched today's meeting.

"Maggie Jennison, check." A smiling Tyler, clipboard in hand, took attendance as we filed in. "Brittany Welles, check."

I handed my envelope to Mr. Martin who pointed to John and Gabe—I couldn't keep their last names straight—but they were seniors, and Alex Moore, a junior—one of Preston's friends—huddled around a desk, sorting change and bills.

"Dude, we have actual dollar bills this time." John grabbed my envelope and dumped the contents. He swiped the change toward Alex and latched on to the bills.

"You'd think it was his." Brittany rolled her eyes as she dropped her handful of money on the desk.

"I was thinking the same thing." I picked up my envelope for the next time and followed her to a corner seat. Even though I knew everyone's first name and felt a little more comfortable, I stayed pretty close to Brittany. I liked the whole she's-going-out-with-Preston's-friend-Zach connection. And she was Chelsea's friend too.

"Nineteen dollars and twenty-six cents," Gabe announced. "Plus the three bucks from last time—"

"Three dollars and eleven cents," Tyler corrected.

"My bad." Gabe scooped the money into a pile. "That makes twenty-two thirty-seven."

"I love how you NHS types can add." Mr. Martin held open a vinyl, zippered bag. "The three eleven is already in here. We'll add to this every week and keep it locked up in the office. From now on, we meet every week. Let's review the awareness campaign. Seems we're on the right track."

Preston

On Friday I swung by Connor's to pick him up for the guys' night out. "You know what we're seein'?"

"Some comedy." He grunted. "Better be good—I'm giving up being with Chelsea."

"You'll survive." I'd had the same thought earlier, about Maggie.

We met up with Zach, Brett and Rob Pruitt, and Alex at the theater. Loaded down with popcorn, candy, and soft drinks, we settled into the top row of seats as the previews started.

The movie *was* funny, really hilarious. We busted up over and over, but then they were in bed—the main character and his girlfriend of like two weeks. Soon laughter roared through the crowd again. But the next bedroom scene was much longer and left nothing to the imagination.

Images of me and Maggie, exploring each other like that, raced through my mind. I grabbed my empty cup and headed for the concession stand.

With the refilled pop in my hand, I leaned against the wall. Already a continuous loop of images—the kind I so did not need—played through my head. How many more bedroom scenes would flash across the screen in the second half of the movie?

My phone vibrated in my pocket.

A text from Zach. "what up?"

Then one from Connor. "where r u?"

Pretty sure I can take care of myself, guys.

I returned to my seat but couldn't get back into the movie. During the next few sex scenes, I fiddled with the lid on my drink to distract myself. When the movie finally ended, I hopped up and stretched. No one mentioned my disappearing act as plans came together to meet at Pizza Hut.

Connor's eyes flitted my way on the drive across town. "It doesn't take fifteen minutes to refill your pop. Even if you hit the john, too."

I focused on the road. "I didn't need to see them . . . that couple in bed."

"Not like you haven't seen it before." He paused. "Not like you haven't done it."

I gripped the steering wheel, white-knuckled. "I don't need you or some stupid movie to remind me of that."

Connor shoved his hands into his sweatshirt pockets and stared out his window.

Air hissed from my mouth. "When I'm with Maggie, that's not the kind of stuff I want parading through my mind."

"So, it's different with her, huh?"

"She's not into that kind of thing, no. And the stuff I used to be all about? That's not what I want anymore."

"Like making out with all those girls—"

"When we were young and stupid," I finished dryly.

"What, now you're old and wise? I was gonna say on Friday nights."

"Huh. Did we think we were cool."

It all began in ninth grade, after football games, but then continued all year. Find out whose parents would be gone, grab some chips or whatever, some music, and hope a good ratio of girls to guys showed up for the pairing off. The idea caught on like crazy. Sometimes, the hangout had to be moved to Saturday night, but we still called it "Friday nights" and almost never cancelled. I hadn't been to one for months. Since last Memorial Day weekend.

"I for one still am cool." Connor grunted like an ape.

I couldn't help but chuckle.

Inside the restaurant, the pizza was good, the conversations loud, but the discussion with Connor replayed in my mind. The party wound down, and we headed out.

After another block or two of silence, Connor cracked his knuckles. "Just so we're clear. Those girls—it's not like they weren't willing. I never forced anyone to do anything." Defensiveness pulsed in his tone.

Memories assaulted my brain. "Yeah . . . talk about willing."

"What?"

"Nothin'."

Caroline, my girlfriend when the hangouts started, was forever unbuttoning her shirt or her jeans, pushing our physical involvement past anything I'd ever done.

"This new attitude about girls and dating and staying away from bedroom scenes—it all has to do with this religious kick you're on, right? His shoulders raised in an exaggerated shrug. "Personally, I thought you'd be over that by now."

"This isn't about being religious. It's about realizing what I want my life to be about." I stopped in front of his house and cut the engine.

"You always went to church, but you were no different than the rest of us. So now you're better than all of us?"

"Nope. Just trying not to mess up again."

"You mean sleeping with Alyssa. You didn't always think it was a mistake."

I dropped my head back against the seat. "Well, it was. A huge mistake—one I don't plan to make again. And one I don't want you and Chelsea to make either."

He snorted. "Your concern has been noted."

"Sex really messed with our relationship—"

"Would you stop it, already? My sex life is none of your business."

"You better not *have* a sex life."

"Dude, enough. You just worry about yourself. Anyway, you and Maggie seem aw·ful·ly cozy lately."

Maggie. The reason I walked out of the theater. I swung my head back and forth across the headrest. "Nothing more than kissing. I'm not going down that road again. I worried night and day that we'd get caught or Alyssa would get pregnant. Not worth it." And Maggie deserved better. I leaned across the steering wheel. "Save yourself a ton of grief."

Connor shrugged. He stretched his arms above his head and popped his neck. His normal expression of cocky confidence returned. "How 'bout we stop by Maggie's so we can say goodnight to the girls?" He held up his hands. "A couple of good·night kisses—that's it. I promise."

"No hidden agenda?"

He slapped his chest with a loud thwack. "I swear."

"Why not?" I started the car and backed onto the street. "Maggie loves surprises." Knowing Connor, I doubted his good·night to Chelsea would consist of a couple of kisses. But seeing Maggie would be great.

After coasting into her driveway with my lights off, I texted her. "how 'bout a surprise?"

Before she could reply, Connor sprinted up the steps ahead of me and rang the doorbell.

"No agenda remember?"

"Dude, stop worrying."

The front door opened about three inches. Two sets of eyes peered through the small space, one above the other.

I opened the screen door so they could see us.

"Preston." Maggie pushed the door open a little more, her face beaming.

"Connor!" Chelsea squealed really loud. The door sprang open, and she flew into his waiting arms.

I rubbed my ringing ear and moved toward Maggie. "Just here to say good night."

"What a nice surprise."

I kissed the top of her head.

Connor backed Chelsea against the porch railing and folded her in his arms, intense making out already underway.

I shook my head and led Maggie inside.

"How was the movie?" She glanced through the screen door at the lovebirds.

"It was okay." I pulled her close, wrapping my arms loosely around her waist. "Hope we're not interfering with your plans."

"Are you kidding? Saying goodnight in person is way better than a text."

I couldn't agree more. I kissed her once . . . then twice more.

Her arms tightened around my neck, and the kisses lengthened.

Watch yourself. I pulled my mouth from hers and brushed each cheek with a kiss.

Connor and Chelsea were still going at it. Chels perched on the railing, her legs wrapped around Connor, his coat slung across her shoulders.

"A couple of good-night kisses, ha." I shook my head.

Maggie giggled. "Them? Yeah, right."

I knocked on the glass. Connor glanced our way. "Time to go." I mouthed.

His eyes narrowed, and he shook his head.

"Oh, yes, it is." I pushed open the screen door, leading Maggie to the porch.

"Okay, okay." He stepped back, and Chelsea's feet slid to the floor.

"Have fun you two." I grazed the back of Maggie's hand with a kiss before letting it go.

Connor leaned in for what I hoped was one last kiss as I headed to the car.

He hopped in a few minutes later as I inched backward down the drive.

"Should've known better than to trust you."

He laughed. "Ah, come on. You enjoyed it. You know you did."

"Promise me you won't go back over there."

He cocked his head to the side. "I won't go back. Satisfied?"

"Yep."

Maggie

In early December, the blue Ford Focus that Mom and I shared died a painful death—painful to me at least. With the pay cut my parents took by coming to the clinic, purchasing another car was out of the question. Three drivers for one minivan meant I almost never got a turn. But when Preston offered to be my personal chauffeur, I decided it might not be so bad after all.

Arriving and leaving together from school each day should leave no doubt in anyone's mind—even *Caroline's*—that we were a couple. At least two other times he'd had to almost peel himself away from her. And I hated that smoldering *come hither* look of hers. He showed nothing but disgust toward her obviously unwanted advances. But jealousy zinged through me every time I even passed her in the hall.

No one other than Nikki had offered me friendly advice about him being a player, but that one, brief encounter had embedded itself in my brain. What had he done to her?

My parents thought he was great, and Michael had warmed right up to him, like having a big brother. They high-fived, fist-bumped, and talked video games, music, and guy stuff. It was cute. Michael probably enjoyed it far more than Preston, but if he thought the soon-to-be-fourteen-year-old was annoying, he never let on. Actually, Michael seemed a little less irritating each day. Maybe he was finally growing up. One could only hope.

Preston

Our last night together before Maggie and her family left for Christmas break in Minnesota had to be special. Already, I dreaded like crazy the seven days we'd be apart. I missed her just thinking about it.

Grabbing her Christmas gift, I ran a hand across my cheek and jaw. Just the right amount of stubble. And she liked it when I dressed up, so I'd traded my usual jeans and t-shirt for khakis and a black plaid button-up shirt. A small price to pay.

She opened the front door before I could ring the bell, and her shoulders scrunched with her trademark excitement. "Ooh, we match."

With a will of their own, my eyes skimmed over every inch of her long, black sweater and tan pants—very fitted tan pants. I forced my gaze back to her face and pulled her close before noticing her parents not more than ten feet away on the living room couch reading the paper. "Oops," I murmured.

"It's okay." Her hair stroked my cheek.

I stepped back from her. "Hi, Cheryl, Tom."

Cheryl peeked over the top of her reading glasses. "Hi, Preston."

"Preston." Tom's voice boomed from behind the newspaper. Cheryl elbowed him. He lowered the paper and nodded.

"See ya." Maggie grabbed the handles of a large gift bag on the floor and pulled me out the door.

After dinner at Guido's, we ended up back at my house. No one was home, and the urge to pull a Connor–Chelsea make out session coursed through me.

Maggie placed an expertly wrapped gift on the coffee table. Covered in red, shiny paper with a huge, gold bow and mounds of curly, red and gold ribbon, it looked amazing. Especially next to my lopsided, red and green striped package that looked like a first grader had wrapped it.

I pulled the boxes to the edge of the table.

"Together on the count of three, okay?" She jiggled her misshapen box.

"Sorry it looks so bad."

Her hand smoothed across the top. "I love stripes."

I smirked. "Yeah, right."

"Come on . . . I can't wait any longer."

"One, two, three," we chanted together. Wrapping paper crumpled to the floor.

I paused before taking the lid from my present to catch Maggie's expression. I'd tossed ideas around for weeks. Picking out gifts was not my thing. I held my breath as she pulled each item from the box. A big stuffed leopard—her favorite animal. A CD I'd burned of our favorite songs with our picture printed on the case insert. Two pair of thick, fuzzy, soft gloves—one a pale purple, the other a deep purple.

"Preston . . . " She rubbed the leopard's soft fur against her cheek, and her finger grazed our image on the CD case.

I picked up the purple gloves. "These are *only* for when I'm not around to keep your hands warm."

A grin tugged at her lip-glossed mouth as her fingertips brushed across the gloves. I guess I'd done okay.

Before she could protest, I ripped the lid from my present and found a 2007 Indianapolis Colts Super Bowl Champions hat and a Colts beanie. "Hey, you remembered I wanted one of these." I put the baseball-type cap on first.

"Ooh, very handsome."

"It fits great." I slipped off the hat and put on the beanie. "This'll be perfect for running this winter."

She pointed to the box. "You missed something."

I pushed the tissue paper aside. "Wow . . . " An incredible, framed picture of the two of us—our foreheads pressed together with a sunset in the background. "When and how did you—"

"I have my ways." She leaned close to see the picture. "For when we're not together." Our eyes met for a long moment. A sigh passed through her full lips before she eased back. "I'll think of you every time I listen to *this,* cuddle *this,* and wear *these.*"

I pulled her MP3 player from my pocket. "Thanks to your mom—the songs are on here, too."

"Mom?" She took the MP3 from my hand. "How?"

"Don't concern yourself with the details." I leaned in for a kiss. Immediately, desire raged through me. I wrapped my arms around her tightly and pulled her body against mine. One intense, hot kiss after another. Breathless, my lips wandered to her neck.

She pressed even closer as her fingertips crept inside the collar of my shirt.

I groaned against her neck.

Take a break.

But I didn't want to stop.

Don't push it.

With will power I didn't know existed, I eased her head onto my chest. I sucked in a deep breath, then let it out slowly. *Wow.*

Maggie snuggled into me. Her hand skimmed over my chest and shoulder.

I kissed her hair. "Are you all packed?"

She sighed. "Mostly."

I squeezed her closer and kissed her hair again. "The sooner you leave, the sooner you'll be back." That's what I kept telling myself anyway.

"I guess." Her voice trembled.

"You'll have a great time—you know you will."

"But I'll miss you so much."

I lifted her chin 'til our eyes met. "I'll miss you too, but it's only a week." *Seven very long days.*

She opened her mouth to protest.

But I cupped her chin and pressed my thumb against her lips. "Shhh . . . " Then silenced her further with a soft kiss that instantly deepened. I forced my mouth from hers.

"My parents want me home kind of early because we're leaving at six a.m. *Ugh.*"

"Wake up just enough to wrap up in your quilt and cuddle up with this guy." I grabbed the stuffed leopard and rubbed it against her cheek. "Then go back to sleep in the van."

"That's what I plan to do." She squeezed the leopard. "Thanks again for the gifts. I love them all."

"You're welcome. The Colts hats are both awesome. And that picture is amazing."

"I kept one for myself, too."

"Good." I pressed her warm body closer despite the *get her home before you do somethin' stupid* alarm pinging in my brain. Finally, I stood and pulled her up with me. "I want to stay on your parent's good side."

"They like you a lot."

"Let's keep it that way."

Maggie

The green road sign announcing eighty long miles to Pine Crossing flew by my window. Nine months ago, the very thought of Pine Crossing made me sick to my stomach, but now I couldn't wait to get back. Not to the town but to Preston—whose arms had better be wrapped around me in less than two hours.

But every thought of us being together stabbed my conscience with a reminder about the white-wedding-dress talk I'd been putting off. Every day the is-it-really-necessary debate circled through my mind. And *not necessary* was clearly in the lead.

"Can't you drive any faster?" I craned my neck to see the speedometer.

"You say something, Maggie?" Dad peered at me through the rearview mirror.

"You're at least going the speed limit, right?"

"Are you in a hurry to get home? I can't imagine why." He snickered.

Mom poked him. "Take a nap, Mags. That will make the time go faster."

I closed my eyes, but then I grabbed my phone to text Preston for the millionth time. "Can't wait to see you."

His response was instant. "meet at your house?"

"YES please!"

"U have plans tonite?"

"YES I plan to be with you!!!!"

"awesome"

I flipped through the pictures on my phone which did nothing but make me miss him more. *I think I love him.*

What else could these crazy-intense feelings mean? It was more than his hot looks, more than his witty personality, more even than how he treated me—which was amazing. All of that mixed with how I felt when we were together and maybe even more important—how I felt when we *weren't* together.

If I loved him, then that talk had to happen.

I closed my eyes as a vision swirled through my mind. A girl in a beautiful white wedding dress being twirled around the dance floor by a tall, tuxedo-clad man.

Me in the white wedding dress. Preston in the black tux with tails.

A smile tugged at my mouth around a sleepy yawn. Maybe a quick nap wasn't a bad idea.

"Thirty miles 'til we're home where I imagine a certain young man will happen to drive up about the time we get there." Dad's laugh echoed through the van.

Had I dozed off?

"Oh, Preston . . . " Michael squeaked in a high-pitched girly voice. He slapped Dad's hand with a high five. Their laughter almost shook the van.

"Ha, ha, very funny." I texted an update to Preston. "30 more miles"

"see ya soon"

Preston

I eased to a stop in front of Maggie's house. Big, puffy flakes of snow drifted to the ground, covering up the dingy piles from last week's snow. The blanket of white sparkled under the light of the street lamp. She would love it.

Headlights approached, and I hopped out before the Chrysler van pulled into the driveway, not caring how anxious it made me look.

When the side door opened, Maggie stepped out, all smiles and giddy excitement. She took a few careful steps toward me on the icy drive.

I covered the distance between us in two seconds and swooped her up. "Man, I missed you." I buried my face in her hair and drank in her amazing scent as I backed us away from the van.

"Me too." She clung to me, obviously as happy to see me as I was to see her.

Michael followed Tom and Cheryl toward the house, arms full of pillows and suitcases. Their voices drifted away from us. The garage door thudded shut behind them.

I eased her to the ground, keeping her close.

Her hands slid from around my neck to grip the front of my jacket.

"Anything left?" Cheryl's voice pierced the night air.

"We've got it." Maggie's grip on my jacket tightened.

The door closed again.

She pulled me down for a long kiss. Her hands pressed against my chest as she smoothed out the front of my jacket.

"We should probably go in." But she stretched up for one more kiss, then tugged on my arm, nodding toward the van.

We carried her stuff and a cooler in, and I waited downstairs, slouched against the family room doorway while she changed.

From his recliner, Tom pinned me with a look I couldn't immediately read. "Maggie insisted we not stop for dinner because she was so anxious to get home. Wanted to see some guy." His expression relaxed, and he chuckled.

I grinned, crossed my arms, and shrugged.

Cheryl stretched out on the couch, phone in hand. "And you promised me food, Mr. Jennison. Our traditional New Year's Eve Chinese dinner?"

Tom nodded, his eyes already closed, as he pushed his recliner back. "Order, and I'll go pick it up."

Maggie pulled on her coat as she hustled down the stairs. She leaned close and whispered, "How late do you think we'll be?"

"I'll bring you back whenever you need me to."

She grasped my arm and pulled me toward the front door. "It's okay if we're out 'til one or . . . " She held up two fingers.

Cheryl frowned.

"Please?" Maggie's mouth pushed into a cute pout.

Cheryl sighed as she glanced at Tom. "I guess. But be careful. The roads are slick with all this snow."

Tom nodded in what I hoped was agreement. He opened his eyes and sent a stern look my way.

I connected with his dark gaze. "We'll be careful, I promise."

Maggie

We ended up at Connors, the only one of the five places we'd been invited that Preston assured me wouldn't have alcohol. Everyone knew his parents were super serious about no drinking. Anyway, I was anxious to see Chelsea.

Cars stretched a block in either direction from his house.

"Preston, dude." Connor yelled at the door over the commotion of the party. "Maggie, am I ever glad you're home." He leaned in close. "He was here like non-stop while you were gone."

"Is that so?" I hooked my arm through Preston's.

"Don't listen to him." He brushed his cheek across my hair as a chuckling Connor returned to his hosting duties.

We mingled, roaming from room to room. I talked him into joining a girls versus guys game of Taboo. He did his best to distract me and my teammates with goofy faces. But his strategy failed, and the girls won.

He tucked me under his arm as we wandered toward the loud strains of karaoke in the garage. Chelsea latched onto me and literally dragged me toward the makeshift stage. Preston's arm dropped from my shoulders, and he didn't follow.

Chelsea waved her hand at him. "You and Maggie have to sing your song."

"Please," I mouthed, donning the pouty little girl face he could never resist.

The Lifehouse song, "You and Me," had become our song after playing on the radio twice the night of our first date and

116

too often after that not to mean something. Which was so weird because it came out forever ago.

Shaking his head, he trudged up on the stage. "I can't believe I'm doin' this."

Clutching his hand, I snuggled up to his side. But one glance at the audience sent waves of nervousness quaking through my body.

Chelsea whispered to the guy working the computer, then whistled to quiet the crowd. "Everyone. This is Maggie and Preston's song."

Preston's lips brushed my temple. "You okay? You're shaking."

Looking up at him, I wobbled my head and sputtered, "N-n-no."

He turned me to face him and pulled me close with his hands on my waist. "We can do this," he whispered.

The music swelled around us, and a hush fell over the crowd.

We sang, eyes locked in a deep almost-embrace, voices blended perfectly. My nervousness melted away. And so did the audience. It was the most romantic thing ever. At the end of the song, he hugged me and kissed my cheek.

I clung to him, never wanting to let go.

Applause and whistles turned our attention back to the crowd that had swelled to include practically every person at the party.

He laced our fingers together and pulled me through the still hooting crowd to a quiet spot in the house.

He stopped, and I bumped into his solid body. The electricity that zinged between us tingled down to my toes. "That was amazing," he said.

I could only nod and stare into the depths of his darkened eyes.

Our private moment slipped away as the crowd rushed in to watch the countdown of the last seconds of the year. *Seven, six, five, four, three, two, one. HAPPY NEW YEAR!*

He pressed me close, and our lips met in the longest kiss we'd ever shared in public as the traditional strains of "Auld Lang Syne" filled the room.

"Happy New Year," he murmured against my cheek.

I could only nod in agreement.

After another amazing kiss, he squeezed me tightly. "You wanna get out of here?"

I found my voice enough to murmur, "If you want to."

He navigated us to the front hall. "We're gonna take off," he called to Connor over the party noise.

"Already?"

"Haven't seen each other for a week, ya know."

"Yeah, yeah." Connor disappeared down the hall and returned with our coats.

Chelsea hurried over for a quick hug. "Thanks for singing, guys. You were great." She cozied up to Connor's side.

Preston helped me with my coat. "When are you two gonna sing?"

"Never." Connor snorted and held the door for us.

"Call me tomorrow!" Chelsea yelled as we headed down the sidewalk.

The wind had picked up, swirling the snow in huge billows of sparkling flakes. By the time we got to Preston's car, white flecks covered us.

He tucked me inside, spread a warm blanket across my lap, and flicked snow from my hair. He reached across me to start the engine. "Warm up while I do something about the snow." He grabbed a scraper and went to work on four or more inches of powdery white flakes blanketing the car.

My shivering had eased up by the time he climbed back inside. "Man, it's really coming down." He rubbed his hands together and blew on them. "We can go to my house, if that's okay."

"Yeah. I was hoping we could talk."

Preston

"This couch is amazing." Maggie ran her hand along the cushion of Dad's Christmas present to Mom.

"I know, right? Who knew Dad had such good taste." I eased down beside her. We were finally alone.

"I love the color."

"Yeah, purple, your favorite."

"Eggplant, actually. Your mom must have picked it out."

"Nope. She said it was a complete surprise. She went on forever about it—as you can imagine—especially the color."

"No more sink hole." She pressed firmly on the cushion.

"I didn't mind sinkin' in with you next to me." I slipped my arm around her shoulders.

"That was kind of fun."

"So, you wanted to talk about something?" I fingered the soft hair hanging down her arm.

She nodded and stared at her lap.

I lifted her chin to find her teeth nibbling on her bottom lip. I eased her lip down. "What?"

She gulped in a shaky breath. "It's just . . . um, I promised myself that if I was ever lucky enough to be in an awesome relationship with an amazing guy, we'd have a little talk. Actually, a really important, uh . . . discussion."

I couldn't help but grin. "Assuming I'm that guy—"

"Of course, you are." She tapped her finger against my chest once, twice . . . a third time. "You see, I've had this dream since I was a little girl about my wedding. The colors, kind of flowers and cake I want, but especially the dress—a sweetheart neckline, a cathedral length train, lots of lace." Her eyes, now wide and serious, flitted around my face. "But most of all, I want it to be *white*."

Planning the wedding already? I swallowed. "Uh . . . most wedding dresses are white, aren't they?"

"Yes. But it has to be white for the right reason."

I shrugged and shook my head.

"I want to be a virgin on my wedding night."

My mouth formed a silent O.

Her hand skimmed over my chest. "I hope this isn't too awkward. I just want us to be on the same page. Not that I think—"

I grabbed and squeezed her hand. "Uh . . . no, it's fine." *She probably wants the groom to be a virgin, too.*

The gold flecks in her eyes brightened. "Oh good, because this is really important to me. Not that I'm trying to rope you into marrying me." She tipped her head and did that cute wrinkled-nose thing. "It's just something I needed to tell you, and it's not because I'm worried that you'll try—"

"I'd been thinkin' maybe we should uh . . . you know, talk about it, too." A shrug rippled across my shoulders as needles of uneasiness pricked my neck.

"Really?" Her head bobbed at a fast pace.

"Yeah, not that I was worried either, but . . . yeah."

Nervous Maggie had morphed into giddy Maggie in a matter of seconds. "I almost talked myself out of bringing it up because I was *sure* it wouldn't be an issue." She leaned close, capturing my gaze. But now a frown tugged at the corners of her mouth. "Is something wrong?"

"Wrong? No, no. Glad you brought it up." The prickles now felt like hot needles.

Her shoulders relaxed, and she sighed. "So, we're good?"

A trickle of sweat slid down my back. "Uh, yeah, we're good." I cleared my throat and put some space between us.

But she edged closer until our lips met.

I forced myself to ease away and grabbed the remote to turn on the TV.

She cuddled into my side, and I went through the motions of surfing for something to watch.

The door from the garage burst open, and for once, I welcomed the interruption. "Oh, I hope Maggie's here." Mom's voice drifted to us as the kitchen light flicked on.

"Maggie! You're back." Mom rushed to the couch, pulled Maggie to her feet, and smothered her in a bear hug. "How was Christmas in Minnesota?"

"Very nice, but it's good to be home."

Mom relaxed her grip. "Poor Preston. He moped around like—"

I shot off the couch and grabbed Maggie's hand to pull her away from Mom. "Okay, Mom, we're all glad she's back." I aimed a pointed look at Dad.

"Nice to see you, Maggie. Jacki, I'm tired. Let's get to bed."

They said good night and headed down the hall. But Dad's head popped back through the doorway. "The snow is really piling up out there. You need to get Maggie home soon—like now."

Maggie pulled her vibrating phone from her pocket. "Maggie, it's Dad. Where are you?" His voice was loud enough I could hear every word.

"At Preston's."

"Well, two cars are stuck in the snow on our street. Are his parents there?"

"Yes, they're here." She turned toward my parents.

"Maybe you should stay there tonight. What do you think?"

"Just a minute." She laid the phone in her lap. "Dad says two cars are stuck in the snow on our street, and he wonders if I should stay here tonight." She looked from me to my parents.

"Absolutely." Mom and Dad answered together.

I nodded in agreement.

"May I?" Dad motioned toward her phone.

She handed it to him.

"Tom, of course Maggie can stay here. We were just talking about the road conditions." We all heard Tom say he would feel better knowing she was safe with us. "No trouble at all—we're happy to have her." He paused. "Happy New Year to you and Cheryl, too. Good night." He handed the phone back to Maggie.

Mom's features froze in one of her gushiest expressions yet. "Oh, you'll be here for brunch in the morning! I'll grab some bedding, and Preston can make you a bed right here on the new couch. Did he tell you this was my Christmas present from Drew? Don't you just love it? Purple's your favorite color, isn't it?"

"Yeah, I love purple."

Mom motioned for me to follow her down the hall. She stopped in front of the linen closet, her hand twisting the door knob. She turned to face me—all the gush suddenly gone and replaced by total seriousness. "I hope this goes without saying, but, I'm going to say it anyway. *Maggie* will be on the couch, and *you* will be in your room."

"Mom." I crossed my arms. "You don't need to worry."

She sighed and patted my arm. "Well, good. I'm not insinuating anything, I just . . ." She shrugged. "You know."

"I know, Mom."

Some gush crept back in. "She's a real sweetheart. I just love her to pieces." She placed a pillow, two sheets, and a blanket across my arms. We headed back to the family room.

"Okay, then." Dad looked at Mom, then back to Maggie and me.

"Good night, you two. Sleep well." Mom blew a kiss in our direction.

I sat down beside Maggie, pushing aside Mom's concern. "So, do you have plans for tomorrow? Or I guess I mean today."

She shrugged, stifling a yawn. "I need to unpack and do some laundry, but that's about it. You?"

"We always have a big family breakfast on New Year's Day. Mom calls it brunch. I have to work at five, but we can do whatever you want until then."

She nodded, covering another yawn with the back of her hand.

"Gettin' sleepy?"

She grinned and shrugged. "You?"

"Nope." Winding my hand through her hair, I pulled her toward me, no longer fighting the urge to kiss her the way I'd wanted to all night. One kiss led to another, and—

Maggie jumped at a loud burst of fireworks from outside.

I dragged my lips from her mouth. "Happy New Year . . . "

She laid her head against my shoulder. "It already is."

Preston

Knowing Maggie's agenda didn't include sex should have left me relieved, stoked even. But it didn't. Because her agenda wasn't the real issue. *I* was the problem.

I could not even fathom a worse conversation than telling her about my past. But now that I knew how important virginity was to her, how could I *not* fess up? Then again, how *could* I?

Why did life have to be so complicated?

At least pending fatherhood wasn't on my plate. During Christmas break, Zach had been worried big time that Brittany was pregnant. Which brought back a lot of unpleasant memories about stuff I never wanted to deal with again.

The first week back to school, he was quiet and kept pretty much to himself. I was afraid of what that meant. But the next week, he sauntered into U.S. History with a huge grin.

"False alarm," he announced, bumping my fist.

"Dude, that's good."

"Man, am I relieved."

"Until next month when you're worried again."

His grin shifted into a scowl.

"You dodged the bullet this time. Might not be so lucky next time."

"You've got a lot to talk about—"

"Whoa. You know me and Maggie aren't having sex."

"Whatever. You live your life, and I'll live mine."

The bell rang, and Zach sank into his seat.

The swarm of memories their pregnancy scare stirred up made it tough to ignore my past like I wanted to. To enjoy being with Maggie and banish from my mind the contradiction between my past and her white-wedding-dress future. Because there wasn't a thing I could do about it anyway.

Soon it was the middle of January, and I realized we'd been together every evening since she came back from Minnesota. I'd loved every second of it.

One night when I slipped in the back door and stomped the snow from my shoes, I glanced at the microwave clock. 10:39

Dad, sitting at the breakfast table, shook the newspaper stretched between his hands and gave me a look. "School night curfew is ten-thirty. Maybe you'd like us to back it up—"

"Sorry. Maggie was going over my AP English assignment."

Mom stood next to him, folding towels. "You and Maggie— you spend a lot of time together. She's a real sweetheart and all, but . . . " Her fingers stilled on the blue towel as her gaze met mine. "It seems like you're with her *a lot.*" Her attention focused again on the towel.

Dad folded the paper. "Just watch yourself, son. That's all we're saying."

Last year my response would have been less than respectful—bordering on extremely rude. But not anymore.

I looked at Mom. "She *is* a sweetheart." My gaze slid to Dad. "And I *am* watching myself." *Really, Dad, I am.* "She means the world to me."

"Aw." Mom sighed and patted my arm. "Well, I just love her to death."

"Tell us something we don't already know." Dad laid the paper down.

Mom grabbed a stack of towels, gave Dad a short nod, and slipped through the doorway.

He folded his arms on the table. "You've dated a lot, but it's more serious with Maggie, isn't it?"

Our eyes met again, and I nodded.

"Which makes getting physical a real temptation." In that moment, we were two men sharing an understanding about guy-girl relationships.

"I know, Dad. We've talked about it."

His eyebrows shot up. "And?"

"We're not gonna do something stupid. I promise."

"Which means what, exactly?"

"We made a commitment not to have sex."

Dad's eyes narrowed. "Really. Well, that's good. But don't push—"

"Dad. I know. I got this."

Maggie

Tyler tallied the weekly collection amounts on the white board. "Sixty-seven dollars and fifty-nine cents." He traced the numbers again, checking his math. "Best week yet."

Mr. Martin stroked his chin and nodded "The total for the year? Maggie, Brittany?"

Brittany and I had somehow been appointed keeper of the project records. "One hundred ninety-three dollars and fifteen cents," I said.

Brittany peeked over my shoulder at the numbers in the notebook.

I held it up so she could see it better. "Pretty impressive, huh?" I whispered.

She sighed and sat back in her seat.

I glanced back to see she'd already checked out as evidenced by her staring-into-space-at-nothing-in-particular look. She slouched further down in her seat and closed her eyes as she twirled a clump of gorgeous, dark brown hair around her finger.

"It's only January, and we're less than seven bucks from our goal." Tyler leaned against the white board, his arms crossed. "We can raise a lot more than two hundred."

"What do the rest of you think?" Mr. Martin's gaze panned across the room.

"I think . . . " Alex strode to the front of the room. "We should put the canisters around town. Posters, too. Wouldn't other people want a chance to give?"

Mr. Martin allowed the brainstorming to continue until the five-minute warning bell rang. "So, how many more canisters?"

"Twenty at least?" Alex turned to Tyler who extended his fist in agreement.

"Alex, you'll assign locations, and you label designers—" He looked around the group. "Erin. How soon can you have more? And Lindsey, how about more posters?"

Erin shrugged. "Maybe Monday?"

"Lindsey?" Mr. Martin pointed at her.

"More posters by Monday."

"Perfect. We're back here on Monday for assignments from Alex to blanket this community with awareness and donation canisters to benefit The Least of These Clinic." Mr. Martin grinned and jerked his thumb over his shoulder. "Great work, guys."

Preston

I'd been guilty of tossing around "I love you" too freely in the past, but I was aching to tell Maggie I loved her. Because I did. I wanted to tell her soon, like today, but the timing had to be perfect and the setting special.

So, it wouldn't be today. But soon.

"He saw his shadow!" Maggie slammed the car door and leaned toward me for a kiss.

"You're probably the only person in the entire Midwest who's happy that pesky groundhog saw his stupid shadow." I tossed her backpack into the back seat.

"Yay, more snow."

I backed onto the street, shaking my head.

"What? No good morning kiss?" She leaned into my side of the car.

"No way." I pushed my lips firmly together and stared straight ahead.

"Just because I want more snow?"

I focused on the road.

"Well, suit yourself." She shrugged, tossing waves of chocolate brown hair over her shoulder.

I stole a glance at her. She didn't look upset—surprised maybe. I walked my fingers across the seat and brushed hers.

"Oh, I don't know." She pulled her hand into her lap.

I grabbed her fingers, lifted them to my mouth, and pressed the inside of her wrist to my lips.

"That's not fair."

"What's not fair?"

"I wanted a real kiss."

"That one felt pretty real to me."

"Well, not that kissing my wrist isn't incredibly sexy, but I wanted to kiss you."

I accelerated through the turn into the parking lot then coasted into the last spot in the back row. "Okay, have your way with me."

She wound her arms around my neck and pressed her incredibly soft mouth against mine in an instantly hot kiss.

I pulled her across the center console and threaded my fingers through the ends of her hair.

She traced a line just above the collar of my coat. Her cool touch on my warm skin was like an electric shock.

She pulled her mouth from mine. "There—a real kiss."

"Talk about sexy." I covered her mouth in another hot kiss.

When she finally eased away, she murmured, "School—remember?"

"Uh, yeah. I think I remember. *Man.*"

She giggled, grabbed her backpack, and reached for the door handle. "Oh, sorry. I forgot."

"Huh?"

"The door. It's your job, not mine."

Preston grabbed his keys and books, hopped out, and sprinted around to my door. "I won't be able to concentrate on anything the rest of the day."

"Is that so?"

He nodded, his eyes wide. "You have no idea."

His prediction proved true for me, too. I spaced half of what every teacher said and had to ask a ton of questions to fill in the blanks.

"Earth to Maggie." Chelsea's fingers snapped in front of my face after lunch. "What has you in such a daze anyway?"

"The amazing kisses in Preston's car this morning."

Her mouth gaped open. "You and Preston?"

I grimaced.

"How long did this hot kissing go on? And why are you here instead of somewhere—"

"For like five minutes. The kissing was hot, but we'd never skip school to make out. And I assure you, it was nothing more than kissing which is all you and Connor had better be doing."

A silent Chelsea stared with narrowed eyes at something behind me.

"Chels . . . "

She wouldn't look at me. "Maybe it is, maybe it isn't. I don't kiss and tell."

"You expected me to kiss and tell."

"Yeah, well, apparently there's nothing to tell."

I brushed her arm with mine. "I'm worried about you two."

She shrugged away from me. "You know how important Connor is to me."

"Yeah, but still. I adore Preston—*you* of all people know that. And I'm pretty sure his feelings are . . . similar."

"Connor says Preston has never been as devoted to anyone as he is to you."

Boy, did I like hearing that. "Okay, then, see? We're very much together, but we aren't having sex."

Something I couldn't quite read clouded Chelsea's eyes. Then she blinked, and her ornery grin returned. "So, will the hot kissing continue on your date tonight?"

I held up my hand to stop her imagination. "We're getting pizza. Why don't you two come with us? Then we'll probably watch TV at his house. There may be a little kissing, but that's it."

She rolled her eyes. "Bor-ing."

"Maybe to you but not to me."

Preston

Connor and Chelsea met us at Pizza Hut where his loud, borderline obnoxious behavior almost got us kicked out. I smoothed things over with the frazzled waitress suggesting his medication had accidentally been flushed down the toilet. She gave me and Maggie a sympathetic look for putting up with him.

He scowled as she walked away with our money.

"Dude, would you rather she thinks you're mentally ill or rude and obnoxious?"

"Whatever, just havin' a little fun. Speaking of which," he slipped his arm around Chelsea. "I hear your plans for the rest of the evening are less than exciting, so I think we'll be on our way." He and Chelsea shared a look about what I didn't have to guess.

"Chels, I don't know how you put up with him."

She smiled and tucked herself closer. "I manage."

~ ~ ~

At home, we slipped through the back door into the dark kitchen. I shrugged out of my coat and tossed my wet shoes aside.

Maggie rubbed her arms and shivered. "I'll keep my coat for now. Where's your mom and dad?"

"I don't know, but I'll grab a blanket, and you'll be warm in no time."

She followed me into the family room still hunched in her coat.

I held up this huge, fuzzy throw that she loved.

Her eyes lit up. "Yes, please." She slipped out of her coat and sank onto the couch.

I sat beside her, dropped the blanket mostly on her, and wrapped my arm around her.

She snuggled into me as I snagged the remote and channel surfed for something decent to watch. "You warming up?"

She smiled, and the gold flecks in her brown eyes twinkled. "Mmm, yes, thank you."

After another fast run through the channels, I dropped the remote on the couch, leaving the TV on some crime drama. I let my eyes skim over her unchecked. Most of her was covered with the throw anyway. When my wandering gaze returned to her face, her eyebrows scrunched and her lips pursed. "What?"

"Nothing." I lifted my hand from her shoulder to trace the curve of her face.

Her head tipped into my hand.

I eased my fingers under her hair and cupped the back of her neck. "You interested in this show?"

Our eyes connected. "Not really."

"Yeah," I angled toward her. "Me either." I leaned in for a kiss. Then another. Immediately, the kissing was hot. A lot like this morning in the car.

Her fingers stroked my hair then inched inside my t-shirt.

My already racing pulse quickened more. I pressed her closer.

Her body molded around me.

Pulling her with me, I slid along the back of the couch, until my shoulders came to rest on the cushioned arm. I stretched out, adjusting her on top of me. All without interrupting the kissing.

Her perfume surrounded me.

I kissed a trail along her jaw, around her chin.

She sighed and her warm breath tickled my ear.

My lips strayed to the skin at the base of her throat.

She arched against my mouth, and a tiny moan escaped her.

I lingered there, kissing her silky skin before marking a path across her neck back to her mouth.

Don't get carried away.

We're only kissing.

Doin' less than Connor and Chelsea probably are.

I lifted her up so I could scoot further down on the couch. My hands slipped under her shirt. The breath caught in my throat as my fingers spread across the warm, soft skin on her sides.

I stroked her back, caught up in the feel of her skin. With a new urgency, my mouth explored hers. Someone groaned—I wasn't sure who. The kissing went on and on. My fingertips slipped inside her jeans.

Maggie pulled her mouth from mine and opened her eyes.

My hands stopped moving but remained on her warm skin. "Sorry . . . " My breath came in ragged gasps. "I'm sorry."

"I know." She rested her head on my chest.

The door from the garage slammed hard and loud. Shuffling feet.

"Whoa." *Patrick.* Heavy footsteps clumped across the room then down the hall.

Maggie eased herself off of me and sat at the opposite end of the couch.

I swung my feet to the floor and raked a hand through my hair.

"The time . . . I need to get home."

A quiet agony filled the car as I drove to her house, all the while wracking my brain for something to say. My hand inched across the seat. Our fingers folded together.

We snuck inside her house like we were late—which we weren't—or guilty. She switched the porch light off.

I gripped her hands together between us. "I'm sorry. I shouldn't have let it go that far."

"I know you are." Her fingers traced the zipper on my coat.

"You mean *so* much to me." Now did not seem like the right time to say those three little words I'd been dying to say.

"You too."

I pulled her close and rested our foreheads together. The silence was so awkward and painful, but I didn't know what else to say. I kissed her one last time and murmured, "'Night."

"Goodnight, Preston."

~ ~ ~

Patrick stood in the kitchen by the sink like he'd been waiting for me. "So much for being careful." His words dripped attitude.

"We didn't do anything."

"Come on, Preston. Kissing is one thing but laying on the couch like that?"

I shouldered past him to open the fridge.

"No—I wanna know. *What* were you thinking?"

I smacked the door closed without getting anything and whipped around. "I don't know, okay? I expected someone to be here, so what?"

"It's not my job or Mom's and Dad's to babysit you two. Take some responsibility. If you can't handle being home alone, you should've walked out the minute you realized no one was here."

I filled a glass with water I didn't want. "Maggie wasn't upset."

He growled. "And that matters why? I thought you woulda figured that out after the last time."

I escaped to my room, the glass of water still gripped in my hand. The accusations from my own conscience were louder and harsher than Patrick's. *Thought you weren't that guy anymore.*

If Patrick hadn't walked in. If we'd started kissing again. Guilt twisted my gut.

Okay, so I'd messed up big time. And I'd used Connor to justify it.

With my arms not wrapped around Maggie, the insanity of comparing us to him and Chelsea was undeniable. I'd been so critical of them. Maybe we had a ways to go to catch up to what they were doing, but that wasn't the point.

Connor was not the one I wanted calling the shots. Not me either. I wanted—no, I *needed*—God to be in the driver's seat.

Maggie

On Monday, bulging Zip-Loc bags of coins and bills dropped on Mr. Martin's desk where Gabe, John, and some new recruits sorted and counted the money. Tyler recorded the group totals on the board. A heavy silence cloaked the room as he did the math. He underlined the weekly total: $201.28.

Mr. Martin's face exploded with a toothy smile. "The grand total, Brittany, Maggie?"

Brittany double-checked the addition, then slid the notebook toward me.

I nodded.

She pushed it closer and sat back in her seat.

Well, okay. "Four hundred fifty-seven dollars and twelve cents."

An ear-splitting cheer erupted. We would probably get Mr. Martin in trouble.

"Quiet down." He stroked his chin below a satisfied smile. "Now what do you think led to this awesome success?"

"Awareness." Tyler announced as he capped the marker. "Getting the word out about the clinic and how it's helping so many people."

"Thank you, Mr. Collins." Mr. Martin leveled his index finger at Tyler, then pointed across the group. "Can we do more?"

"I've thought of ten or so more places to put canisters." Alex tapped the piece of paper on the desk in front of him. "And we need more of those book mark things. My locations were all out." The poster makers had created bookmark-sized fliers to place beside each canister.

"Good. Good." Mr. Martin nodded.

"Hey, Maggie. Do you think the clinic could use volunteers? I need more community service stuff for my college apps." Lindsey's hand fluttered in front of her. "I know, I'm a little behind, but hey, better late than never."

"They always need help with something. I'll ask my parents and let you know." I'd gladly give her or anyone the Saturday morning receptionist job.

The five-minute bell rang.

Mr. Martin stood. "Erin's group will get more canisters ready. Alex will divide the additional locations among the collection teams. Lindsey and company will provide us with many more bookmark fliers. Maggie will put together a list of volunteer tasks—Lindsey gets first dibs." His hand swept toward the door in dismissal. "Until next week, crew."

~ ~ ~

The week was crazy busy with no time for Preston and me to be together until Thursday night after he got off work.

Before he cleared the porch steps, I opened the door and reached out to him.

He laced his fingers with mine, smiled his signature smile, and kissed me hello.

He followed me to the kitchen where I grabbed a Mountain Dew and a Diet Coke.

"Where is everyone?"

"Mom and Dad took Michael shopping for his birthday. We all went to dinner, but I asked them to bring me back after we ate."

We settled on the couch. I offered him the drink, but he motioned toward the coffee table. He tipped his head back and closed his eyes.

"You're kind a quiet."

"Just tired. It's been a hectic week."

"I've missed you."

"Mmm, me too." He found my hand and laced his fingers with mine without opening his eyes.

"Maybe you need a nap."

His eyes popped open. "I didn't come over here to nap."

"Oh?"

He wrapped his arms around me and eased my head onto his chest. "I definitely plan to stay awake."

"Did you remember my grandparents' anniversary dinner tomorrow night?"

"Yep."

"Thanks for going with me, by the way."

"What—you were going to ask someone else?"

"Of course not." I smacked his chest lightly. "But you could have had other plans or whatever."

"Why would I do that?"

"Getting dressed up isn't your favorite thing."

He raised my chin until our eyes met. "My very favorite thing is being with you. Getting dressed up is nothin'." The look in his eyes shifted my heartbeat into a fast, erratic pattern. "Will you be there with me?"

I nodded.

"Then I'll love every minute of it." His hushed whisper sent shivers down my back.

His hand threaded through my hair as our lips came together. Immediately, the kissing was intense. He pressed me closer with a hand on my lower back.

I let my fingers glide across his neck and the hard muscles along his shoulder. The heat from his skin warmed my hands even through his shirt.

His hand slipped from my hair and drew a slow line down to my elbow then grazed along my side to my waist. A gentle tug at the hem of my shirt, first on one side then the other, raised the fabric. Warm fingertips brushed across my skin seconds before his hands pressed flat against my bare back. His lips wandered along my jaw then nestled at the base of my throat.

Waves of hot tingles shot all the way to my toes. *This is okay, right?*

A barely-there debate trickled through my mind, but all thoughts dissolved when his mouth captured mine again. He had to be the most amazing kisser ever. His warm touch moved to caress my stomach.

The phone didn't ring. No one came home. Nothing interrupted us. I had no idea how long we'd been kissing, but I wanted it to go on forever.

As his lips again scorched a path across my neck, his fingertips eased under the side of my bra.

Uhh . . .

His other hand dipped inside my jeans.

I pulled away from him, breathless.

His hands jerked from my body as he slumped backward, his breath coming in short gasps. Regret washed over his face. "Maggie." He breathed out my name in a hoarse whisper. "Sweetheart, I'm sorry." He closed his eyes, shaking his head.

"It's okay—we stopped."

His breathing still a little ragged, he laced his fingers through mine and looked into my eyes. He took a deep breath and opened his mouth just as footsteps and voices filled the kitchen. He flattened his back against the couch, putting space between us.

Michael and Dad laughed hysterically.

"You guys crack me up," Mom chimed in.

Preston's face went blank as he pressed his lips together.

"Maggie." From the kitchen doorway, Dad's gaze darted from me to Preston. "Preston."

"Hey." I forced a cheery smile.

Preston only nodded. He angled toward me and away from Dad. A look of guilt crept across his features like a shadow.

I gripped his hand. "What's so funny?"

Mom joined Dad in the doorway. "Oh, it's not half as funny as they think it is."

"Preston will think it's hilarious." Michael pushed past them and planted himself on the coffee table right in front of us. I half listened as he recounted a crazy situation they'd witnessed at the mall. Something about a guy with a mask. Funny, yes but not as funny as Michael obviously thought. Preston laughed anyway, and his face relaxed.

With Dad and Michael still chuckling and Mom shushing them, they headed upstairs.

Preston squeezed my hand. "I need to go."

But it was only ten. "Why?"

"I still have some homework."

"Ah, really? Not much, I hope."

"Nah." He stood, pulling me up with him. Our eyes met. "It's okay, Preston, really."

He leaned his forehead against mine. "I'm still sorry."

"I know you are."

We walked to the front door. I bit my lip hard to keep the words I love you from spilling out. If he didn't say it soon, I would say it first.

He squeezed me tight then his hand curved around my face, and he brought my forehead to his lips.

"Don't stay up too late."

"'Course not." His ornery grin didn't live up to its usual dazzle.

His hand dropped to his side, and he shuffled out the front door.

Minutes later as I changed into my favorite pj's, our super long make out session replayed in my mind. I gulped and closed my eyes against the surge of feelings the memories unleashed. Then Preston's apology, his guilty expression, his obvious remorse crowded into my mind as I pulled the covers over my head against the cool chill in my room. Clutching my phone to my chest, I waited for his goodnight text and tried to ignore the uneasy dread churning in my stomach.

But why? No clothes came off, nothing was even unbuttoned or unzipped. And we'd stopped before anything major happened. Wasn't that the important thing?

I pressed a shaky hand against my stomach, and with a lot of effort, pulled my thoughts away from the debate about the wrong or right of what had or hadn't happened. I was lucky to be in this amazing relationship with such an awesome guy.

We are fine. End of story.

Preston

The blare of my alarm jerked me awake. How could it be morning already?

I jabbed at the snooze button blindly, my eyes refusing to open. A tangle of sheets and blankets wrapped around my feet kept me from yanking the bedding over my head. I hit snooze a second time, feeling like I hadn't slept at all.

My blurry vision finally focused on the suit hanging from my closet door. Maggie's grandparents' fiftieth anniversary dinner was tonight.

The alarm sounded for a third time. I slammed it with my fist, and a post-it note stuck to my hand.

German field trip leaves 7:30 am sharp. Do not be late.

"Aw, *man.*" I bounded from bed and tripped on the tangled bedding. I swallowed back a word I hadn't uttered in a long time.

Great. Now I wouldn't see Maggie all day.

I climbed on the bus with one minute to spare and sank into the empty second row.

Frau Koch walked the aisle taking attendance. "Just made it, *Herr* Jacoby."

I nodded and pulled out my phone to text Maggie. "Dumb German field trip miss u already"

"I remembered. Miss you too. Have a great day! ☺"

I traced her picture on my phone's screen, popped in my ear buds, leaned back, and closed my eyes. Music filled my head but couldn't crowd out the vivid memories of being with her last night. A surge of guilt clashed with a strong wave of desire.

Last night had proved one thing—I wasn't handling the physical part of our relationship just fine. And staying upright? That hadn't helped at all.

I yanked the ear buds out and tossed them on the seat. I scooted to the window and leaned against the cold glass. My phone vibrated with a text from Maggie. "Are you there yet?"

"almost"

"Have fun."

"not likely"

I wandered through the huge convention center alone, trying to focus on the World War II exhibit. My notes should have been an easy ten points, but I'd be lucky to get five.

Maggie texted me throughout the day. She seemed fine, not upset or anything. Maybe it wasn't that big of a deal.

I squirmed into the most comfortable position possible to catch a few z's on the way back to school. The next thing I knew, Frau Koch tapped my shoulder. "Preston, we're here." She smiled and moved to the next row.

I grabbed my stuff and pulled my vibrating phone from my pocket as I hopped off the bus.

Maggie. "Still picking me up at 6?"

"yes can't wait to see U"

"Me too."

"going for a run"

"Ok ☺"

Despite the cheery, normal conversation throughout the day, a massive weight settled on me. No more pretending or denying it. We had a problem. Maybe a run would help me think.

I hit the familiar path at Montgomery Park in an easy jog. My legs complained after half a lap around the running path. Spending all my free time with Maggie had cut big time into my running routine. I had to push myself to sprint for two laps, then struggled through one more at a jog before slowing to a walk. The intense burning in my legs was nothing compared to the guilt squeezing my chest. And I was no closer to a solution.

Preston

I couldn't breathe at all as Maggie descended the stairs, gorgeous in a knee length dress the same chocolate brown as her hair and eyes. Matching spiky heels showed off her legs, and a mass of curls swept to the top of her head completed the incredibly sexy look. "Wow."

Her gaze roamed over me. "Aren't you extremely handsome?"

I grabbed her hand and twirled her around. "*You* are stunning."

"We make a pretty hot couple, huh?"

My hand skimmed up her arm. "Mmm hmm."

"Time to hit the road." Tom called from the kitchen.

Cheryl poked her head into the living room. "Look at you two. You're riding with Preston, right?"

"We'll be right behind you." Maggie fussed with my tie, her shiny fingernails skimming the tie's textured pattern.

The door to the garage closed with a thud.

She tugged on my suit jacket's lapels. "Who knew a charcoal gray suit, white shirt, and black tie could look this amazing?"

I rested my hands on her waist. The fabric of her dress was thin and clingy. All the wrong thoughts raged through my mind. I stepped back for some breathing space. "You are beyond gorgeous."

She stretched up for a quick kiss that I didn't allow to linger, and then we headed to the car. On the way, she chatted about her day and asked about mine all while stroking the back of my hand resting on the center console. Further proof she wasn't upset about last night. I let myself relax, psyched and relieved that I'd obviously made too much of what had happened.

At the party, she paraded us around, introducing me to more relatives than I would ever remember. I'd never been that great with names, but my poor memory had little to do with that tonight. It was all I could do to force my attention away from Maggie. She'd never looked more beautiful.

When the home movies began, she pushed her chair as close to mine as possible and snuggled against me.

I wound my arm around her shoulders.

Her soft, warm body practically melted into me. Her sexy scent surrounded me.

My pulse sped up. After a couple of minutes, I pulled my arm from around her shoulders and laced our fingers together instead.

She glanced at me from the corner of her eye.

I winked and swallowed back a sigh. As the black and white movies transitioned to colored images, my mind wandered back to the mental battle that had kept me up half of last night. Despite how normal everything seemed today, I couldn't shake the negative vibe that being with me was bad for Maggie. That I was the wrong guy for her.

Even the thought of hurting her in any way sucked all the breath from my lungs. Sweat beaded across my forehead, along my neck.

She looked up at me with narrowed eyes.

I leaned into her hair and whispered the need to excuse myself to the men's room.

Her gaze attached to me as I slipped out of the side door.

The cooler air in the hallway hit me like an arctic blast, especially breezy against my wet forehead. In the restroom, I splashed cold water on my face and across my neck, and ended up dotting the front of my shirt with wet spots. Pressing a paper towel to the splotches, I considered how long I could be gone before she came looking for me. Probably not long.

I stole back into my seat as light flooded the room.

"You okay?" Her narrowed eyes were in full study mode as she looked me over.

"Yeah. What did I miss?"

"Just some very unflattering shots of me at that awkward pre-teen stage."

"Ah, man. Maybe I could convince them to rewind."

She punched my arm lightly. "Not a chance, buddy."

People stood to give tribute or share a memory which allowed my mental battle to continue. In the worst way, I wanted to go with the assumption that everything was cool, but the guilt ripping at my gut told a different story.

Maggie leaned toward me and whispered, "Hangin' in there? I hope it's about over."

I grazed her hair with my nose. "Doin' fine."

As soon as we could break away from her enthusiastic relatives, we hurried to my car. I fiddled with the heat controls and radio, feeling her eyes on me.

"Well, at least the food was good." Maggie's finger again traced a pattern on the back of my hand. She tugged on my hand until it rested on her leg.

"It was great." I failed at holding in a long yawn.

Her eyes flitted toward me every couple of seconds.

Say something. "Was a nice celebration."

"You sure you're okay?"

"Just a little tired." I lifted my fingers to lace with hers and flashed a big, dimple-included smile.

She continued to watch me. "Can't wait to see the pictures from tonight."

"Can I get one for my mom? She tried to sneak one of those strips of pictures we got at the mall out of my room. Always telling me what a cute couple we are."

"We're a *hot* couple."

"You're tellin' me." *Too hot . . .*

I pulled into her driveway and shifted into park.

"You want to come in?"

"Uh, maybe not, if that's okay." I gripped her pinkie with my thumb. "I'm beat."

"I can walk myself in."

"I'm not that tired."

"Really, it's okay." She leaned against my arm.

I gathered her close, grateful for the layers her coat put between us. I trailed kisses across her cheek and into her hair.

"You sure you're alright?"

I placed a lingering kiss on her mouth. "Yes." My arm unwound from her body, and I reached for the door handle.

Maggie shook her head. "Really, let me walk myself in."

"No—"

Her finger pressed against my mouth. "It's fine, Preston."

I sighed. "Okay, this one time."

~ ~ ~

The faint sound of an incoming text barely registered in my groggy brain. Rolling toward the bedside table, I groped for the phone. It slid to the floor with a thunk. I pawed the carpet until my hand wrapped around it.

It was Maggie. "Are you sure you're not upset with me?"

The phone buzzed again. "Please just tell me."

I typed a fast reply. "not upset with u"

Hers came back faster. "I know something's up. Why won't you tell me?"

I raked a hand through my hair and jabbed one to speed-dial her number. "Maggie, I'm not upset with you."

"I know the anniversary dinner wasn't exactly fun—"

"It was fine, and I loved being with you."

"Okay, then what?"

Quiet sniffling interrupted my attempts to put together a decent answer. "Are you crying?"

She sniffed again and mumbled something that sounded like "no."

I swung my legs over the side of the bed. "Sweetheart, please don't cry. I'm not upset with you, I promise."

She sighed, obviously not convinced.

"I didn't get much sleep last night. I'm just tired."

Silence.

"Please believe me."

"I want to believe you, but you're scaring me."

"It's nothing. Stop worrying."

Maggie

I blew my drippy nose for the fifth time and threw the wad of tissue at the wastebasket. As much as I wanted to believe Preston and collapse in relief, it wasn't happening. And now, I wouldn't get any sleep which would make my clinic shift tomorrow ten times worse.

Most Friday nights about this time, that dumb Saturday morning shift loomed ahead like the biggest inconvenience in my life. It would have been different if I got paid for getting up that early every single Saturday morning.

As I trudged from the bathroom, a familiar voice wafted up the stairs.

"Tom, Cheryl, I'm sorry to bother you so late, but I need to see Maggie."

Preston is here?

"Well, Preston." Dad's tone was hesitant. "A few minutes will be fine."

I dashed back into my room and latched the door with as little noise as possible.

Footsteps thudded up the stairway, then a light tap rattled my door. "Maggie, it's me."

I opened the door a crack. "What are you doing here?"

"I had to see you." Dark circles dulled the usual brilliance of his blue eyes. He nudged the door open more.

As I backed away, he lunged forward, instantly wrapping me in his arms. "I'm sorry I made you cry," he murmured, his mouth pressed against the top of my head.

I burrowed into him, my hunched shoulders pressed against his chest, soaking in his warmth as relief flooded through me.

"We need to talk about . . . last night."

So that's what's bothering him. I took one step back and wrapped my hands around his arms. "Okay . . . "

"But not tonight. It's too late."

I pushed off his arms and backed out of his embrace. "Now wait a minute—"

His strong shoulders squared. "Let's have dinner tomorrow night, and we'll talk. I promise."

I crossed my arms and shook my head.

"Come on, don't you trust me?" His hand curved around my face.

My cheek fell automatically into his warm palm. "You know I do." I closed the space between us and traced the letters on his Madison High t-shirt.

He lifted my face until our eyes met. "I need to get outta here before your parents toss me out."

"Don't go," I pleaded, all pouty.

"I promise, tomorrow night we'll figure this out." His lips lingered on my forehead. "I love you so much."

My head jerked up. "I love you too!"

"I've been wanting to say that for so long."

"Me too." Now I really didn't want him to leave.

He exhaled a deep breath. "I *have* to go."

I somehow pressed closer.

"Not because I want to, but, really I do." He backed toward the door. "Tomorrow night, you and me, dinner at Guido's."

Preston

After my Saturday shift, I hit the park at a full sprint. I pushed myself to go three full laps, then slowed to a fast walk.

Coach Thomas jogged toward me. "I'm impressed, Mr. Jacoby. You training for something? Saw you out here last night, too."

"Nah, got a lot on my mind. Running helps clear my head."

"I got three more laps. If you don't mind slowing it down—"

"Yeah, I need to cool down anyway." And the plan for tonight's talk had yet to come together.

"Nice running weather, huh?"

"Yep."

"New season will be underway before we know it." Fresh out of college, he'd been an awesome Little League coach, and now he headed up the community's parks and rec programs. I umped for him and helped out wherever else he needed me. To me and the other guys, he'd always be Coach.

"Yep, comin' up soon."

Our feet pounded the asphalt in rhythm.

"Junior year been as tough as you thought it would be?" Coach slowed his pace a little.

"Not too bad."

"Still seeing Maggie?"

I nodded.

Coach slowed a little more. "Sometimes it helps to talk."

By the end of the first practice, every kid he ever coached knew two things about Nick Thomas. He was an unashamed

Christian who cared about people in a huge way. A great combination of coolness and caring, his picture could have been next to the word *genuine* in the dictionary.

Last summer, while I tried to get my act together, I could have talked to him. But I didn't want help—his or anyone's. At a football game last fall, I'd introduced him and his wife, Kristen, to Maggie. She had loved them both immediately.

"You doing okay?" His gaze that night had demanded more than a "yeah."

"A lot better, Coach, thanks."

His thumbs up approval of me and Maggie meant a lot. We'd bumped into them several times at basketball games in the last couple of months, too.

Maybe running into him tonight wasn't a coincidence. My gaze flitted his way. "Maggie and I are having dinner tonight . . . and a talk about relationship stuff."

"Talks are good."

"I guess, if you know what the heck you're supposed to say."

"That would probably help." He gestured toward a park bench, and we sat down.

"We've got a problem." I shook my head. "No, *I've* got a problem." I stared across the park at the leafless trees. "I was attracted to Maggie the second I laid eyes on her, but I didn't rush to ask her out even though it about killed me. I let our friendship grow first. Got permission before I held her hand *and* before I kissed her. We even decided sex would not be a part of our relationship. Saving sex for marriage is huge to Maggie, like a life goal." I tugged my Colt's beanie down on my forehead.

"So far so good. What's the problem?" He mopped his face with a hankie and stuffed it back in his pocket.

"It was never about the physical stuff, and I guess I assumed it wouldn't be an issue. Because our relationship was based on so much more than *that*." I kicked at a stone, sending it flying into the park. "But I was wrong."

156

Coach crossed his arms, nodding slowly. "A commitment not to have sex is great. But it takes more than that. Couples fall off the 'abstinence cliff' all the time because they don't have a game plan to keep sex out of the relationship."

I turned to face him, and a silent question hung in the air between us.

I pulled my gaze from his and stared straight ahead. "Her shirt was kind a short, her jeans were kind a low—" I shook my head hard. "*Man*, no they weren't, not really. It was my fault, not hers, and now I can't get the feel of her *incredible* skin out of my head."

No shock in his steady nod. "Maggie's reaction?"

"She stopped the kissing, and then Patrick walked in. So that was it. But I've imagined what *might* have happened a thousand times. She wasn't upset at all. So I told myself as long as there was no more laying down, we'd be okay. But the next time was even worse." I yanked my hat off and tossed it on the bench.

He ran a hand across the stubble-length hair on his head. Good way to hide his seriously receding hairline. "There's nothing really wrong with kissing. But a kiss is something special—should be anyway—and kissing is *meant* to lead to other things." He leaned forward, his clasped hands swinging between his knees. "Kristen and I went to the mall last weekend, and everywhere I looked, teenage couples were all over each other. I don't want to even imagine what goes on when those couples are alone."

Me either. I shoved my hands into the pockets of my sweatshirt.

"You're a seventeen-year-old guy in an exclusive relationship with a girl you're very attracted to and care about a lot."

"Mmm hmm."

"You live in a sex-crazed world, surrounded by messages that are anything but pure. Now if that's not a recipe for temptation, I don't know what is."

"Tell me somethin' I don't know. Like what to do about it."

He angled toward me. "Do you want things to change? Are you serious about it?"

"Yeah."

"You're miserable and that's good. The question is, are you miserable enough to do whatever it takes to protect you and Maggie?"

"Sure, but I don't know how."

"It's time to get that game plan in order. You . . . "—he leveled his finger at me—"are taking action sooner than a lot of guys. Too often they wait until they're already so close to having sex it's like stopping a runaway train. You ready to get serious?"

"I am." I straightened my back against the bench.

"What do you think needs to happen?"

I shrugged.

"Come on. You're a smart guy—figure it out."

"I don't know where to draw the line."

"Physical intimacy is a slippery slope. Once you start to slide—"

"I get that but how far is too far?"

"That's what everyone wants to know, the million-dollar question."

"Yep."

"Think about it. Where should your focus be? On how close you can get and still be in the clear?"

"Probably not." Memories assaulted my brain, proof that Coach was right. "The further away the better, I suppose."

"That's right. Where exactly you draw the line is entirely up to you and Maggie but those long make out sessions—" Coach shook his head. He didn't need to finish the sentence. "What else?"

"No more bare skin for sure."

"You got that right. How much are you two alone?"

"Probably too much."

"If you can't handle being alone with her, then own up to it."

"But what do I say? How do I explain it?"

"Be man enough to say, 'I can't handle it, can't trust myself', whatever."

A heavy sigh puffed from my mouth. "That sounds so, I don't know, so *weak* or something."

"You're not weak—you're human." He paused. "Tell her that because you're serious about the commitment not to have sex, things have to change."

That sounded okay. "But shouldn't she be more upset? She acts like everything's fine."

"At this point, it's not having the same effect on her that it is on you, but you can't rely on her to say no. The responsibility has to belong to both of you."

"What if she thinks it's dumb?"

"Why would she? My guess is she'll think more of you, not less."

"Man, I hope you're right." Hope shot through me like a burst of adrenaline.

"You gotta be honest with her." He glanced at his watch. "What time are you picking her up?"

I pulled out my phone. "Uh, wow, in a little over an hour. Better get going." I stood and stretched my hand toward his.

He shook my hand, then pulled me toward him in a bro hug. "Thanks, Coach."

Preston

Maggie's hair fell across her cheek as she cut her fettuccini. She pushed the loose strands behind her ear. "Oh, I almost forgot. Grandma and Grandpa said to thank you for coming to their dinner last night. They said any guy willing to spend a Friday night with a bunch of old people must be a keeper."

"A keeper, huh? Probably shouldn't tell them about my late night visit. Did your parents say anything?"

"Not a word. The door stayed open, and anyway, they trust you."

Guilt jabbed my chest like a dagger. "Well, good."

The conversation lulled as the food on our plates disappeared. I signaled our favorite waitress, Becky, for drink refills.

Maggie pushed the last clump of noodles around her plate. She glanced up. Our eyes met for a moment before she focused again on her fettuccini. She finally pushed her plate to the table's edge with several bites left that, any other night, I would have scarfed down.

Becky swooped in again, all smiles, to take our plates and tempt us with dessert that neither of us wanted.

The space between us was suddenly heavy, like when a coming storm makes the air almost too thick to breath. My food sat like a rock in the pit of my stomach, and my pounding heart could probably be heard in the next booth.

"So, are you ready to talk?" Maggie propped her elbow on the table and rested her chin on her hand. The fingernails of her other hand tapped lightly against the table.

I huffed out a breath. "I'm sorry for letting things go so far."

Her fingers stilled on the tabletop. "I know, but nothing really happened."

"It may have seemed like nothing to you, but to me, it was definitely something."

Surprise widened her eyes. "Oh, um, I didn't, uh . . . " She pulled her hand back and dropped it in her lap.

"If we'd stayed on that couch even a few more minutes . . . " I shook my head.

Maggie's eyes widened more, and she lifted her quivering chin from her hand.

"You *should* be upset with me. That's why things have to change."

"Change, like how?" Her voice was barely above a whisper.

"All the making out we've been doing." I shook my head.

Her arm dropped to the table with a thud. "Don't break up with me over this, Preston, please."

"No, *no*. Of course, I'm not breaking up with you." I snatched up her hand.

She squeezed my fingers so hard, sharp tingles danced down the back of my hand. Her eyes closed as she sucked in a deep breath.

"Maggie."

She nodded and swiped at a tear.

"Things have to change, but I'm *not* suggesting we break up." That was the last thing I wanted.

She nodded again, pulling in another shaky breath. "I didn't know the situation was so . . . so—"

"Tempting?"

"I was going to say serious."

"It's serious all right."

Her thin eyebrows shot up over teary eyes filled with questions. "So, what kind of changes?"

"We've been home alone way too much and no more being in your room, door open or not. That was a bad idea."

She unwrapped her hand from around mine to dab at her eyes and wipe her nose with a napkin. "All of that's fine—whatever needs to change—just so we're not breaking up."

I leaned closer. "I absolutely do not want to break up. I'm sorry you thought that."

She nodded, then swiped a napkin across her nose again.

I was not at all sure I'd convinced her. "You okay?"

A weak nod. Her shaky smile didn't boost my confidence either.

I pulled her hands together in the center of the table. "I love you, remember?"

Finally, a real smile. "I love you too."

"I know my parents are home tonight, so how 'bout we hang out there?"

"Yeah, sure."

Still holding one of her hands, I dug in my pocket for money.

She pulled her hand loose and reached for her coat.

"Hey there, my job, remember?" I slapped bills on the table and grabbed my own coat as I slid from the booth.

A mere whisper from Maggie, "I remember."

Maggie

We climbed the porch steps, and Preston pulled me against his solid chest. "Don't ask me to come in," he whispered next to my ear.

I gripped the front of his jacket. "I won't." But I wanted to.

His warm, strong embrace protected me from the cold night air. Our lips came together in one hungry kiss after another.

I held tighter to his jacket.

"Gotta go," he murmured against my cheek. He took a step back.

A wave of freezing air filled the space between us. A huge shiver rippled through me.

"Better go in before you freeze." He backed up further, then pressed his lips to the back of my hand. "I love you."

"Love you, too." I squeezed his fingers until the distance between us pulled our hands apart. Shivering, I scampered inside and tiptoed to my room.

Being kissed by Preston was like nothing I'd imagined even in my wildest dreams. My insides completely melted every time his fingertips caressed my face or threaded through my hair. Goose bumps raced down my arms just thinking about his strong arms wrapped around me, his lips pressed against mine.

Scenes from the last couple of times we'd been alone played through my mind, shooting warmth down to my toes. Was he being overly cautious? Or was I in denial?

If he found me *that* tempting . . . How incredibly flattering. But it was sort of scary, too.

Would more have happened if Patrick hadn't come home?

But more didn't happen.
We stopped.
It won't happen again.
Everything will be fine.

Preston

Questions bounced around inside my head like a ping pong ball on steroids. Did Maggie need to know more? Like everything? Were we at that point in the relationship? I was desperate for sleep, but my mind refused to shut off. This was the absolute last thing I wanted to be stressing over the night before my big Valentine's Day plans.

Considering how she freaked out about breaking up, there was no way I could tell her now. But maybe I could come clean to Coach. As much as I dreaded tarnishing my reputation with him, that wouldn't be a tenth as bad as confessing to Maggie.

He used to be proud of me and hold me up as a team player, good sportsmanship—all that kind of stuff. Not disappointing him was important to me back then. Still was now. But if he could help me figure this out, I had to tell him.

I hit the park the next day right after church, half hoping I'd see him. Half hoping I wouldn't.

When I spotted him rounding the north end of the jogging path, my heart hammered. How do you tell someone who's proud of you that you messed up bad?

I jogged in place, matching his pace until he reached me. "Coach."

"Preston." We continued along the park's perimeter

Too much sweat trickled down my back for the short time I'd been jogging. Especially in forty-degree weather.

"How'd it go with Maggie last night?"

"Went really well, actually." Our pace slowed to a fast walk. "I admitted I can't handle so much alone time and definitely no more being in her room together."

Coach jerked to a stop. His narrowed eyes pierced through me. "You were in her *room*?"

"Not like that. Just for a few minutes to talk and only once. Her parents were home, the door stayed open, but, *man*, there was something so enticing about it. No more of that."

He grunted and resumed walking. "I'll say. So, what was Maggie's reaction?"

"Surprise mostly, and then she freaked out, thinking that I wanted to break up, which of course I don't. Said whatever needs to change is fine by her as long as we don't break up."

"Sounds good. Proud of you."

An all too familiar pang of guilt shot through me. He wouldn't be proud of me in a minute. I stuffed my hands into my sweatshirt pockets and sucked in a deep breath. "There's some stuff I left out the other night. Not about Maggie and me, but it's pretty relevant to what's going on."

"Have anything to do with that rough patch you went through last year?"

"What?"

"You and Alyssa broke up, and your life kind of spiraled out of control." A shrug rippled across his shoulders. "You don't do your best field repair work when you're hung over."

"I . . . uh . . . ." I slowed our pace to a stroll.

"Thought you kept the whole mess under wraps, didn't you? Well, you're lousy at lying. 'Doin' fine, Coach.' If I had a buck for every time you spouted that line . . . I wanted to wring your neck and make you fess up. But instead I prayed for you."

My mouth gaped open, but no words found their way out.

"I care about you—you know that." He elbowed my side. "Man, was I psyched when the story circulated that Preston Jacoby 'got religious big time'. I could see you'd changed. Your attitude was different, and you had a new depth. It was obvious

God was working on you. I hoped you'd talk to me about it, but you didn't. So I just kept praying for you."

I stopped and turned to face him. "Wow, Coach. I don't even know what to say."

He shook his head. "Simply looking out for a friend."

A wall of doubt slammed into me. Why not just leave it at "a rough patch"? Would it really help to spill all the details? A picture of Maggie, innocent and trusting, filled my mind. Nope. I had to go through with it.

"About that rough patch. I should probably fill in the gaps."

Coach pointed to the same bench we'd sat on last night.

I huffed out a breath. "You mentioned Alyssa." I swallowed. "My life got real complicated after Alyssa and I . . . slept together."

His eyebrows arched, but he continued to look straight ahead, saying nothing.

"No big let's-do-it plan. It just happened. And continued to happen despite massive guilt that hammered me day and night. When Alyssa's dad announced his transfer to a plant a couple of hours from here, she freaked out about leaving and got incredibly clingy. The clingier she got, the more I pulled away. It hit me, here I was, a sixteen-year-old guy having sex with his fifteen-year-old girlfriend. What was I *doing*? This move could be my ticket out." Memories flooded my mind in a slow-moving parade. "I really liked her, but after we had sex, the guilt and the worry someone would find out or that she'd get pregnant—it weighed on me like a ton of bricks.

"I said no to a long-distance relationship, which broke her heart. She begged to stay here with her grandparents, but her parents refused. The breakup got really ugly, awful things were said. And then she was gone." That last argument rewound in my mind as if it had happened yesterday. The yelling. The name calling. The utter devastation on her face.

"Even after she left, I kept up this huge front with the guys about how sex was so great. Course I continued my good guy routine, too. Went to church every week with the family, same as I'd always done, all the while hitting the bottle more each week." I shook my head at how ridiculous it all sounded.

"One day I hit rock bottom. I can't remember exactly what set me off, but I yelled—swore actually—at God and blamed Him for my screwed-up life. And in a voice I could *hear*, Coach, He said, 'Give me the pieces of your life, and I'll put it all back together.'"

Coach cocked his head and studied me. "Guess you took him up on His offer?"

I met his gaze. "For the first time in my life, I got serious about a relationship with God. Suddenly, I cared a lot less about being cool and popular. This desire to be more than a sure-I-go-to-church kind of Christian consumed me. But that meant a lot of things in my life had to change. And they have. Just wish I hadn't jacked things up so bad before I came to my senses."

Coach was quiet for a good minute. Probably deciding which of my issues to address first. Finally, he cocked his head in my direction. "We all mess up. What matters is that we learn from our mistakes and head in a new direction."

"That's what I've been trying to do—move on and let Him call the shots."

A firm, short nod confirmed his approval. Then he sighed. "So, you and Alyssa, huh?"

I nodded grimly.

"I'm assuming Maggie doesn't know."

I shook my head.

"That does complicate things."

I exhaled. "I should have told you before. Is this a game changer?"

"I'd have said all the same things—talk about boundaries, know your limits, get a handle on it early." Coach crossed his arms. "It will be tough, but it *is* possible."

"Man, I hope so."

"Depends on how committed you are. What you need is someone to hold you accountable who'll be tough. Someone you'll listen to even when you don't want to hear what he's saying."

"I know the perfect person."

"Who?"

"You."

A slight grin tugged at Coach's mouth.

"You already know my story. And there's no one I trust and respect more."

His eyes narrowed. "I'm willing, but you have to understand, I'll be tough on you like you can't even imagine."

"I know you will. I need someone who's not afraid to lay it on the line."

His hand jutted toward me. "You've got a deal."

If him being tough on me was anything like his handshake, I might regret this arrangement.

"We'll get together once or twice a week, more if you need to. And you and Maggie go back on my prayer list." Coach pointed up. "Because it's His strength that will help you keep that commitment."

Creases formed across his forehead as he refolded his arms across his chest. "Now, tell me about the alcohol."

"Ever hear guys talk about Friday nights?" I crooked my fingers in the air.

"Sounds vaguely familiar."

"Started out after football games during freshman year and basically amounted to make out parties. Find a house with very inattentive or absent parents, snag some snacks, crank up the music, and let the pairing off begin. Pretty innocent stuff to begin with, but once alcohol started showing up, the parties got hard core. By the middle of last year, the houses with the most *bedrooms* were the party favorites."

Coach frowned and shook his head. "That's awful."

"It seems totally ridiculous now—the whole setup. I made out with more girls than I care to remember. Fairly innocent stuff with most, but with a couple . . . " I shook my head against the flashbacks flooding my mind. "Being with Maggie now, I can't even imagine what the appeal was to all that. And *man*, what I wouldn't do to get rid of the memories."

"Too bad it doesn't work that way. So, at a party—"

"Not there." I sighed and shoved my hands deeper into my pockets. "After the party, at her house. And then, wherever we could be alone, but never at a party." I kicked a stone and watched it skitter into the grass. "After Alyssa and I broke up, I didn't hook up or date anyone but, boy, did I drink. Even arranged for the alcohol a couple of times."

Coach's jaw tensed. "Almost nothing makes me madder than people who supply teenagers with alcohol. And it bothers me just as much when the popular, fun kids lead scores of their friends astray."

I raised my hand above my head. "Guilty as charged. That's another thing that bugs me. I can't erase the terrible example I spread around so thick." I kicked another stone.

"Those parties still going on?"

"Yep. Haven't been to one for a long time. It's mostly a freshman and sophomore thing now. A lot of the older couples want more privacy than make out parties provide."

A yikes expression pulled at his face.

Yep. That kind of thing was huge in the junior and senior class.

"Maybe you *can* do something about that lousy example."

"Like what?"

"That's your first assignment. Give it some thought, pray about it, too, and let me know what you come up with next time we get together."

"Homework?"

"Told you I'd be tough. Can you handle it?"

"I can handle it."

"Good. Part of accountability is mending fences and righting wrongs."

Preston

I'd begged to have Valentine's Day off and roped Mom into helping me cook a special dinner for Maggie. While she fussed over the finishing touches on the food, I set the dining room table with her best china, candles, and a dozen red roses.

Dad strode past me into the kitchen. "Can Preston handle it from here?"

I backed up to catch him and Mom through the doorway.

"Well . . . " Mom frowned and squinted up at Dad. "I don't know."

Dad's gaze shifted to me. "Preston?"

I shrugged. "Yeah, I guess."

"Great, because I'm taking you out to dinner, Mrs. Jacoby." He backed Mom up against the counter and leaned toward her. "Can you be ready in, say, a half hour?"

Mom giggled like a teenager. "Well, I suppose I can be, but I want everything to be just right for Maggie."

Dad shot me a look.

"Mom, it's cool. Show me what to do. It'll be fine."

Mom kissed Dad's cheek, then swatted him away. "Okay, come here, Preston. Now the chicken alfredo is almost done—it's simmering. The Caesar salad's in the fridge—toss it before you serve it."

I nodded.

"The rolls have to be baked." She shook her head. "I don't know about this."

"I can bake the rolls, Mom. How long?"

She checked the oven temperature. "About twelve minutes. Maybe more, but not a second longer than fifteen. You'll have to watch them closely." She opened the fridge and pointed at desert. "You found a great raspberry cheesecake recipe. Save us a piece?"

"Maybe. What about the appetizers?"

"Oh, I almost forgot the stuffed mushrooms. They're in the fridge too—bake them for twelve to thirteen minutes before the rolls." She put her hand on my arm. "Eat those first, Preston, before you serve the salad."

"Duh, Mom. I know when to eat the appetizer." I shook my head.

Dad snagged her arm and pulled her toward the door. "Jacki, he'll be fine. Go get ready."

She resisted Dad's tug. "I'll have my phone. If you need anything, just call."

"I will." I lifted the lid and peeked at the pasta.

Dad came back to the kitchen after making sure Mom made it to the bedroom. "Great job on the table."

"Watched a YouTube video like five times. Does it look okay?"

"Looks perfect to me. If you served Maggie a Big Mac and fries with those roses, she'd love it."

"Mom said you two would be around all evening."

"Which I'm sure you were thrilled about."

"I don't mind." In fact, it felt safer that way.

"Well, what can I say? She likes surprises."

"Can you keep an eye on all this while I get Maggie?"

He nodded, peeking under the lid at the alfredo.

"No eating—just watching." I socked his arm.

"Yeah, yeah. Just get your girlfriend."

I wanted everything to be perfect for Maggie's first Valentine's Day with a guy. I hadn't been alone on Valentine's since like 6th grade, a fact I planned to keep to myself.

Maggie

⬥⟶≈≈⟵⬥

O ne more mushroom. You want it?" Preston stabbed the last stuffed mushroom with his fork.

"Those little things are almost too cute to eat."

"I'm pretty sure you ate like four already."

"Don't remind me. But no, I couldn't eat another bite." I leaned toward him. "The table, the roses, the food—all of it was so amazing. You're incredible."

The dimple danced across his right cheek. "We're not finished yet." He strode to the kitchen and returned with two big slices of a gooey-looking desert.

"That looks incredibly yummy."

"Raspberry swirled chocolate cheesecake. I found the recipe, but Mom made it."

I savored a bite of pure velvety smoothness. "Tastes even better than it looks. Chocolate and raspberries—two of my favorites."

"I know." He took a big bite himself. "It is good. Hey, before I forget, Thursday after school, I'll have to drop you off quick. I'm gettin' together with Coach."

"Working on Little League stuff already?"

"Uh, no. We're gonna get together on Thursdays to hang out and talk. Kind of an accountability thing."

I paused, my fork in mid-air. "Really."

He carefully cut several bites of his cheesecake and nodded, without looking at me. "Yeah."

My fingers inched across the table to his hand. "I think that's wonderful."

174

His eyes met mine. "Might invite some of the guys to join us at some point, maybe."

"What a great idea." I squeezed his hand. "You're such a good friend."

~ ~ ~

Mr. Martin scanned the list of volunteer clinic jobs Mom and Dad had come up with. "They need all kinds of help."

I pointed to the last line on the list. "The woman doing the cleaning quit last week, so Mom's been doing it after she closes up. She didn't get home last night until eight-thirty. The budget's so tight, they can't hire a replacement for a while."

"We'll see how the group wants to handle this." He handed the list back to me. "You're up first, Maggie."

I took a couple of bites of my mixed berry yogurt as the NHS members filed in. By now, everyone brought a lunch to what had become weekly meetings because it was impossible to wait in the lunch line and make the meeting on time.

Mr. Martin whistled. "Listen up—Maggie's got an impressive list of volunteer positions."

I gulped some of my bottled water and slid onto the desktop. "Some are weekly, some daily, some are one-time or occasional things. I made copies."

Alex grabbed the stack of papers and passed them out. "This should beef up your resume, Lindsey. How many jobs you want?"

"Just a couple," she murmured.

"There have to be other procrastinators still looking for stuff to pad their college apps," Tyler said.

"I imagine so." Mr. Martin rocked on his heels.

"Why not put in the morning announcements that the clinic needs volunteers and give their phone number so whoever wants to help can call them," Erin suggested.

Mr. Martin's gaze shifted to me.

I shook my head. "That sounds good, but the staff is so small, they can barely handle all the calls coming in now. A bunch of volunteers calling in would push them over the edge."

Mr. Martin rubbed his stubbly chin. "Maggie's got a point. They don't need more work."

"So, *we'll* organize the volunteers. Set up a table at lunch for people to sign up." Tyler emptied the crumbs from a bag of chips into his mouth.

Heads nodded around the group.

"Tyler and Maggie—you two want to organize something? And Lindsey gets to pick the first five jobs."

Lindsey blinked and held up five fingers. "Five?"

"That's right. Tyler?" Mr. Martin pointed to him.

Tyler shrugged and nodded. "Sure. Maggie?"

"Okay." I stared at the long list. This would probably take more time than I was willing to give. But what could I say?

"Great. Now who's in the bulletin board group? I'd like you to change up the one by the gym. New pictures or something. And another board's available at the south entrance. Get something fantastic on it by Thursday." Mr. Martin rubbed his palms together as the five-minute bell rang. "And all of you— see Maggie and Tyler. I expect every one of your names to appear on this list." His thumb jerked over his shoulder in his usual gesture of dismissal.

"I'll get with you later, Maggie." Tyler grabbed a couple of extra copies of the job list on his way out.

Preston

Operation "work on Preston's lousy example" kicked off the second week of meeting with Coach when we invited the guys to join us. We sweetened the deal with the promise of pizza. Still, I had no idea if they'd show. But thanks to a really crummy school lunch, growling stomachs interrupted class all afternoon,

By 3:15, Coach's office looked like a reunion of our eighth-grade traveling baseball team. Alex and Brett sprawled on the old leather couch next to me, and Connor, Robb, and Zach straddled folding chairs. Coach perched on the corner of his desk. "Man, you guys eat like hogs!" He shook his head at three already empty pizza boxes on the counter next to his desk.

"What—you're only having two slices? Coach, I'm disappointed." Zach held up his empty plate that had tipped with the weight of six pieces of pizza two minutes ago.

"My wife's expecting me to eat her home-cooked meal in about two hours. And besides that, at my request, she holds me accountable for what I eat, and her look of disappointment practically breaks my heart."

Snickers and sarcastic "Aw's," echoed around the room.

Coach waved away the sarcasm. "Which brings us to the reason for this pizza fest." He nodded my direction.

"Thought you just missed us, Coach." Rob stuffed half a slice of pepperoni pizza in his mouth.

"Course I do. But there's more to it than that." Coach's gaze drilled into me.

I sucked in a deep breath and leaned forward. "Some of you know that Coach and I are gettin' together to talk about stuff. A kind of accountability setup."

A quick scan around the room revealed every eye was fixed on me. I swallowed.

Coach nodded and crossed his arms.

"We're getting together on Thursdays, and any of you are welcome to stop by, if you want. The only requirement is that anything shared here, stays here. We keep it between us."

No one said a word. But no one got up to leave either.

Coach crunched his paper plate into a ball and tossed it at the trash can across the room. He pumped his fist as the white blob hit the target. "Yes."

"You still got it," Brett quipped.

"You bet." He rubbed his hands together and settled back on the desk. "So, how many of you gentlemen are currently seeing someone?"

Every guy's hand went up.

Coach nodded. "Okay, I have a question for you. Something to make you think." His gaze scrutinized us through the dramatic pause. "Would you still want to be in a relationship with this girl if—for whatever reason—you couldn't touch her for . . . let's say the next month."

Things were about to get real interesting. Only Coach could get away with seriously posing that kind of question.

"For whatever reason? What's that supposed to mean?" Connor rocked back on his chair, frowning.

"The reason isn't important—that's what it means," Coach explained.

"That's ridiculous." Rob huffed and rolled his eyes.

"That's the dumbest thing I've ever heard, Coach." Zach's arms crossed over his broad chest.

Yep, just what I expected. Actually, they were less rude and obnoxious than I thought.

"Alex, Brett, Preston, what do you think?"

I jerked my head left toward Alex.

He shrugged. "I don't know if we'll be together that long."

Coach slid to his feet off the corner of the desk. "Might not be together for the next month, huh?"

Alex's shoulders rose in a long shrug. "Dunno. Maybe, maybe not."

"Okay, then. Is there a physical aspect to your relationship with—" He pointed to Alex then spun his hand in a circular motion.

"Gracie Keller." Alex grinned, all proud-like. "Well, sure."

"It sounds like you don't know how much you really *like* her. Yet there's something physical about the relationship?"

Alex frowned. "Not like *that*, just kissing and stuff."

"Kissing and stuff." Coach nodded then pointed at Brett. "How about you?"

Brett, who was nothing like his older brother Rob, had always had a ton of girls for friends but never a *girlfriend* until now. "I'd be willing to give it a try."

Coach nodded. "Preston?"

"Absolutely no question. I'd want to be with Maggie."

Zach's dark eyes challenged me. "How do you even *be* in a relationship with a girl without touching?" He drew out the word relationship, making it sound stupid.

"It would be tough, but given the option of being with Maggie or not being with her, it's not even a choice."

Rob rocked his chair back on two legs. "Why even bother if it's gonna be strictly hands off?" He brought the chair back down with a loud thud.

"That sounds bad," I muttered, shaking my head.

"Maybe to you, church boy, but Coach wants us to be honest, right Coach?"

"That's why we're here, Rob." Seconds ticked by as Coach seemed to examine each one of us with a stone-like expression. "It's a scenario you'll probably never run into, I know, but what point do you think I'm trying to make?"

"It shouldn't be all about the physical, duh. But no touching at all?" Connor turned his palms up.

I followed Coach's gaze past the circle of guys to the doorway.

"Tucker. Come on in." Coach motioned to a big guy in a backward baseball cap and a letter jacket from Washington, the neighboring school.

The guy covered the distance to Coach's desk in huge strides then bumped fists with him. "Coach." He took a seat on the opposite corner of Coach's desk.

"Guys, I'd like you to meet Tucker McIntire. He goes to my church."

"Hey." A murmured, unison greeting and jutting chins acknowledged him.

"The looks on your faces." Tucker slapped his knee. "Coach just posed his if-you-couldn't-touch-your-girlfriend question, right?" His eyes widened as a grin splashed across his stubbly face.

"We all failed except for Brett and Preston." Rob pointed an accusing finger at me.

"That's not true." Coach pointed back at Rob. "You all passed because you were honest and took a moment to consider it."

Tucker shrugged out of his jacket. "It *is* possible to have a girl/guy relationship without the physical."

"But why would you even want to?" Zach's voice taunted.

Tucker's grin became a serious straight line. "Guess it depends on what you want from the relationship."

"Tuck has an interesting perspective." Coach grabbed Tucker's coat and tossed it on the chair behind the desk.

Tucker clasped his hands together, let them fall into his lap, and took a deep breath. "I had sex for the first time when I was fourteen. Cami was fourteen, too. Most days we went to her house after school—her parents were never home. And one day we did it. As I walked home, brilliant thoughts like 'Now I'm a man' paraded just ahead of real scary ones like 'Hope I didn't get her pregnant.' I locked myself in my room and prayed that she wouldn't get pregnant, and then I swore that it would *not* happen again." He slouched and sighed. "But, the next day, guess what? It's not like I'd asked my *mom* to drive me to the store to buy condoms, so I prayed even harder walking home that night. Promised God I'd never have sex again if He'd keep her from gettin' pregnant." He flipped his hat around and pulled it low on his forehead.

"But we kept doin' it, and even though I eventually got some condoms, Cami got pregnant. I thought her dad was gonna string me up, and my mom came this close to having a nervous breakdown." He held his thumb and index finger about an eighth of an inch apart.

Tucker looked over us, like he was studying the light hanging in the far corner or something. His jaw twitched. "Cami lost the baby. We spent my fifteenth birthday in the ER. No matter how long I live, I'll never forget the sound of her sobbing the night our daughter died."

It was like all the air got sucked from the room and was replaced with an incredibly loud and suffocating silence.

Tucker flexed his hands, and his knuckles popped. "Cami and I didn't stay together long after that. Talk about baggage weighing down a relationship." He jerked his head toward Zach. "So. Why did I wait two months to kiss my girlfriend Claire? Why is our relationship one of the least physical you've probably ever seen? Because I *never* wanna go through anything like that again. And, I gotta believe there's something better than fourteen-year-olds sneaking around to have sex."

"How do you and Claire make it work?" Coach's question was for Tucker, but his eyes drilled into mine when he asked it.

Tucker glanced at Coach, then seemed to direct his focus to me, too. "We do a lot of stuff together, like going to things at church and school. We cook dinner or chill with her family or mine. But we don't hang out at home unless we know people will be around." An ornery grin lit up his face. "We keep it strictly PG rated, like if Grandma was across from us."

Snorts and rolled eyes all around.

"My grandma's so out of it, she wouldn't have a clue," Rob smirked.

Tucker shrugged. "Maybe it's your parents, a younger brother or sister, your pastor, whoever. If you wouldn't do somethin' with them in the room, then don't do it. My grandma's always been there for me. She's taken a huge interest in me and Claire, and man, I'd hate to disappoint her again."

He pointed to Coach. "This guy's been an incredible help, too. I wouldn't be where I am today without him. And he keeps gettin' me to tell my story. Guess if I can help even one person avoid what I went through, then it's worth it."

Coach's gaze shifted from Tucker to pan across us guys. "Like my wife watching what I eat. Challenging a person to high expectations can have a powerful impact." Coach pointed at me. "Preston's serious about the no sex commitment he made to Maggie. And you better believe, I'm holdin' him to it. We'll be here every Thursday, and like he said, you guys are welcome to join us anytime. Anything else you want to say, Preston?"

I shook my head.

Coach moved behind his desk and began shuffling papers. "I've got a meeting to get ready for. But feel free to hang out as long as you like."

I motioned to Tucker. "There's a couple of pieces of pizza left. Help yourself."

"Don't mind if I do." Tucker slid off the desk and slapped the remaining pieces on a paper plate.

"Thanks for the food." Connor stretched and grabbed for his coat.

"Hey, no problem." Coach clapped Connor on the shoulder and then walked with Tucker toward the door.

Connor nodded toward them and murmured, "Some story, huh?"

"I'll say."

Zach shook his head in disbelief or awe, I wasn't sure.

Rob's face held no expression.

Brett and Alex both looked about half sick.

Coach and Tucker walked back toward the group. "Nice to meet you all." Tucker tossed his empty plate and grabbed his coat.

"You too." Connor held out his fist to bump with Tucker's.

Rob asked about Washington's last football season, and Tucker shared a quick recount of the winning play at the regional finals.

The rest of the guys chimed in their thanks and headed toward the door.

Coach motioned me behind his desk. "Tuck needs a ride—you mind dropping him off?" Our eyes met. And his had lots to say. "He's a good guy, and he's been where you are right now."

"See ya later," Rob called as he and Brett headed out.

"Yep." My eyes remained locked with Coach's.

Tucker, his hands shoved in his pockets, appeared beside me. "Hey, uh, Preston, right?"

I nodded.

"Would you mind giving me a ride? Coach said you don't live that far from me. My car's in the shop again." He grunted and rolled his eyes.

"Sure, no problem."

We drove in silence for three blocks. There was so much I wanted to ask him, yet it felt weird talking to a stranger about personal stuff. "You've got quite a story."

Tucker lowered the radio volume. "If I hadn't lived through it, I probably wouldn't believe it myself."

"I'm assuming your girlfriend, uh—"

"Claire."

"She knows about your past?"

"Hard to keep something like that a secret."

"If you don't mind my asking—"

"Coach says I've been where you are now. Thought it would help if we talked."

I nodded. "That's what he said to me, too."

"I don't wanna think where I'd be if he hadn't walked into my life and stayed there."

"Yeah, he's the best." I sucked in a calming breath. "So, Claire. Is she okay with . . . everything?"

"At first, she wasn't even sure about being *friends*. But with my incredible charm—" He flashed an ornery grin. "I convinced her there was no harm in friendship. Then I wooed her like crazy before asking her out. It took a lot of convincing, believe me."

"I can't imagine Maggie ever being okay with my past." I braked at the light. "Do you need to be anywhere soon?"

"Not until six. Claire and I have a date to bake cookies. I know—how will we handle the excitement?" His deep laughter filled the car.

"Sounds fun, actually." I pointed to the McDonald's ahead. "Mind if we have a Coke and talk?"

"That's cool, but I'd rather have a Dr. Pepper."

~ ~ ~

I paid for two drinks, and we settled in a corner booth.

"So, tell me about Maggie." Tucker jammed his straw through the ice.

A smile tugged at my mouth. "She's amazing—the best thing to ever happen to me, right behind my decision to get serious about a relationship with Christ. She's a Christian, too. We've been together since October, and early on we made a commitment not to have sex." I twisted my straw paper into a knot.

"How's that going for you?"

"The temptation is huge, for me anyway. And considering I had sex with my last girlfriend—" My eyebrows shot up. "We talked about being careful, and that's helped, but . . . " I exhaled.

"It's tough—especially because you've already opened that door."

"Yep." I nodded.

"You started something, and now it's hard to turn it off."

"Exactly." I pressed my palms flat on the table. "I can't stand the idea of telling her about my past, except I kind a feel like I'm not being honest if I say nothing. Although I'm pretty certain it would break her heart."

"You sure about that?"

"Saving sex for marriage is so important to her, like a life goal. Her plan is to someday wear a white wedding dress that stands for purity."

Tucker nodded. "Good plan."

"But she'll want a groom who waited, too. And it's not like we're engaged or anything, still." I flung the wadded-up straw paper across the table. It bounced and Tucker caught it.

"You didn't tell her you never had sex, did you?"

"No, but I'm pretty sure she assumes. I told her I think sex should be saved for marriage, which I do, *now*."

"I understand not wanting to bring it up, but her knowing could be helpful." His gaze drilled into me.

My shoulders slumped. "I suppose, but telling Coach was bad enough. Telling Maggie . . ." I shook my head. "I can't even think about it without my stomach heaving."

"It would be tough, no doubt about it."

"Don't know if I could do it." I leaned back in the booth. "New subject. How are you makin' it work with Claire? I know you said you aren't alone that much."

"I didn't get it all figured out right away."

"Yeah?"

"After Cami, I had sex with two other girls—all before I turned sixteen. I could *not* believe how fast those relationships went there."

"Because you started something that was hard to turn off."

"Exactly." He folded his arms and leaned on the table. "That's when Coach walked into my life. He helped me retrain my mind, my body, my whole thought process about girls and dating and life. It was hard work, and Coach was tough as a grizzly bear. And God . . . was God." A far-away look clouded his eyes, like he was reliving something big or traumatic.

He shook his head and took a deep breath before his eyes focused on me again. "Uh, sorry about that. Sometimes the memories are right there, like it happened yesterday." He pushed out a big breath. "It's those memories that drive me to make sure God's the one in charge. Because *that's* what makes it possible for me not to pursue sex with Claire."

We really are in the same place.

Tucker relaxed back in his seat. "Anyway, Claire knew about Cami, so the subject came up like the third date, way before I even kissed her. It was a major, serious discussion let me tell ya. I told her everything, ending with my commitment not to have sex again until I find and marry the woman I wanted to spend the rest of my life with."

"Did she freak out about the other girls?"

"For a minute, I thought we were through, but I promised her our relationship would be different—it already *was* different. So, she agreed to give us a shot."

He fiddled with his hat. "Once I finally did kiss Claire, *man*, that's all I wanted to do. No way could I handle being alone with her for hours at a time or night after night. That's why we hang out at her house with her brothers, sister, her parents, whoever. Knowing someone could walk through the room at any moment." He knocked his fist against the tabletop. "We're together like all the time but without the temptations that go with being alone."

"There's gotta be times when no one else is around."

"Sometimes. But we make a point of having a plan for the evening. Like tonight we're—"

"Baking cookies." I chuckled.

"And her little sister will probably help. Her parents kind a plant the little ones around us. It's their way of contributing to the effort."

"They know too?" My mouth hung open.

"About Cami."

"Are you kiddin' me?"

"When you mess up as bad as I did, pretty much everyone knows about it."

"Man, I don't think I could deal with that."

"Actually, they've been pretty cool about it. They let me know right from the start what their expectations were—no sex, no alcohol, no drugs, no encouraging Claire to go against family rules. They knew about her commitment to wait, and let's just say, I was forewarned that I would treat her in the most gentlemanly manner possible." He tapped the table again. "Parental involvement is a good thing, Preston. If either my parents or Cami's had paid *any* attention, the situation might not have gotten so out of control." He held up his hands. "Not saying it was their fault, but a little awareness would have helped."

"Both my parents and Maggie's are pretty involved, but mine don't know about Alyssa. I hope they never have to find out. My brother Patrick knows, and he's on me all the time."

Tucker stared at me but said nothing.

I wanted to look away but couldn't. "You think I should tell them?"

"Not my decision." He drummed his fingers on the table. "Whatever helps you stick to your commitment. Telling Maggie, telling your parents." He shrugged. "Telling *her* parents. I guess it all depends on how serious you are."

I closed my eyes. *Anything but that.*

"Dude, I'm not trying to be the heavy."

A low growl escaped my throat. "I know."

His expression became a mask of seriousness. "Whether or not you tell and who you tell is up to you, but if you're serious about waiting, you've got to figure out what gets to you. And Maggie needs to know, too."

"Well, she's a real snuggler, which I love. But man, when she's all soft and warm and smells so awesome, my mind wanders to all kinds of places it shouldn't go."

"Tell me about it. Sometimes, I have to consciously put space between me and Claire."

"Does she understand?"

"At first she'd look at me like 'what's going on?' if I scooted away or stood up and wandered into the kitchen. But she gets it that I need room to breathe."

"Claire sounds amazing."

"Don't I know it."

I glanced behind Tucker at the clock on the far wall. "Hey, don't want to make you late for cookie baking."

He swatted at my arm.

"Coach was right—I needed to talk to you."

"Anytime, just give me a call."

We exchanged numbers.

"Maybe we could double sometime, you and Maggie, me and Claire."

"Yeah, sure." I stood up and stretched. "You have no idea how much this helped."

"Yeah, I do. I've been there. I'm still there—just a little further down the road maybe."

Maggie

I grabbed the ringing phone for the thirty-fourth time at 9:34 a.m., adding another tick mark to the tally of calls. If I survived the rest of this Saturday morning shift, it would be a miracle. "Good morning, The Least of These Clinic. How may I help you?" My gaze strayed to the crowded waiting room where twenty bodies pressed into a space with a dozen mismatched chairs and an overflowing toy chest. "No appointments left today. I can get you in Monday afternoon at—"

"Ryleigh cried half the night." The teenaged female voice trembled, like on-the-verge-of-panic trembled. "I'm going home tomorrow and back to school on Monday. Can't you squeeze her in?"

I swallowed a rude groan. If I had a quarter for every time someone begged to be *squeezed in*. "I'm sorry but—"

Mom's hand pressed on my shoulder. "Who is it?"

"May I have your name?"

"My baby is Ryleigh Anderson. She's seen Mrs. Jennison a few times."

My hand clamped over the mouthpiece. "Ryleigh Anderson."

Mom sighed and nodded. "Squeeze her in."

"Where?" I zig-zagged my finger up and down the full schedule.

"At noon." Her raised hand silenced the protest clawing up my throat. "When do we ever get out of here right at noon?" She patted my arm and rushed off to her next patient.

"We can see Ryleigh at noon," I grumbled into the phone.

"Oh, thank you. We'll be there."

I cradled the phone and stretched as Preston's text notification sounded from my cell. I snatched it from my pocket and pressed the silence button. "free for lunch?"

"You bet. That will get me through the morning!"

"noon?"

"Make it 12:30, please."

"C U then"

"☺"

The ringing phone, call number thirty-five, tried to pull my attention away from Preston. I only half listened to a long, whiney list of symptoms because Preston was never really out of my thoughts.

By the time the whimpering Ryleigh, wrapped in a dingy pink blanket, and her very young mom arrived at 11:55, I was desperate to escape. Both blonde, the baby was adorable and her mother very pretty in spite of the dark circles under her bright blue eyes. "She can't be more than seventeen," I murmured as they settled into a chair. Soon the whimpering turned to actual crying. The young mom stood and, patting the baby's back, paced a slow circle around the now empty waiting area.

Twenty minutes later, Mom held the door open and motioned mom and baby to exam room one. "Mags, please pull the charts for the Monday morning appointments."

"Ugh, I'm already so far behind. I still have three things to do on the closing list, and Preston will be here in less than ten minutes for lunch."

The knob on the waiting room door slipped through Mom's fingers, then she poked her head through the inner office window. "I'm pretty sure he'll wait. No, I'm certain he'll wait." Her dark eyes connected with mine. "It helps the craziness of Monday morning so much when the charts get pulled."

"Fine." I flipped the appointment book to Monday and grabbed a pen. "Of course, he'll wait. He's the most amazing boyfriend ever."

Mom's voice floated from down the hall. "Might have to agree with you on that."

Preston

Maggie's text at 12:35 came as no surprise. "Ten more minutes, please. I'm hurrying."

"no prob" I tossed my phone on her seat. Figuring it would probably be more like twenty minutes, I leaned my seat back and closed my eyes. The sound of a baby crying interrupted my half-consciousness. I blinked at the radio clock: 12:50.

I sat up as a blonde in a black coat walked by my window, a squirming baby wrapped in pink in her arms. She plopped a bag on the trunk of an old, green Ford parked crooked in the space in front of mine. Switching the bundle of baby to her other arm, she opened the back door and leaned inside.

Something about her seemed familiar, but I shrugged it off. Just as I leaned back to catch a few more z's, she stood up and slammed the door. Big blue eyes. Tousled blonde hair. *Alyssa.*

My body fell back on the lowered seat. "What in the—" My wrist dropped across my forehead. Had she seen me?

A tap on the glass confirmed my worst fear. Alyssa, all wide-eyed, motioned for me to roll down the window.

Ignore her. Sit up, and drive away. But my muscles refused to move.

She tapped again, louder, hugging her coat close.

The last two minutes replayed, in painfully slow motion, through my frantic mind. She'd been carrying a very small baby.

I jerked upright and opened the door, pushing her out of the way. "That baby, is it yours?"

She backed up against the car next to me. "Yeah, she's mine."

"Is she . . . " Words jammed together in my throat.

Her fists clenched. "No 'How are you? How's life in Cedar Hills?'"

"Who's the father, Alyssa?" My raised voice threatened in a way I didn't want it to. Or did I? "Is she mine?"

Her expression morphed from a glare to a frown to the quivering lip I'd witnessed all too often. She sniffed and hugged herself. "Her name is Ryleigh."

"But is she *my* baby?" I hissed, the threat in my voice even stronger now. Gripping the open car door was all that kept me on my feet.

She garbled a response. " . . . wish . . . "

Wait, what? I peered into those blue eyes I used to think I couldn't get enough of. "Wish *what?*"

She swiped at a tear trickling down her cheek. "I have to go."

Before I could process what had happened, her car sped away.

"Sorry I'm so late." Maggie's voice pierced the fog in my brain. "Thanks for waiting." Her gloved hand squeezed my arm. "Preston?"

I blinked hard and turned away from the disappearing Ford to Maggie's bright smile. "Uh . . . hey." I searched her face, struck by the trust and innocence in her bottomless, brown eyes. My heart raced, and sweat broke out across my forehead. On autopilot, I took her hand, led her to the passenger side, and opened her door.

"What are you hungry for?" She asked. "I got up too late for breakfast. Bet I could eat as much as you."

"Hungry? Uh, yeah, always."

Preston

You're quiet. Guess I haven't given you much chance to get in a word, huh?"

"Hmm?" I zoned back in as Maggie dropped her empty wrappers on the tray.

"Something wrong with your sandwich?" She snagged one of my fries, then another.

"Nope." I pushed a big bite of my barely touched burger into my mouth.

"It was soooo hectic this morning, I thought I'd lose my mind."

I nodded and forced another bite.

"Oh, you should have seen this baby. She was the cutest thing. Her mom couldn't have been much older than us, if that. I felt sorry for her. She said Ryleigh cried half the night. I wonder what . . . "

My hand froze in mid-air, french fries dangling. *She's talking about Alyssa's baby.* I dropped the fries on the tray and shoved it aside.

"Wow, you sure you're not sick? You never leave fries." Maggie snatched them up.

"I'm, uh, fine but I need to go. Mom asked me to . . . clean up the garage, like yesterday and I forgot, so—" I grabbed my coat and Maggie's and stood up.

"I need a nap anyway. Call me later?" Maggie slipped into her coat and arranged her hair across its hood.

"Uh, yeah, sure."

~ ~ ~

"Coach wants to meet tonight do you mind?" My finger hovered before hitting send.

Coach *did* want to meet. But it was my idea not his. Did that mean I was lying to Maggie? At the moment, that seemed the least of my worries.

I jabbed send. She loved the whole accountability setup with Coach, and she'd be okay with us not hanging out if that was the reason. Besides, I'd be awful company tonight. And she'd want to know why.

She answered in less than a minute. "I'll miss you, but that's cool. Text me later."

"will do love u" That's all she needed to know now.

"Love you too! ☺" That's all I needed to know.

I pushed through Coach's office door, said nothing to him or Tucker, and collapsed on his worn leather couch. I dropped my head back and focused on the water stain on the ceiling.

"How's Alyssa doing?" Coach asked.

"How should I know? Before I could recover from the shock, she was gone."

"Boy or girl?" Tucker spun a basketball on his index finger.

"Girl."

"Could she be yours? How old is she?" Coach picked up his desk calendar.

I jerked forward. "Alyssa muttered 'I wish or you wish' or something like that when I asked if she was mine. And get this, at lunch Maggie tells me about this really cute baby whose mom wasn't any older than us." I jumped to my feet and paced. "Maggie *talked* to Alyssa, but she didn't put it together because I'm sure she would have said something."

I braced my arms on Coach's desk and leaned toward him. "What if Alyssa's moved back? What if she keeps going to the clinic? What if Maggie figures it out?" I was shouting by the last question, my gaze boring into him like answers would appear across his forehead any second.

Coach's thumb jerked toward the couch.

"Dude, calm down." Tucker dribbled the ball once, then sank into the chair across from Coach's desk.

"I can't calm down until I know what's going on." My fist connected with a stack of files on the desk.

Coach stood.

I backed up. "Sorry."

He walked around the desk, jabbed my chest, then pointed to the couch.

I backed up but remained standing.

He perched on the corner of the desk and crossed his arms. "How old is the baby?"

"I don't know, small. She was wrapped in a blanket."

"When did you and Alyssa break up?"

"Early March—a year ago like next week."

He flicked his fingers through the calendar pages. "If the baby's like a newborn, she's not yours, but if she's older—"

"She can't be mine." I ground out the words through clenched teeth.

"Why? Because you don't want her to be? Doesn't work that way." Tucker dropped the basketball and scooted forward. "This pretty much ends the tell-Maggie-don't-tell-Maggie debate."

"Now wait a minute—"

"Preston." Coach tossed the calendar on his desk and stood well within my personal space. "If Alyssa needs the services of the clinic, it's probably not a one-time thing. She'll be back."

Tucker hopped up and formed the third side to the triangle. "Maggie has to hear about this from you. She *will* find out who Alyssa is, and if there's even a remote chance that baby's yours"—his head wagged back and forth—"Dude, you're out of options."

Maggie

"Hey, Jacoby." Zach waved as Preston and I headed out after school on Monday. "Wait up."

As Zach weaved through the crowd, I adjusted the collar on Preston's shirt and peeked up at his serious expression and darkened eyes. *What's wrong with him?*

His major issue—whatever it was—worried me more by the hour. Since lunch on Saturday, he'd been quiet, withdrawn, even spacey. "Doing fine," he'd insisted when I couldn't help asking if something was wrong.

Yeah, right.

Preston bumped Zach's fist. "What's up?"

As we merged into the hall traffic, Zach's eyes darted around as he glanced over one shoulder then the other. "Need a favor."

"Sure." Preston fished his keys from his pocket and handed them to me.

I gripped his fingers for a second before taking the keys. "I'll meet you at the car. See ya, Zach."

Zach nodded as Preston pushed open the door for all of us.

I waved the guys ahead and pulled my phone from my purse, pretending to check for messages so I could keep an eye on them. They stopped at Zach's car where Preston propped himself against the bumper, my backpack slung across his shoulder. Zach paced in the narrow space between cars.

Now something was up with Zach, too.

Preston

I'm not gonna be here tomorrow." Zach's pacing between the cars halted. "Can I get a copy of your notes from history? I'm barely passing."

"Yeah, sure, no problem. You okay?"

He shrugged but said nothing.

"What's up?"

He exhaled a loud sigh and glanced at me for just a second. "Brittany's pregnant."

"Aw, man. That's . . . rough." Wait, what about his relieved announcement a few weeks ago? "But I thought you said—"

"It wasn't a false alarm after all."

"Hey, I'm sorry."

He jerked his head in a quick nod. "We're taking care of it."

"You guys'll figure it out."

He stared at me, his face grim. "I said we're taking care of it."

I stepped in front of him. "What do you mean?"

He dropped his head and murmured, "She's having an abortion tomorrow."

"Are you serious?"

His head snapped up. "We're not ready to be parents. Heck, I'm not that great at takin' care of myself, let alone a baby. Besides, who wants to be saddled with a kid for senior year? And then there's college."

"But an abortion?"

His angry eyes flitted across my face. "What do you want us to do? Put our entire lives on hold because of a baby we didn't plan and don't want?"

"Look, when you have sex, you know this can happen, right?"

A growl rumbled from his throat, and his glare could have melted the asphalt. "I don't need you preachin' at me. I need your history notes. Can you do that?"

I sighed. "Yeah, I'll share my notes." I stared into his still seething eyes. "Don't do something you'll regret."

"We've thought about it, and that's our decision."

Gripping the back of my neck, I took a step back. "Do her parents know? Do yours?"

"Just her sister. She's covering for Britt at school. And now you." The set of his mouth silently ordered, *Keep it that way.*

"I won't say anything."

"Not even to Maggie."

I nodded. "How's Brittany doin'?"

He kicked his car's front tire. "She's scared half to death."

"Are you sure she wants to do this?"

"I'm not forcing her, if that's what you're insinuating." His jaw clenched. His eyes blazed.

"That's not what I mean. But she'd better be sure and you too. 'Cause once it's done—"

"I know, I know." Irritation coated his words.

"Let's go somewhere to talk—"

"Nah. Gotta get home." His shoulders slumped like an inflatable that someone had pulled the plug on. He slouched against the driver's door, hands jammed into his pockets.

I leaned on the door beside him.

He scraped the toe of his shoe across the bottom of the car next to us.

What could I say or do? "Let me know if . . . if Brittany's okay and everything."

He straightened up and turned around.

"Later, if you want to hang out or—"

"I'm good." The set of his jaw told me the subject was closed.

A baby. An abortion. And I couldn't tell Maggie.

Maggie

W hat's up with Brittany?" Mr. Martin peered over my shoulder at the new donation total. "Third meeting she's missed, right?"

"I have no idea, but I plan to find out."

His finger rubbed across the number on the notebook page. "*This* is amazing." He stood and sighed. "Thanks for checking on her. If there's anything I can do . . ." His palms splayed and tilted up.

"I'll let you know."

He gave me a double thumbs-up, then whistled and drew his hand across his throat. "Drum roll, please."

The guys drummed a fast, very loud beat on the desk tops, their favorite part of weekly meetings.

A smirking Mr. Martin again slashed a hand in front of his throat and pointed to me.

"Six hundred eighty-four dollars and fifty-six cents."

When the cheering subsided, Tyler hopped on the desk beside me. "So, when do we actually give them the money?"

Mr. Martin shrugged. "What are your thoughts?"

Lindsey raised her hand. "How about a group presentation? We all go there, maybe get a tour. It's a pretty cool place."

"We can make one of those giant checks. It would be fun," Erin chimed in.

A chant broke out. "Field trip, field trip."

Mr. Martin slashed across his throat again. "Terrific idea. Can you set it up for us, Maggie?"

"Sure."

"Let's shoot for next Tuesday, seven a.m.—"

"Whoa. Seven a.m.?" Alex shook his head. "You've got to be kidding."

"We can't tour when the place is full of patients. The staff would be too busy, not to mention privacy issues." Mr. Martin cocked his head and shrugged. "Do you still want to make a group presentation?"

"Course we do." Tyler hopped to the floor, sporting a big smile. "I'll spring for donuts."

Alex hooted. "In that case, I think I can make it. Jelly filled. With vanilla frosting."

Shouts of donut favorites drowned out the ringing bell. I backed away from the expanding group of donut lovers surrounding Tyler.

"Brittany," Mr. Martin reminded me as I slipped by him.

"I won't forget."

Tyler sprinted to my side in the hall. "Maggie, hey, I need your donut preference, you know, for the tour next week." He cleared his throat and jerked a quick nod to Preston who appeared on my other side.

"Anything chocolate, I guess."

"Chocolate. Check." He pretended to scribble on his notebook cover. "Hey, I think we need to man the volunteer table at lunch tomorrow. Tons more people sign up when someone—"

"Calls them out and won't take no for an answer." Preston smirked.

"Whatever works." Tyler grinned and tilted his head toward me. "You'll help me out tomorrow, right?"

"Sure. Maybe I'll get someone to take some of my Saturday shifts."

Preston curled his arm around my waist and whispered into my hair, "That would be nice."

~ ~ ~

"We're all set for a tour next Tuesday at seven a.m." I reported to Tyler the next day as I peeled the top from my raspberry cheesecake yogurt. "Mom and Dad love the idea."

"Yes!" Tyler dropped his sandwich and slapped my hand with a high five. "We'll get all these volunteer spots filled and present them with a host of eager helpers to go along with that giant check." He snapped the pages listing the volunteer positions.

"Bummer Mom said a big N-O to my generous offer to share my Saturday morning shifts."

Tyler scanned the lunch line for draftees. "Guess you're too good to be replaced. Indispensable Maggie."

"Yeah, well." I quirked an eyebrow and sighed.

"I'd be willing to give it a shot sometime, if you have an emergency or something."

"Are you serious? I already told both Mom *and* Dad there's no way I can work the day of prom." Proof of Tyler's multi-tasking abilities surrounded me at this very moment. As he finished his sandwich, he counted the open spots on the list and perused the students eating at nearby tables on one sideof us as well as those still in line on the other side. He'd be a perfect replacement.

"No problem. Clinic's open 'til noon?"

I nodded, slipping in a bite of yogurt.

"Consider it done as long as your parents say it's okay."

"I'll convince them. Don't you worry about that."

I stretched and craned my neck to see Preston eating with some of his friends. Or rather sitting. His hand was wrapped around a bottle of Gatorade, but he didn't have any food. Even in his profile, the strain of whatever was bugging him couldn't be hidden. What could it be? I pushed my napkin into my half-full yogurt carton.

He couldn't be thinking about breaking up, could he?

Anything, *anything* but that.

~ ~ ~

Preston worked late both Thursday and Friday but promised we'd do something on Saturday night. He'd gotten a little quieter each day, and my twitching stomach had grown into a nauseous pit. When I suggested we have a quiet evening at his place, he agreed and actually seemed relieved.

After we ate, everyone settled in to watch a DVR'd episode of *America's Got Talent*. I snuggled against Preston, who pulled me close and winked. His usual witty commentary boiled down to a couple of generic statements. Jacki's banter filled in the gaps, and no one but me noticed his lack of enthusiasm.

When the show ended, Jacki wandered to the kitchen while Patrick surfed for something to watch next. Drew dozed in the recliner.

Preston rested his head on the back of the couch, his darker-than-normal blue eyes fixed on the ceiling.

I leaned close and tapped the letters on his old Little League staff t-shirt. "We need to talk."

His expression was blank. "Hmm?"

I stood and tugged him to his feet. "You and me, in the other room. It's time for a talk." I scurried to the kitchen for a Mountain Dew and a Diet Coke, then led the way to the living room.

I sat and patted the sofa beside me. "You're not fine—no matter how many times you tell me you are. You've been so withdrawn, you're barely eating and—"

"There's something you need to know."

Preston

I stood by the couch, heart pounding, mind racing. *What do I say?*

Maggie tugged on my arm, to sit beside her, but I pulled from her grasp and walked to the window.

"Preston, you're scaring me."

I turned around, but I couldn't make even a sound come from my closed-up throat.

Worry poured from her wide-eyed expression. "What is wrong?"

Wooden legs carried me back to the couch. I lowered myself next to her.

Her nails bit into my arm.

The sensation snapped my brain into gear. I rescued my skin from her grip and cradled both of her hands in my lap. "The baby at the clinic last Saturday. She belongs to Alyssa, my ex-girlfriend."

Maggie's eyes narrowed and then widened. "Ryleigh Anderson belongs to *that* Alyssa?"

"Yeah."

"But why was she at the clinic? Is she back in town?"

"Don't know. She didn't say."

"*Say?* You talked to her?" Her nails found my hand again.

"In the parking lot. Before you came out."

"Why didn't you tell me?"

I shrugged. "I . . ."

Maggie snatched her hands away. "If you didn't tell me then, why are you telling me now?"

Here we go. "I know I should have told you right away, but I was in shock. I'm telling you now in case it comes up again or whatever."

Her shoulders relaxed. "Oh. So that's what's been bugging you all week? That your ex-girlfriend has a baby?" Her fingers rapped against her palm. "Ryleigh's like three months old, so Alyssa must have found a new boyfriend—and slept with him—super fast."

"The baby's three months old? Is that what you said?"

"Something like that. I didn't look at her birthday. Why?"

"Uh . . . " I rolled my shoulders in what I hoped was a "whatever" motion. "She didn't come back to the clinic today, did she?"

"No. We had a record number of patients but no Ryleigh or Alyssa. Ryleigh's last name is Anderson. Is that Alyssa's last name?"

"Mm hmm." Panic no longer clouded Maggie's eyes. Did I have to say anything more? As long as Ryleigh wasn't mine—

"Aw. Now I really feel bad for her. She's pretty. Is she our age?"

"A year younger." Every reason for spilling the details of my past had faded almost to nothingness. Maggie was better off not knowing. *Why* would I knowingly break her heart?

". . . a mother at sixteen. I hope she has a lot of support. Wonder what their story is, you know, if the father's still in the picture or what." She tucked herself close to my side and leaned on my shoulder. "I'm glad I heard it from you." She turned her head and peered up into my eyes. "Why were you so worried about telling me? It's not like Ryleigh's *your* baby. Now that . . ."

Air rushed up my throat, and my heartbeat hammered in my ears drowning out Maggie's voice. Where relief had flowed only moments ago, guilt now raged.

"Preston. Hey."

I shook my head. "Hmm?"

"Boy, are you spacey. You obviously need some sleep." She stood and held her hand out to me. "I'll keep an eye out for Alyssa."

I sprang to my feet. "No, no. You don't need to do that."

Maggie folded her arms and studied me. "She's your ex. I'm okay with that."

"I doubt she'll be back, anyway. End of story." I forced a smile and pulled her close. "Let's get you home."

Maggie

❧

"**B**ack to school tomorrow"

Brittany's text answered only one of the many questions I'd asked in ten texts and five phone messages since last Tuesday. All unanswered until now.

"Great! Did you get the message about the NHS field trip to the clinic Tuesday at 7 am? Tyler is bringing donuts! ☺"

"Yeah"

"Want to sit with me at the volunteer table at lunch tomorrow?"

"homework to catch up"

"Oh sure. Find me tomorrow so we can talk."

Who missed four days of school because of cramps? Zach had sulked silently all week. Maybe they were fighting. Or worse, maybe they'd broken up.

I sank deeper into my bed and closed my eyes, waiting for her to text back. Or maybe I'd hear from Preston.

In a super short call this morning before church, he said he didn't feel well and thought he shouldn't come over today. "I'll sleep it off. Don't want you to get whatever I have," he'd insisted.

I still couldn't figure out why he'd been so upset about Alyssa and her baby. Did he think I'd be mad his ex-girlfriend came to the clinic? It was kind of odd if she lived a couple of hours away. But whatever. Maybe Brittany knew the story. I opened my eyes to text her. "You know Preston's ex, Alyssa?"

It took a couple of minutes, but she responded, "what about her?"

"She came to the clinic a week ago with a baby girl. Did you know she had a baby?"

"no"

"Neither did Preston. The baby is so cute. Where does she live?"

"idk who is the father?"

"Baby has Alyssa's last name so maybe the guy's not in the picture. She looks just like Alyssa."

Brittany didn't text back, so I tossed my phone on the pillow beside me and curled onto my side. My stomach did that twitchy thing it had been doing a lot lately. Worry about whatever was going on with Preston or some stomach bug he'd shared with me? At this point, I'd rather be sick—throwing up even—than deal with the worry that something was off between us.

Preston

I dropped my head onto my crossed arms during home room, the only class where catching a few z's was allowed. But I needed to think more than I needed sleep. Avoiding Maggie yesterday did nothing but intensify my guilt. She'd been all sweet and caring when the only thing wrong with me was a raging conscience. And this morning, she'd fussed over me like a mother hen. How much longer could I go on like this?

I flopped my head to the right and got an up-close look at Brittany one row over. Red, puffy eyes and incredibly pale with a blank expression frozen on her face. A stone-faced Zach hovered behind her.

Anger and frustration boiled inside me. For their situation and for mine.

The bell rang, and I bolted, jogging three doors down to find Maggie waiting for me. The worry lines creased even deeper into her forehead than when I'd picked her up this morning.

I pulled her close and hugged her tightly.

She relaxed against me and sighed. "You okay?"

"Mmm hmm." I kissed her hair, inhaling her familiar scent. Another lie.

Except it wasn't, 'cause for those few seconds, I felt incredible.

I kissed her forehead then her cheek. The anxiety melted from her face and body.

She pressed herself close, bubbling with chatter about something I couldn't focus on enough to remember for even two seconds. But I left her at Accounting, smiling, and for the moment, that was all that mattered.

In German, I tapped Zach on the shoulder when Frau Koch stepped out to take a phone call. "Brit looks awful. Do her parents know yet?"

Without turning around, he shook his head.

"Aren't they suspicious?"

He faced me, and he didn't look much better than her. "She told them she had cramps. Don't know how much longer that excuse will hold up."

"Is she okay? I mean, physically. Is she just upset?"

His eyes wide, he shrugged. "She's healing. I guess. But man, she's a *basket case*. I have no clue what to do."

I leaned closer. "Dude, she needs help. She at least needs her friends if she can't talk to her parents."

His expression didn't change.

"Let me tell Maggie." I moved right in front of his face. "Girls need each other for stuff like this."

His jaw twitched, but then he nodded. "But let me say something to her first."

"Do it right away 'cause Maggie can probably get with her after school."

He grunted. "You're pushy, you know that?"

"You doin' okay?"

"I'm fine."

How fine could he be? It was his baby too.

~ ~ ~

"I need to talk to you."

The crease lines instantly reappeared across Maggie's forehead when I pointed to the far corner table in the cafeteria.

"Don't worry," I added, regretting the use of the phrase, "we need to talk."

Her teeth sank into her lip as she arranged our food in front of us.

"Hey, stop." I brushed my thumb across her chin. "I was just wonderin' if you got with Brittany over the weekend."

"She finally answered my texts on Sunday afternoon. Have you seen her today?"

I shook her juice and opened it. "She looks awful." I leaned toward her and lowered my voice. "She had an abortion last Tuesday."

Her jaw dropped as her eyes grew huge. "What? You've got to be kidding!"

"Nope. No one knows except her sister. Zach says she's a mess—he doesn't have a clue what to do."

"So, did you know they were . . . you know."

I nodded.

Maggie

I propped my face against my palm and toyed with my sandwich, tearing off the cheese sticking out of the bun and nibbling on the shredded pieces.

"Are you gonna eat that sandwich or dissect it?"

My appetite was gone. I shoved the sandwich toward him. "I can't imagine how horrible it had to be. It gives me goose bumps to even think about it." I closed my eyes and scrunched my shoulders against the chill that rippled through me.

"I hope you don't mind. I thought maybe you could talk to her."

What would I say? "So, I heard you had an abortion," didn't sound like the best way to start a conversation. "Guess I can grab her after the special NHS meeting with the reporter."

Preston studied his sandwich before he took a small bite. Seemed his appetite still hadn't returned. Any other day, by now he'd be done with his food and questioning what I didn't plan to eat. Any day prior to the last two weeks.

"How's Zach?"

He shrugged as he chugged his Gatorade. "Not good."

~ ~ ~

I caught up with Brittany outside Mr. Martin's classroom. "Hey, Brittany."

She turned around.

I swallowed the gasp pushing up my throat. Her deathly pale face held no expression at all. She blinked red, swollen eyes and pressed her lips into a tight line. A lot more blinking followed, and then she looked away.

A huge lump stretched my throat as I grasped her arm and pulled her toward the wall. "Let's talk after the meeting, okay?"

She looked at the floor, her lips trembling. A nod-shrug rippled through her.

I wanted to hug her, but then we'd both be bawling for sure.

She pressed her back against the wall. "I'm not sure . . . I can go in there."

"It shouldn't take that long. We'll sit in the back."

We slipped into the last row, unnoticed by the students swarming around the *Pine Crossing Times* reporter.

Brittany fiddled with one rolled-up sleeve and then the other. The normal brightness of her sky-blue eyes had been replaced with a vacant, far-away look. The dark circles smudged beneath her lifeless eyes accentuated her paleness. She glanced at me with what I could only describe as quiet desperation.

Mr. Martin shook the reporter's hand again and slapped him on the shoulder. "Thanks for covering our project."

The guy agreed to be at the clinic the next morning to take a photo of the official check presentation. "Thanks for sharing about your project," he said as he shook hands with some of the guys. "Hopefully my story will boost your success even more."

Mr. Martin issued last-minute instructions about the field trip, reminding us the bus would leave at 6:45 a.m. sharp. He strode to the doorway before issuing his usual over-the-shoulder dismissal. Then beaming a huge smile, he fist-bumped each student on the way out.

"Good to see you, Brittany."

She ignored his extended fist, brushing by like she couldn't leave fast enough.

His gaze shifted to me.

I pasted on a brave smile and bumped his fist, totally ignoring his questioning eyes.

Brittany had escaped half way to the exit before I caught up with her. "How about we talk in the courtyard?"

She shrugged as if she couldn't care less.

We sat at a round table on the all-weather patio outside the cafeteria. "If you're cold, we can go inside, but it's more private here."

She zipped her sweatshirt, pulled her hands inside her sleeves, and crossed her arms on the table.

I pulled gloves on, wishing I'd borrowed one of Preston's sweatshirts to wear over my coat. "Are you okay? I mean, are you in pain?"

She blinked hard, breaking the trance-like stare. "The pain's mostly gone, just a little cramping, but the emptiness . . . Do you think that will ever go away?" Her shoulders lifted with a deep breath. "Because I don't know if I can go on if it never goes away."

I gulped down a wave of panic as I reached for her hand. "You have to tell your mom so she can help you."

She jerked her back straight, pulling her hand out of reach. "She'd just be mad. She told me 'Have sex if you want, but don't you dare get pregnant.' Great advice, huh?"

Horrible advice. Especially from a parent.

Her gaze turned toward the football field on the other side of the campus. "Zach doesn't understand—he doesn't get any of it. He thinks by now I should be fine. He wants normal back. Like I'll ever feel normal again." Her gaze drifted back to me. "He stayed pretty close the first couple of days after—" A visible tremor shook her body. "But now he's so impatient. And when he realizes I'm done having sex . . ." She bit into her bottom lip as tears pooled in her eyes. "I could never go through this again."

I gripped the fingers peeking out of her sleeve. This time she didn't pull away. "Oh Brittany."

"I thought he loved me. Hoped he did, I guess. But all I know now is the emptiness is sucking the life right out of me." Tears streaked down her cheeks. She yanked her hand from my grasp and pressed the edge of her sleeve against her mouth. Her eyes squeezed shut as tears soaked into her sweatshirt.

I scooted around the bench and wrapped my arms around her, barely able to breathe around the massive lump clogging my throat.

Her body was stiff at first but relaxed as the quiet tears turned into body-shaking sobs.

I held her tight, my tears pouring out as fast as hers. I wanted so much to make her pain go away, to tell her everything would be okay, that she would be fine *really soon.* But I couldn't.

When her sobbing and shaking eased up, I loosened my embrace. "I'm here, whatever you need. You don't have to face this alone." I dug in my backpack for tissues. "Are you supposed to go back for a checkup or anything?"

"Next Wednesday, but Zach says he can't miss school again. He's barely passing."

"I think you should tell your mom. Or someone else who can go with you and help you get through this."

She scooted away and shook her head firmly. "You don't know my mom."

"Okay, then we'll come up with someone else. In the meantime, you're stuck with me."

Brittany wiped her nose and blotted her cheeks.

"And I'll get Preston to talk to Zach."

Her eyebrows shot up as she blew her nose.

"He's got to be hurting, too." Right? At least he should be.

"If he is, it looks a lot different on him than it does on me."

"A lot of guys aren't good at expressing their feelings."

"That's Zach all right. But maybe he'll open up to Preston." A flicker of hope flashed across her face but was gone so fast I wondered if I'd imagined it.

"Preston's waiting in the parking lot. We can take you home, or you could come to my house, whatever you want."

"I just want to go home."

"Maybe later we can grab something to eat?" I let my eyes rove across her. "Have you been eating at all?" Her cheeks looked hollow, and her collar bone almost poked through her skin.

"I've had almost no appetite since I found out I was pregnant." Haunted eyes stared at me. "I couldn't have come to you on my own."

The lump swelled in my throat again. "Thank Preston. It was his idea."

~ ~ ~

Moments after the car door shut behind Brittany, Preston turned to me. "So?"

"She's a disaster all right, and as worried as I am about her, I'm even more ticked at Zach. He doesn't understand why she can't move on, right now, with the rest of their lives. *And* she says there won't be any more sex, which she knows he won't like."

His jaw twitched, and his grip on the steering wheel tightened. "I guess it's different for him."

"Yeah, no one cut or suctioned or whatever a baby out of his body." I squeezed my eyes shut against the vivid images swarming my brain.

His hand covered mine.

I spread my fingers, letting his fall between mine. "Will you talk to him?"

"I can try."

He pulled into my driveway, and for just a second, the warmth and pressure of his hand disappeared. He turned off the car then linked our fingers together again and angled his body toward me. "I'm sure talking to you helped her."

"I hope so."

Preston

Zach's confession played through my mind as I headed back to Maggie's later that night. "To me it wasn't a baby yet. I just wanna get past this." I could understand how he wanted to think that. I might be tempted to lean that way too if—

A picture of Alyssa tucking a pink bundle into the back seat of her car seared my memory. My hands gripped the steering wheel. Every hour of the past nine days had crept by so slowly it seemed like nine months. Ugh, *nine months.* A number I did not want to be reminded of.

She's not my baby.

Because wouldn't Alyssa have come to me right away if the baby was mine? That's what made the most sense, so that's what I was banking on. Still, the thought that she hated my guts so much she chose to go it alone could not be completely ignored either.

With a growl and a firm shake of my head, I shut down the mental discussion. It would no doubt invade my brain later, making it impossible to sleep, but now I wanted—no *needed*—some uninterrupted time with Maggie. Her creased-forehead, lip-chewing concern had all but disappeared. Apparently, I'd gotten better at hiding my turmoil. And she hadn't mentioned Alyssa or Ryleigh in days.

I sprinted up the walk, glancing at the time on my phone, hoping her parents wouldn't mind me stopping by so late on a school night. Pushing a lingering image of Alyssa and the baby out of my mind, I rang the doorbell.

"It's just Preston! I'll get it." Maggie called out as she opened the door, wearing a big smile.

"Just Preston, huh?" I pushed my lips into a pout but couldn't suppress a lopsided grin.

"Most awesome boyfriend ever." She grabbed my hand and pulled me inside.

I settled my hands on her waist. "Awesome, huh?" As I gazed into her chocolate brown eyes, I snapped shut the lid on everything else.

"That's right."

"Can we talk somewhere? Maybe on the porch?"

"Let me grab a sweatshirt." She disappeared in the direction of the family room.

Cheryl poked her head through the doorway. "Hey, Preston."

"I promise not to keep her too long."

She nodded and disappeared with a wave.

Maggie returned, pulling a sweatshirt—one of mine—over her head. "It's fine, she doesn't mind." She grabbed a throw from the couch.

Maggie

I snuggled in close to Preston on the porch swing. Threading my arm through his, I tucked my legs underneath me and spread the throw across our laps. "Did you talk with Zach?"

He nodded.

"And?"

"To him it didn't seem like a real baby yet. He's super worried about Brittany, though. He really does care about her."

"He better."

"He's hoping you talking to her will help a lot. Even thanked me for us getting involved. And from Zach, that's really somethin'."

I pulled at a loose thread on the throw. "Did you mention, you know."

"I reminded him there's a way to guarantee this won't happen again. And he knows I wasn't suggesting condoms or the Pill."

"What'd he say?"

"Nothing. He knows—it's just that old habits are hard to break."

I turned wide eyes to peer at him. "Old habits? Are you saying he's slept with other girls?"

He nodded.

"Really. Wow."

"Hey, that's just between you and me, okay?"

"Oh, yeah, sure."

He picked up my hand. "Is she doing any better?"

"I think so, a little. She told me about the procedure." A chill zig-zagged across my shoulders. "I can't imagine going through anything like that. I'll be surprised if she ever has sex again."

He wrapped his arm around me and nudged me closer.

I rested my head on his shoulder. "It's scary the way sex can mess up your life."

The muscles in his shoulder, his arm, and his chest tensed beneath me. "'Bout time I headed home."

I faced him with a pouty frown. "What? You just got here. Can't you stay a little longer?"

"It's late. I should go." He lifted his arm from around my shoulders and stood in one swift motion.

"Ah, come on." I grabbed his hand.

He leaned down, brushed his lips across my cheek, and backed away.

My heart pounded. The pouty look had done nothing. What was going on?

"I'll see ya tomorrow."

Preston

My mind buzzed on overdrive the next couple of days. Not coming clean with Maggie about Alyssa and Ryleigh zinged my conscience on an hourly basis. Watching the growing misery between Zach and Brittany tore me up. In spite of Maggie spending a lot of time with Brittany, she was still a mess. And Zach seemed to grow angrier by the minute. Worse than that, it looked like they were about an inch from breaking up. And there was nothing we could do about it.

By Thursday, I was in serious need of some time with Coach. If I could just make it to three o'clock.

Connor and Chelsea caught up with me and Maggie on the way to lunch.

"Since your girlfriend hijacked my girlfriend to man the clinic table, the least you can do is keep me company and offer me half your lunch." Connor smirked.

"Company, yes. Half my lunch—" I shook my head "—no way."

We left the girls with their sack lunches, sprinted to the food line, and headed for a corner table.

I unwrapped my sandwich, wondering how much of it I'd be able to get down.

Connor shook his Gatorade, then downed most of it. "Going to Coach's after school today?"

"Yep."

"Anyone else been showing up?"

"Just Tucker. You should come."

A shrug spanned his shoulders as he grabbed some fries. "Tucker seemed cool. You met his girlfriend yet?"

"Yeah, she's great. We're doubling with them Friday night." I took a bite of my burger.

Connor bobbed his head, chewing slowly.

"Maggie loved them both right away. She and Claire really hit it off."

"Nice." His sandwich dropped to the tray with a splat. He pushed it aside and crossed his arms on the table. "Chelsea's been dropping hints that she'd be willing to, you know, if I want to."

I frowned and shook my head. "Bad idea."

"That's what you're always sayin', but I'm not so sure waiting matters that much."

"It does." What little appetite I'd had hit the road. I tossed my sandwich back on the tray. "Alyssa showed up at the clinic with a baby girl."

"A baby? Whoa, dude."

"Couple of Saturdays ago, I saw her in the parking lot. Maggie checked her in, not knowing who she was. Thought the baby was so cute."

"Who's the father?"

"I don't care as long as it's not me—"

"Could it be?"

"I'm pretty sure Alyssa would've pounded on my door a long time ago if she was mine."

Connor shook his head. "Don't know, man. She was madder at you than anything I'd ever—"

"Don't remind me." I shoved my tray aside.

"You gonna pursue it?"

I couldn't help but look toward Maggie and Chelsea across the cafeteria. "I don't want to." Because even thinking about it made the possibility too real.

Connor's gaze followed mine. "You ever gonna tell her about you and Alyssa?"

"I already told her Alyssa's the one with the baby, but that's it. She doesn't suspect anything because . . ." I shrugged.

"She thinks you're a virgin, too." He snagged a few more fries.

The uneasiness in my chest swelled. *You're a jerk, Preston.* I tore my gaze from Maggie. "So, what'd Chelsea say?"

Connor sighed. "It's not what she *said*." His suggestive grin filled in the gaps. "It's so weird, her being the one to push. Well, not exactly push, but she's obviously willing." He exhaled loudly. "I'm tempted big time, and I'm not very strong in the resistance department."

If only I could tell him about Zach and Brittany. "You like her a lot, right? Sex could really mess that up."

"I've thought of that. But when we're alone and her willingness is so evident—" He shook his head. "Actually, I'm not sure why we haven't done it already. Aren't you even tempted?"

"Course I'm tempted. That's why we're limiting the making out and alone time."

Connor snorted. "That doesn't sound fun at all."

"Listen, don't just let it happen. If she's that willing, and you don't do something about it—"

"Yeah, yeah."

"Tell Chelsea you don't want to make one of the most important decisions of your life in your car or on her parents' couch." I knew the picture I'd just painted in his mind.

The five-minute warning bell rang.

"Come with me to Coach's office."

"I'll think about it."

~ ~ ~

Before I even crossed the threshold into Coach's office, I got my confession out of the way. "I bailed on telling Maggie the whole truth." There. I'd said it.

Coach's hello-smile morphed into one of his glarey-eyed disapproving looks. "You know, it's not what either of us thinks that matters."

Tucker shrugged. "It's not my decision. Or my relationship. Or my commitment." The bounce of the basketball punctuated each word. "Or *my* potential baby girl."

I gritted my teeth. "Listen—I'd have heard from Alyssa again if that baby was mine. It's been almost two weeks and not a word." Every hour that passed stoked my theory that Ryleigh did not belong to me.

"If it were me," Tucker glanced at Coach before drilling me with a steely gaze. "I'd wanna be one hundred percent sure she wasn't mine."

"I *am almost* one hundred percent sure," I muttered through a loud sigh. "But I'm really feeling led—no pushed—to tell Maggie everything. I just don't know *how* can I tell her that not only did I already have sex, but there's a slight chance I fathered a child."

I paced the length of the long room, every muscle in my body achingly tense.

"She'll be upset, but give her a chance to deal with it. Claire came to terms with my past, and it's worse than yours." Tucker cleared his throat. "I, uh, shared your situation with her—no names or details of course. But I asked her if she'd want to know."

I perched on the corner of Coach's desk. "And?"

"She said if she was in a serious relationship, she'd definitely want to know. Is it serious between you and Maggie?"

"I think so." I studied a snag in the carpet rather than face either Tucker or Coach.

Coach rapped his knuckles on his desk. "You do not want Maggie to hear *any* of this from someone else."

"I know." Even I couldn't deny that.

"You can do this, Preston. You're praying, right? God won't let you down." Coach reached across the desk and gripped my arm.

"You'll do the right thing." Tucker's head shook with a firm nod.

Wished I had as much confidence in me as they did. "Be honest and break her heart. Do nothing and hope she doesn't hear about it from someone else? Those are my only options, right?"

Tucker shrugged. "Not the way I would word it but basically, yeah."

Maggie

⁓⧖⁓

Claire swatted Tucker's arm. "Tell us, right now, or—"

"Or what?" Tucker smirked as he swung the car into The Pines miniature golf course. "I thought you trusted me."

"It's not a matter of trust."

"Stop worrying. It's just a little friendly guys versus girls competition, right Preston?"

"Yep." Preston squeezed my hand from our cozy spot in the backseat. Both of us being passengers had its advantages.

The plans for our double date unfolded. Miniature golf. Bowling. And something called A Need for Speed. Preston and Tucker versus me and Claire through all of it.

I pulled Claire aside while the guys picked up our clubs and balls. "I'm not very good at stuff like this."

"Just have fun. But do try." Her brown eyes sparked with an infectious enthusiasm. "It would be awesome if we beat them."

By some incredible stroke of luck, we nailed miniature golf, beating the guys by ten strokes. But they beat us by forty-three pins in bowling. It all came down to the Need for Speed—whatever that was.

"A video game?" I bit down on my bottom lip. "My brother got all the video game skills."

"It's not that hard." Preston's arm reached across my shoulders. "Watch them, and you'll do fine."

My jaw dropped—and I completely forgot to pay attention to how the game worked—as Tucker edged Claire by half a second in the fiercest competition I'd ever seen.

Wow, Preston mouthed, his eyes huge.

"You almost had me," Tucker murmured as he offered Claire a high five.

"Next time, buddy." She slapped his hand, hard. "I'll get you yet."

Their fingers folded together. "You probably will. But not tonight."

Preston gave me a thirty second explanation which got lost inside my non-techy brain. I did terrible, losing horribly to his impressive skills, even though I was pretty sure he didn't give it his all. "Sorry." His mouth turned down in an only half-sorry frown.

Tucker bumped Preston's fist. "That's fifty points for Preston's win and another fifty for mine. And, if I'm not mistaken, that means the guys win."

Preston scribbled in a small notepad then circled the final scores. "Yep. By one hundred thirty-three points."

"Not so fast. I think the girls should choose a competition." I whispered my idea in Claire's ear.

She bobbed her head fast. "Yeah, you guys wouldn't object to one more, little contest, would you?"

Tucker turned narrowed eyes to Preston. "It's only fair we allow the girls to choose one contest, don't ya think?"

Preston stroked his stubbly chin and shrugged. "I'm game."

Claire and I slid across the icy parking lot, whispering, plotting our strategy. She hopped in the driver's seat.

Three blocks from the bowling alley, when Claire clicked on the turn signal, Tucker snorted. "McDonald's? What—an eating contest? We've got this hands down, Preston."

Preston frowned. "I don't think it's an eating contest, dude." He tugged on my arm, but I brushed his hand away. "Let's hurry in."

Claire and I sauntered across the restaurant to the video game console in the corner. I caught pieces of the guys' conversation behind us.

" . . . was afraid of. Wordster," Preston moaned. "Maggie's unbelievably awesome . . ."

"Great." Tucker walked up behind Claire. "So, what have we here?"

"A super fun game where you make words from random letters. We'll play three rounds and add the scores to each team's total. Deal?"

The guys exchanged what-have-we-gotten-ourselves-into looks. Preston crossed his arms. Tucker's hands plunged deep into his pockets, but with a shrug he announced, "Sure, why not?"

Preston's grim expression matched Tucker's as Claire and I posted a new high score for two of our three rounds. By the time our turn ended, Tucker had lost the gleam in his eye from winning the Need for Speed. And Preston's scowl suggested a forfeit would be less painful than actually playing and losing.

I almost choked trying not to laugh at their muttering, the correcting of each other's spelling, and the growling at their dismal scores. Claire and I racked up twice as many points as the guys, pushing the girls to a huge win.

"So, what do we win?" I questioned as we settled into the car.

"Who says you win anything?" Tucker grumbled.

"Oh, and if you guys had won, you wouldn't have expected a prize?"

Their silence seemed to admit that I had a point.

"Okay, a prize. Let's see." Preston looked around inside Tucker's car.

"Don't even think you'll stumble across something in here that will work for a prize." I poked him with my elbow.

"That's right." Claire got nose-to-nose with Tucker. "We want a *real* prize."

"Well, honestly, aren't we prize enough?" Preston leaned toward the front seat. "You got to spend the evening with two handsome guys. It doesn't get much better than that."

"I admit that might have worked like five months ago but not a chance now." I still considered Preston the prize. I just wouldn't admit it at *this* moment.

Tucker pulled from the parking lot. "So, what if we cook you a romantic dinner?" He glanced over his shoulder at Preston. "Will that be prize enough for you Wordster champs?"

Claire glanced from Tucker's profile to me. "What do you say, Maggie?"

"You've got a deal." I extended my hand to Preston.

Claire held hers out to Tucker. "Emphasis on *romantic*, and you two do the cooking. No bribing your moms to do all the work."

"Agreed." Preston thrust his fist across the front seat to bump with Tucker's.

We settled into separate quiet conversations for the drive home. When Tucker turned into my drive, he glanced back at Preston. "Claire and I can say our good-byes right here if you and Maggie want to go in."

"Give us maybe fifteen minutes?" Preston suggested.

"Fifteen it is." Tucker tapped the screen of his phone.

Preston jabbed a few buttons on his own phone. "Let us at least get to the porch."

"Yeah, yeah, stop whining. And don't make me come in after you."

Preston swiped at Tucker's arm wrapped around Claire's shoulders. "I'll come out, don't you worry."

"Bye, guys." I led Preston into the house and peeked into the family room. Dad snoring in the recliner—Mom asleep on the couch. We tiptoed back to the dimly lit front room.

He pulled me close on the couch. "So, did you have fun tonight?"

"I had a lot of fun."

He closed his eyes and rested his forehead against mine. "Me, too."

"Too bad you have to work so early tomorrow."

He opened his eyes. "Why?"

"I wanted to be with you longer tonight." I kissed his dimple.

"I'm not sure your intentions are honorable, Miss."

"I'm not sure either." I kissed along his stubbled jaw.

He captured my chin in his palm, drawing my mouth to his for a long kiss.

I relaxed against his chest as his strong arms wrapped around me. If only I could stay like this forever.

In what couldn't have been more than five minutes, the phone's alarm sounded between us. A quick swipe from Preston's finger silenced it.

"Love you," he whispered, kissing my cheek.

I nestled into his neck. "I love you, too."

He pulled me to my feet.

I stretched up for another kiss.

When he eased his mouth away, I held his head close. "Maggie."

I stepped back, letting my arms fall to my sides. "Time's up. I know."

Preston

S o?" Tucker snapped the radio off when I hopped back in beside him.

"She had a great time. We both did."

"Not what I'm askin'."

"What?"

"Don't *what* me. Have you got a plan?"

A wave of dread washed away every bit of the night's enjoyment. *Thanks, Tuck.* "I'm telling her tomorrow night, okay? Maybe Sunday afternoon. This weekend for sure."

"The sooner the better."

I studied his profile. "You sure about that? 'Cause I don't know—"

"Stop it. Unless you're not interested in staying in this relationship. If that's the case, I guess it doesn't matter. Go ahead and talk yourself out of telling her the truth."

Why did he always have to be right? I exhaled a long, steady breath.

"Dude, get it over with. When the dust settles, have her talk to Claire."

~ ~ ~

Late Saturday afternoon, I found Maggie at the front door, juggling a large bag of groceries.

"Hey, what's all this?" I scooped the bag from her arms.

"Night of fun number two. You seemed so relaxed last night, but already this morning you lapsed back into quiet, sulking Preston. Which made me sad, so I decided we needed a second night of crazy fun." On tiptoe, she peeked into the grocery bag. "All the ingredients for your favorite cookies—Ultimate Peanut Butter Chocolate Chip—and those stuffed mushrooms you made for us on Valentine's Day that I loved so much. Oh, and I checked. Your mom will be around all evening."

How sweet of her. I shifted the bag to my other arm and pulled her close. "What about that pizza you've been craving that—"

"Already ordered. It's being delivered at six-thirty or we can change it to seven if you want."

I kissed her forehead. "That's perfect." *No way I can tell her tonight.*

In the kitchen, Maggie slipped an apron over her head and held up a black one like the one I wore at work.

I shook my head.

"Oh, come on. It's my dad's—he wears it when he grills. I already know you look *hot* in an apron." Her eyebrows danced across her forehead. "Please?"

I snagged it from her and slipped it over my head.

She scampered behind me, tugged on the strings as she tied them, and pressed a kiss to my shoulder.

Soon she had me measuring sugar and manning the mixer.

She peered into the mixing bowl. "Doing a great job there." She patted my cheek and let her fingers slide down my face, along my chin, and across my neck. "I'll get the eggs." She moved toward the refrigerator.

I rubbed at something on my cheek. "What the heck?"

Girly giggles burst from Maggie before she clamped a hand over her mouth.

A bunch of white powder coated my hand. "Flour?"

She nodded, pressing her lips together against another wave of giggles.

"Oh, very funny." I ran my hand slowly across my cheek then with the other hand, grabbed Maggie's wrist, and pulled her toward me.

"Preston, the eggs! Don't break the eggs."

I massaged her cheek with my floury hand.

Her face wrinkled, and she tried to pull away.

"You don't like flour on your face?"

She yanked from my grip and rubbed her still floury hand across my jaw, smirking as the white powder stuck to my stubble.

Mom cleared her throat several times from the doorway.

"Hey, what's up?" I asked.

"Preston, come here." She disappeared back into the family room.

"Be right back." I brushed Maggie's cheek with a kiss that left flour sticking to my lips. I found Mom tapping her foot in the next room. "What is it?"

"There's someone here to see you." She paused then whispered, "It's Alyssa and a baby."

"Who?"

"*Alyssa* and a *baby*."

I bolted to the front door.

Alyssa, her mouth creased in a nervous smile, held the small baby covered from head to toe in pink.

"What are you doing here?"

"What's on your face?"

I rubbed my hand across my cheek. "It's flour. We're baking cookies." I crossed my arms and closed the distance between us. "Why are you here?"

"I came to talk to you—"

"About what?"

Alyssa adjusted Ryleigh higher on her shoulder. "We didn't get much of a chance to talk when I saw you at the clinic."

I backed her closer to the door, reached around her, and pushed the door open. I pointed outside, nudging her backward, giving her no choice but to step out. "What do we have to talk about?"

"Us."

I shook my head firmly. "There's no us, Alyssa."

"But there could be. See, I've been staying at my grandparents a lot so the long-distance thing wouldn't be an issue anymore."

Ryleigh's tiny face turned toward me, deep blue eyes above a toothless smile even I couldn't deny was really cute.

I jerked my gaze back to Alyssa. "No, no. *Why* would you think that?"

"Because we were great together." Shiny tears filled her eyes.

I groaned.

"Won't you just think about it? That's all I'm asking. Think about it."

I hated it, but I couldn't tear my gaze from Ryleigh's face as the question hammered in my brain: *Who is her father?*

"Who—" I gulped a breath down my dry throat. "Who is Ryleigh's father?"

She shifted the baby to her other arm. Her eyes darted from me to Ryleigh. "I don't know for sure."

My arms shot into the air. "Are you kidding me? How can you not know?"

Ryleigh whimpered and squirmed.

Tears threatened to spill from Alyssa's wide eyes.

"But she's not mine, right?"

A shrug rolled across Alyssa's shoulders.

"What?" I pressed forward, backing her to the edge of the steps. "It could be me?"

Alyssa cringed at my harsh tone. "I'm not sure."

"Then why am I just hearing about it now?" I raked my hands through my hair and paced the small strip of porch between the door and Alyssa. "Why didn't you come to me when you found out you were pregnant?"

"Well, I . . . She sniffled.

I whipped around, half expecting to see Maggie peeking through the small window in the door. "Listen, I can't do this now. Are you staying at your grandparents?"

She nodded as Ryleigh let out a whiney cry.

I gripped the door knob. "We can talk tomorrow. Give me your number."

Her expression brightened. "It's the same."

I spun the knob back and forth. "I don't have it." I'd erased her number long ago.

"555-2121."

Yep. That was it. I turned my back to her, done with this conversation.

"Don't forget to call me tomorrow, so we can talk."

Like I'll forget. I opened the door, stepped inside, and closed it behind me in less than twenty seconds.

"Preston?" Maggie's cheery voice called above the ballgame sounds from the TV.

I sprinted to the kitchen, my heart pounding.

"Hey, I thought you got lost. Everything okay?" Maggie pushed a cookie sheet into the oven.

"Um . . . yeah. Fine." Willing my pulse to return to normal, I sauntered toward her.

"What did your mom need?" She dropped the hot pad on the counter.

I shrugged. "Nothin' important." Another lie.

"Well, let's get to work on these stuffed mushrooms."

"Hmm? Oh, yeah, the mushrooms." I wrapped my arms around her waist and turned her around.

She relaxed against me.

I closed my eyes, breathing in her familiar scent. Desperate to erase the last few minutes, I buried my face in her hair and pressed her closer. A loud, heavy sigh brought me back to the reality of the moment. Mom, her arms crossed, her eyes full of questions, stood silently in the doorway.

I raised a thumb's up to her. *Lying to Mom, too.*

Her arms dropped to her side and relief flooded her face. She tiptoed away.

I kissed Maggie's forehead, then pressed my lips against the hair framing her face.

"Mushrooms, remember?"

"I'm pretty sure—" I lifted her chin "—they can wait a few more minutes."

Her arms slipped around my neck. "Maybe."

Her warm body pressed closer. But the questions, the fears, the uncertainty raging in my brain would not be silenced.

What if Ryleigh is my baby?

Preston

Patches of bare ground peeked between the melting snow drifts in the fields outside of town. White snow capped the hills in the distance. I inched up the long lane at Alyssa's grandparents' farm, winding through the fields of Christmas trees they raised and sold.

Forcing each footstep, I trudged to the house. I tapped my feet against the old wooden porch to loosen the snow from my shoes.

The door creaked open, and my breathing hitched. Alyssa, holding the baby that might be mine, held the door open.

I focused over her shoulder at a picture on the far wall. "Are your grandparents home?" I couldn't be one of their favorite people at the moment.

"They're not here." She motioned me in.

I strode into the familiar "sitting room" as her grandma called it and sank onto the flowered couch. I rested my elbows on my legs, my hands flexing between my knees.

Alyssa pulled a rocking chair closer to the couch, sat down, and perched Ryleigh on her knee. Her finger brushed the baby's cheek, and Ryleigh's face—a miniature copy of Alyssa's—lit up with a toothless smile.

I tore my eyes from the baby to look at Alyssa. Gone were the dark circles and fatigue from two weeks ago. Covered by makeup, probably. Her blue eyes sparkled. Her shiny lips held a hint of the mischievous smile she was known for, framed by blond hair carefully styled in the tousled-no-style look she'd perfected. And wow—she was wearing the same tight-fitting, blue-striped shirt that I'd made no secret about liking. A lot. I averted my eyes as memories flooded my brain.

I cleared my sand-paper dry throat. "Okay, let's get this figured out. When was she born?"

"December 20."

January. February. March.

Drool dripped from the corner of Ryleigh's mouth.

I scraped at the stubble across my chin, trying to control the anger boiling through me. "Then why in the world didn't you call me?" I sprang to my feet. "If she's that old—is she mine or were you sleeping with someone else, too?"

Alyssa's back straightened. "Only you—you know that."

I paced the length of the room. "Do your parents assume it's me? Your grandparents? Man, Alyssa. Everyone knows but me?" I ground to a halt right in front of her.

She laid Ryleigh face up across her lap. The baby's hands each wrapped around one of her mom's fingers. "I had no idea when my last period was, and I didn't realize I was pregnant until I was pretty far along." Without looking up and in a voice ten times calmer than the situation called for, she continued. "I only had one ultrasound, early on. When she was born, she was small yet big enough to be full term, but other things—like being so sleepy and having trouble eating—made the doctor think she might have been early. That's why I'm not sure who her father is."

Unbelievable. "But you slept with someone there in Cedar Hills? So maybe it's him?"

"I was with this guy for a little while, so maybe." Still, she avoided looking at me, focusing on swinging the baby's tiny arms.

"How can you *not* know who got you pregnant?" I hissed down at her.

Her head snapped up, and her blue eyes blazed. "Listen—I don't need this attitude, okay? I convinced myself in the beginning I didn't need you or any guy. But it's a lot harder doing the single parent thing than I thought it would be, especially with my family falling apart and—" Her voice cracked. She shook her head, pressing her eyes shut.

Ryleigh let out a loud cry.

Alyssa propped the baby against her shoulder and patted her back. She swallowed hard and met my angry gaze with teary eyes. "Seeing you at the clinic brought back all these memories, ya know? We had a lot of good times, Preston, don't you remember?"

"That was a long time ago. I've moved on."

"Yeah, well, I tried to move on. I tried really hard. But you know what? I compared every guy I met to you, Preston Jacoby." She pointed her finger in my face. "The first guy I ever loved, the first guy I slept with, the first guy to totally smash my heart. Then I tried hating you, which worked for a while, but then I saw you at the clinic." She shook her head. "All I could think about was how I used to feel safe and protected when I was with you. And how great it would be if we got back together."

Ryleigh began to cry for real. Alyssa stood up, thrust the baby into my arms and tossed a pink blanket across my shoulder. "Hold her while I make a bottle."

I sat down as my hands molded around the tiny body. The baby's cries turned to wailing. I bounced her on my lap. When that didn't work, I pressed her to my shoulder, like I'd seen Alyssa do. I patted her and rocked back and forth. *This is unreal.*

When Alyssa finally returned, I almost tossed the baby back to her. She settled into the rocking chair, adjusting Ryleigh in the crook of her arm.

"I guess you were right, there's no 'us' anymore. I'm sorry I bothered you." The sparkle had left her eyes. She blinked fast against the tears that thickened her voice.

An ache gripped the center of my chest. I'd hurt her again. "Hey, I'm sorry for yelling. It's just that I *hate* having all this sprung on me. If I'd known—"

"What would you have done? It's obvious you don't care about me anymore." Her eyes squeezed shut again.

Ugh. "I understand why you'd hate me. I treated you bad when we broke up." I scooted to the edge of the couch. "And pushing you to have sex was wrong, too."

"You didn't force me."

"I know, but still, we shouldn't have done it." I exhaled a big breath. "So I guess the next step is a paternity test to find out who her father is."

Alyssa shook her head. "Not necessary. You don't want to be with us so it doesn't matter."

"Uh, yeah, it does matter. If she's mine, I need to know."

"I'll manage. My grandparents will help me—they're really good with her."

"But—"

"It's fine." She sniffed a couple of times as she propped Ryleigh up to burp.

I shot to my feet. "I want to know. Don't you get that? I need to know if she's mine."

She carried Ryleigh to a small baby bed in the corner and laid her down, then walked to the front door and pulled it open. "Thanks for coming to talk. And for the apology."

I blocked the door with my foot. "Wait a minute. We are not done here."

She crossed her arms. "Are you willing to give *us* a second chance?"

"No, but—"

"No buts, Preston." She squared her shoulders. "If you're not interested in Ryleigh and *me,* then I'm not interested in continuing this conversation."

I'd seen that determined set to her mouth, that fierce look in her eyes before. "This is not over, Alyssa. Not by a long shot." I strode through the door, yanking it shut behind me with a loud thud.

Maggie

I scrolled through my text inbox to Preston's message. "Tied up with Coach tonight will pick U up for school tomorrow k?"

Two unexpected meetings with Coach in a week. Technically, eight days.

I'd responded, "Sure. I LOVE you!" To which he wrote back, "love U"

But something didn't feel quite right. No "Can we change plans?" or even "Sorry to change our plans." Not that we'd planned anything all that special, but still. I hated the nauseous yuckiness that had set up a permanent home in the pit of my stomach.

But considering how much making out went on last night, how could anything be seriously wrong? He'd seemed especially snuggly after coming back from whatever Jacki needed him for. But hey, I'd take that over the mounting tension of the last few weeks. Distracted, moody Preston or hold-me-close Preston? No contest. Unless all the making out was the reason for the meeting.

If he skipped our goodnight text, then I'd worry.

I flipped open my laptop and stretched out on my bed. Now I'd have time to work on a better system for tracking the clinic volunteers. Non-NHS students looking to pad their college apps had been lining up at the registration table, too, complicating the situation but in a good way. There was plenty of work to go around. I fiddled with a couple of spreadsheet set-ups before finding the perfect one to keep the growing project in check. I added a section for adult volunteers, remembering that Mom had asked about teachers or administrators who might be interested in mentoring teenage mothers, single parents, or those simply struggling with life.

A picture of Alyssa and Ryleigh filled my mind. I bet she fit all those categories. Yesterday morning, I'd glanced through next week's clinic appointments, looking for either of their names but found nothing.

Chelsea had almost fainted when I told her about Alyssa. Honestly, she got really pale, and her eyes kind of glazed over.

"Were the two of you close before she moved?"

"No. I'm surprised she has a baby that's all."

"So was Preston. She's really adorable—tiny and blonde, looks exactly like Alyssa."

Maybe she was hurt Alyssa hadn't told her. Anyway, Chelsea had nodded and changed the subject fast, leaving me with a strange feeling that lingered all day.

My phone shook under my pillow where I'd thrown it to keep me from checking every ten seconds for a text from Preston.

Chelsea. "what's up w/ emergency meeting w/ coach?"

My stomach did a major flip. Who'd used the word emergency? Preston? Coach? Connor? "I don't know. Who called the meeting?"

"Preston begged Connor to come"

Why would Preston call an emergency meeting? And insist Connor be there? "What did Connor tell you?"

"only that its big"

Icy rivers of panic raced through my veins. I buried my face in the pillow.

My phone vibrated inside my closed fist. "bored can i come over?"

I jabbed the save button and closed my laptop. Did I want to be alone? Yes. Not really. *No.*

With shaking fingers, I texted Preston, "Call me when you're done, please." He owed me an explanation.

Then to Chelsea, "Sure come over."

Preston

━━━━━⟨⟩━━━━━

"You're more than out of options now, Dude." Tucker twirled that same stupid basketball on his index finger. "You need to *run*—not walk—to Maggie right now and tell her the entire story."

"But if Alyssa's not going to push for paternity . . ." Connor shrugged.

"Maybe not now." Coach leaned forward from his perch on the corner of his desk. "She's hurt you don't want to be with her, but being a single parent won't get any easier."

"Do you want to live the rest of your life wondering if Ryleigh is your daughter? Man, I wouldn't." Tucker flung the basketball at me.

I caught it in the air. "I have to find out, which means telling Maggie and maybe my parents." I dropped the ball to the floor and fished my buzzing phone from my pocket. "Maggie wants me to call her when I'm done here."

All eyes drilled into me.

Coach stood and motioned us around his desk. "Let's pray."

~ ~ ~

Maggie waited at the open door as I dodged patches of ice on her front sidewalk. A welcome excuse for my slow approach to the house.

"Preston, what's going on?" Her wide, round eyes darted across my face as her freezing fingers slipped between mine.

I pressed a kiss to her forehead. Then another.

"My parents are out with some friends. But Michael's here somewhere."

I nodded. Not that we'd have to worry about that tonight.

I pulled in a deep breath, but my heart continued to pound like I was sprinting around the park. "We need to talk."

With a slight nod, she pulled me to the couch. Still clutching my hand, she collapsed, crisscrossed her legs, and fixed me with a look that left no doubt I wouldn't be leaving until she knew everything.

My sweaty palm stuck to her cold skin. When I tried to unlace our hands, her grip tightened. "It's okay—hold on." I pried my hand lose and wiped both across my jeans then folded my hands around her icicle-like fingers.

Where do I start? I'd driven around the block three times, racking my brain for how to begin the most dreaded conversation of my life. I still had no clue.

"Just tell me . . . please." I hadn't said a word yet, but already her lips trembled and tears threatened to spill over her bottom lashes.

I cleared my throat and forced my gaze to connect with hers. "When Mom called me into the other room last night, it's because Alyssa and Ryleigh were there."

Maggie's eyes became huge. "At your house? Why?"

"Because there's a chance I'm Ryleigh's father."

———————⟡———————

The room began to spin. "Her *father?*"

"I'm sorry, Maggie, I—"

"That can't be, Preston. Because that would mean you and Alyssa had sex." I shook my arms against his hold on my hands.

"I wish it'd never happened, but it did."

Thrashing against his grip on me, I tried to shove him away.

Finally, his hands fell to his lap. An anguished look tugged down the corners of his mouth.

"No. It. Didn't." Tears trickled down my cheeks.

His silence said everything.

"And Ryleigh might be yours?" I choked. "How could you keep something like this from me?" I hugged myself as ice cold chills rippled down my back and arms.

"I had no idea there was a baby—not until I saw her at the clinic."

I scooted away from him until the arm of the couch jutted into my ribs. *He's not a virgin . . . and he might be a dad.* "I don't know what to say."

Preston inched toward me. Had his eyes ever been this dark? His expression this serious, so full of regret?

"You lied to me." I spat the accusation through clenched teeth.

A loud sigh sputtered from his pressed together lips. He shook his head. "No, Maggie, I didn't lie to you. I committed to *us* not having sex. I never said I was a virgin. You just assumed."

"Well, yes," I screeched. "Didn't you assume the same about *me*—even before the white-wedding-dress speech?"

"Yeah, I guess. But I didn't lie."

I crossed my arms and glared at him. "It's the same as a lie."

"No, it's not." He raked his hands through his hair. "I didn't see the need to bring it up so early in our relationship." His soft, sweet tone—the one that always melted my defenses— threatened to dampen my anger.

"We were careful. I had no reason to think she might be pregnant."

What? Oh, there'd be no melting of my defenses tonight. I pinched my eyes shut and shook my head. Pushing down the nausea that crept up my throat, I drew my knees to my chest and wrapped my arms around them. They were careful. *Nice.*

I peeked at him, barely opening my eyes.

His gaze remained fixed on me.

I rested my chin on my knees.

"Her parents announced they were moving because of her dad's job. She freaked out, didn't want us to break up. I didn't handle it very well. We both ended up really angry, and then it was over." His hands clenched and opened in his lap.

"That's it? You dumped her because they moved?"

"It was more than that. Listen . . ." He reached toward me.

I rocked back away from him, squeezing my legs closer to my body.

"None of that matters. Alyssa and I are history. There's nothing between us anymore."

"Except maybe a baby girl."

He shook his head fast. "Alyssa was with some other guy after me. Ryleigh might be his."

"How old is she?"

"She'll be three months on the twentieth."

"The twentieth was yesterday."

Preston

A tear streaked down Maggie's cheek. "More than once?"

I dared to shift a fraction of an inch closer to her. "What do you mean?"

She studied me with watery eyes. "You did it more than once?"

I nodded.

Her expression wilted even more.

I scooted closer. "My feelings for her were nothing compared to how much I love you."

"Is that supposed to make me feel better?" She dropped her forehead to her knees.

I traced the back of her hand with two fingertips. She didn't flinch or pull away, so I stroked each finger. "I'm sorry, Maggie."

Her shoulders trembled, then shook.

Guilt and regret flooded through me like hot lava. "I would give anything to change this."

The door from the garage banged shut.

Maggie jumped, then swiped her hands across her eyes and down her cheeks.

"Is that Preston's car?" Tom's voice drifted from the kitchen.

"Yeah, they're in the living room," Michael mumbled around a mouthful of something.

Two seconds later, Cheryl poked her head through the doorway. "Hey, guys."

Thankfully, Maggie's tear-streaked cheeks faced me, not the door. She tossed a wave over her shoulder with one hand and continued to swipe at her eyes with the other.

"Hi, Cheryl." I waved—something I never did—and pasted on a smile.

"Brought home leftover pizza. Want some?" She held up a takeout box.

Maggie mouthed 'no,' her eyes begging me to get rid of her mom.

My gaze darted from Maggie to Cheryl. "No thanks. We're good." I almost never turned down food.

"You sure? It was really good."

"I'll take it if they don't want it." Michael appeared and snatched the box from her.

Cheryl shrugged out of her coat. "You had your chance."

"We're good, Mom." Maggie's voice only shook a little. She stood and grabbed a couple of throws from the couch. "Porch," she whispered.

I followed her out and latched the door quietly behind me.

Maggie wrapped one throw high around her shoulders and back, sank onto the swing, and covered herself with the other one.

I sat beside her.

She scooted, putting several cold inches between us.

I stared ahead at a full moon that would have gotten plenty of oohs and ahhs from her if I hadn't just smashed her heart.

She pulled up her knees, overlapping both throws in a mish-mash of fabric.

How much should I tell her? Considering I'd gotten this far and hadn't been kicked off the property, I might as well get it all out. "Alyssa doesn't want a paternity test. She said if I'm not interested in being with her, she's not interested in knowing if Ryleigh's mine."

"Seriously?" Maggie's head rolled across the back of the swing's cushion. "But *you* want to know, don't you?"

"Of course."

Maggie's head stopped moving. "I know why she said that. Do you?"

I shrugged.

"She wants you back. Obviously, she wants that more than she wants to know who the father of her baby is." Maggie's head jerked up. "Maybe you aren't Ryleigh's dad, but she's pretending *not to* know so you'll get back with her."

I'd never considered Alyssa to be manipulative. Clingy, yes. Consumed with our relationship, yeah. Devastated at the breakup—completely. *Oh, boy.*

I pictured Ryleigh in my arms this afternoon. "Does she seem the right size? For a three-month-old, I mean."

"I guess. Why?"

"Alyssa said she didn't find out she was pregnant for quite a while. She may have been full term or early—no one knows. Which makes the whole father issue more complicated."

The front door opened with a creak. Cheryl poked her head out. "'Night you two. Ooh, aren't you cold?"

"We're fine, Mom. Goodnight." In the dim light of the porch, Maggie's red eyes weren't very noticeable. She met her mom's gaze and smiled enough to be convincing.

"'Night." I nodded, producing another fake smile, as if it could make everything okay.

Maggie angled toward me as the door shut and pulled the throw tighter around her knees. "Would you consider it—getting back together with her?"

"Never. I want to be with you." I draped my arm around her shoulders, more on the cushions than on her.

Maggie's back stiffened.

I stroked the hair on her shoulder and leaned in. "Sweetheart, I love you."

Tears shined in her still puffy eyes. Several long, slow blinks pushed a stream of teardrops down each cheek.

My thumb traced the wetness on the left, then the right cheek. "I *love* you," I whispered, "And I'm sorry."

Her knees fell to my lap as she collapsed against me, her face pressed into my chest.

I folded her into my arms. Tunneled my fingers through her hair. Kissed the top of her head.

Her nails bit into my arm. "What now, Preston?" She sniffled and gulped a swallow. "What do we do now?"

Preston

If she breaks up with me because of this—something that happened before I even knew her . . . "Please, God, don't let it end over this."

Rain splattered across the windshield. A horn blared behind me. The light had turned green. Gripping the steering wheel, I pulled into the intersection.

The longer we'd talked, the more Maggie had cried. I'd expected tears but not that many. I'd completely broken her heart.

I drove through the empty streets to the edge of town and turned around. I maneuvered back through town, past the high school, then headed the opposite direction out of town, too restless to go home.

My frustration had mounted as she'd pushed for answers. Answers I didn't have. But leaving her with everything so up in the air scared the heck out of me.

She loved me. She knew how much I loved her. Would that be enough?

I turned down the next country road and found myself driving past Alyssa's grandparent's farm on the right. Two dim lights glowed from the old farmhouse. Are three-month-old babies up at 1 a.m.?

I parked at the end of the lane, the weight of a thousand regrets ripping through me. My fist connected with the steering wheel again and again until the stinging reached my elbow.

Maggie's question throbbed in my brain, "What do we do now?" So did the guys' comments from earlier.

"You can't do this on your own, Preston. You need God's direction." Coach had years of wisdom on me.

"Don't do anything you'll regret later." Already I'd come to rely on Tucker. He hadn't missed yet.

"Alyssa's giving you a pass, dude—take it." Connor was known for taking the easy way out. Still, his suggestion tempted me.

But could I live with myself if I walked away? And as devastated as Maggie was by the whole situation, I was pretty sure she'd never let me turn my back on it. Somehow, *some way,* I had to find out if Ryleigh was my baby.

"Okay, God, I'm seeking. You better be answering—and soon."

The low gas warning pinged. I pulled back onto the road and headed home.

Turning off the headlights, I coasted into the driveway at 1:22 a.m. I'd have to be extra quiet sneaking in this late.

Maggie

If Mom didn't consider Sunday a "school" night, I'd have begged for Chelsea to stay over. Instead, I burrowed deep under the covers of my bed and texted her the "emergency" news. "It's bigger than you'd ever imagine—I hope you're lying down."

"oh?"

"Preston may be Ryleigh's dad."

A full minute passed before she responded. "NO WAY"

"YES." Like I'd kid about *that.* I pulled my quilt up to my chin. The cold had seeped into my bones on the porch, and if I ever warmed up, it would be a miracle. Any other night, Preston could have warmed me up, but not tonight.

"Connor said nothing. details please"

"She might be his baby or not but Alyssa isn't interested in a paternity test unless Preston wants to get back with her."

"WHAT???"

"Crazy. right? She said she'll manage by herself with grandparents help."

"wow"

"WOW for sure. Connor really said nothing?"

"not a word"

"I'm so upset that Preston lied to me."

"did he say he was a virgin?"

"Not exactly but he made me think he was."

"being a virgin isn't the most important thing"

Of course, that's what she'd say. Every time the subject came up, her big green eyes practically rolled out of her head.

"It's important to me."
"so what now?"
"No idea."

Preston

Torrential rain poured down, making it hard to see on the way to Maggie's the next morning. The dreary sky promised a rainy, miserable day. Just what we needed. I pulled into her drive, as close to the house as I could get. A wave of relief swept through me to see her at the front door waiting. I pushed her door open from the inside and grabbed her backpack as she slid in.

She glanced at me for a second, then dropped her gaze to her lap.

"Hey." I tipped her chin up with my finger. Any other day, I would have kissed her, almost without a thought. But maybe not today. "How are you?"

"Fine." Not even a fleeting smile before she turned her pale face toward the window.

An awkward silence surrounded us for a couple of blocks.

"So, I've got this test in Algebra II that I'm not looking forward to at all."

Her head snapped back toward me, her eyes huge as she glared daggers at me. "You've got to be kidding! You may have *fathered* Alyssa's three-month-old baby, and you want to talk about algebra tests?"

"The algebra test I can do something about. The other thing is out of my hands."

Maggie hugged herself tightly. Her short, gaspy breaths told me she was trying not to cry.

I pulled into the fourth row of the school parking lot and killed the engine. Gripping the steering wheel, I watched students with happy, uncomplicated lives stream by.

Maggie swiped at a couple of tears on her cheeks.

School started in twenty minutes. "You gonna be okay?" I reached for her hand.

She pressed herself against the window and shrugged.

"Maggie." I tugged lightly on her sleeve. "Come here, please?"

Stiffly, she leaned toward me.

I cradled her chin in my palm and pressed my thumb against her trembling lips. "We'll figure this out."

Maggie

The warmth from my mug of caramel cappuccino soaked into my freezing fingers. I held my favorite coffee to my face, sniffing the sweet fragrance but too afraid my nauseous stomach would reject it to actually take a drink.

I cringed at Preston's grip on his vanilla latte, expecting the mug to shatter any second.

After the longest day at school ever, he'd suggested we kill time at the coffee shop across from Coach's office. Tucked in our favorite corner booth—away from the listening ears at home— we had until his five o'clock shift to figure out the next step.

He pushed his untouched latte aside. "It's a lot to take in, I get that. You're disappointed. You have every right to be. But that doesn't mean things between us have to change." His fingertips brushed across my wrist. "How I feel about you or what I want for us—none of that's changed."

Seriously? "How can this change nothing?"

"Because I still want us to be together." He exhaled a loud sigh and pulled his hand across the table, away from me. "That's why I don't want there to be any more secrets between us."

I swallowed hard. More?

Preston focused on his fingers tapping against the coffee-cup patterned tablecloth. "In the past, I had a lot of girlfriends and unfortunately, I made out with a bunch of other girls. Didn't think there was anything wrong with my course-I'm-a-Christian-cause-I-go-to- church attitude either. But one day all that changed, and God became *so* real to me." His eyes finally connected with mine, dark and troubled.

"I knew a lot of other stuff had to change too. That's why I didn't date anyone after Alyssa until you." He pulled his latte back in front of him, studying it as if he'd never seen creamy whip before.

A heavy numbness hung over me like a hazy bubble umbrella. How many girls? Five? Ten? Fifty? All the looks, the little comments. Caroline falling all over him. Nikki pronouncing him a player. Now it all made perfect sense in a horrible, sad way.

He leaned in close, his voice barely above a whisper. "Alyssa is the only one I had sex with—I promise."

That was probably supposed to make me feel better. It didn't. I peered into his eyes, missing the silvery flecks.

"Do you remember how long I waited to kiss you?"

An instant memory, as clear as if it had happened yesterday, sped my mind back to that night at the park. I resisted the tug on the corner of my mouth and purposefully sunk my teeth into my bottom lip.

"I've changed, Maggie. I'm not the same guy I used to be." He slipped my fingers from around my cappuccino and cradled both my hands in his. Since the day we met, I'd loved his hands. How big they were compared to mine, how safe and protected I felt when their warmth wrapped around mine. How, despite the size difference, they fit perfectly with mine, like they were meant to be laced together forever. "You mean the world to me, and it kills me that my bad choices have hurt you."

I opened my mouth to say something, but nothing came out.

Preston's mouth stretched into a thin line. His eyes narrowed. He gripped my hands tighter.

Say something.

His eyes pierced through me. Honest, vulnerable, nothing held back.

"Okay." The only word I could force from my mouth. I hoped he wouldn't ask what it meant because I had no idea.

Disappointment crept across his face like a cloud hiding the sun. He eased me closer. "Okay?"

I pulled back, blinking back tears for the hundredth time.

"Maggie, I'm sorry."

I knew that. I nodded which spilled tears over my eyelashes.

His thumb stroked my wet cheeks. "I should probably tell you to just walk away, save yourself a lot of grief. But I can't because I want so much to be with you."

Until yesterday, I honestly believed Preston was perfect, that *we* were perfect. Not only was he beyond amazing, but being in this relationship was the most incredible thing ever. But in one split second "perfect" had vanished. How could he say nothing had changed? Everything was different now. *Everything.*

"Sweetheart, say something, *please.*"

I gulped and sniffled and batted my eyes to clear my vision. "I . . . I need to think. I just . . . need some time."

"What do you need to think about?"

"Us."

Preston

I swung into Guido's parking lot with less than two minutes to get clocked in. The old Preston would have ditched this shift without a second thought. More proof that I'd changed, but would Maggie believe it?

The last hour rewound in my mind. So, she needed time to think. No biggie, right? Sweat beaded across my forehead, and my stomach tightened. Who was I kidding? This was huge.

Was I still willing to let God call the shots if it meant losing Maggie? Just letting those words fall into place in my brain clamped a vise around my chest 'til I could barely breathe. It had never been this hard to seek His direction before. Why now?

Because the stakes had never been this high. I'd never wanted anything more than I wanted to be with Maggie.

I'd get through this shift somehow then beat it back to her house.

Thank goodness we weren't busy 'cause I couldn't have handled a lot of orders. My lack of attention led to a nice grill burn on my right arm a couple of inches above my wrist. I brushed it off as nothing to keep my boss from freaking out. But every time I reached across the grill, the heat seared the quarter-sized blister even though I'd covered it. *Ouch.*

I shot a text to Tucker on break. "Maggie is falling apart could Claire call her?"

"I'll ask. you ok?"

"nope call u later"

~ ~ ~

I'd never closed the grill so fast. I called Tucker on the fast sprint to my car. "She needs time to think about us," I blurted when he answered. "And I'm terrified."

"That's understandable."

"Which?"

"Both."

"I told her I should let her walk away, but now, I'm afraid she will. I can't lose her."

"You're praying, right?"

"Trying to. Did Claire call her?"

"Said she would. Anything more from Alyssa?"

"Nope."

"Hang in there. And keep praying."

Maggie

N o matter how much I massaged my temples, the killer "crying" headache didn't ease up. I pulled the cool sheet over my face and tried to stop thinking about everything. Preston. Alyssa and Ryleigh. Brittany and Zach.

The ringing phone coaxed me to uncover my head. Without opening my eyes, I answered with a hoarse, "Hello?"

"Hey, Maggie, it's Claire. Heard you could use a friend."

"Oh, hi." I propped another pillow under my head. "Wait, how did you know—"

"Preston texted Tucker. Asked if I could call you."

"Not surprised. He's pretty worried." As evidenced by his creased-forehead, tensed-jaw, and super dark eyes. I rolled to my side. "So, how much do you know?"

"Preston's ex has a baby that may or may not be his. She wants him back whether or not he's the baby daddy. And," she let out a breathy sigh, "you thought he was a virgin, like you, but he's not."

"Yes! One minute we're the happiest couple ever, not a care in the world. Then wham! It's like being caught in a tornado that won't put me down. Tell me what to do, Claire, because I can barely put two coherent thoughts together."

"Well . . ." The silence stretched on making me nervous. "Seems to me there are two separate issues here. Who's the baby daddy, for one. Preston wants to know, doesn't he?"

"Yes, but how much can he do if Alyssa says no to a test?"

"I'm not sure how all that works. Maybe your parents know about that stuff?"

"Oh no, there's *no* way we're talking to them about this."

"Well, somehow he has to figure it out. Then there's the other issue."

"He lied."

"I get it that you're disappointed that he's not a virgin, but did he really lie?"

First Chelsea, now Claire? "Well, he listened to me go on and on about how important waiting was to me and let me think he was a virgin, too."

"Okay, that seems less than honest. But it wasn't actually a lie."

"Maybe not, but—"

"The choice is yours. You'll either get over it, or you won't."

Is she kidding? I flopped onto my back and flung off the covers. "It's not that simple. At least, it's not for me." Another round of tears stung my eyes. Maybe I didn't want to talk to her.

"Listen, I know how you feel. God and I had some pretty intense conversations about why I had to fall so hard for a guy who didn't wait. I cried and yelled and cut Tucker's picture into tiny little pieces. Then God said, 'get back to me when you become perfect' or something like that." She chuckled.

An unwelcome grin tugged at my lips.

"Anyway, I decided Tucker deserved a chance. The more we were together, the more I wanted to be with him. And once I understood how committed he was *now* to waiting, I made the choice to get over it."

"You make it sound so easy."

"It wasn't. It was hard. And it didn't happen overnight. I had a lot of feelings to sort through. But once I decided I wanted him in my life, I had to stop going over every possible scenario that might come up and take one day at a time. It was tough, but for me, it was the right decision."

"So, your advice is just get over it." Was that even possible?

"What I'm saying is put a lot of thought and prayer into your decision. Preston seems like a great guy. Tucker thinks a lot of him. And the two of you have a good thing going, right?"

"*Had* a good thing. And if Ryleigh is his baby—"

"What if she is? Will that change your feelings for him?"

"Maybe. I don't know. I can't even think anymore."

Nothing from Claire except quiet, calm breathing. Of course, she was calm. It was my life falling apart, not hers.

I squirmed as my bed suddenly wasn't all that comfortable anymore. "It would complicate things, okay? My parents would find out. Everyone would know he slept with her."

"I get that. One of the toughest parts for me was that everyone knew Tucker's past. But you have to ask yourself, would you walk away from this relationship just because people knew he had sex with someone else?"

A heavy sigh passed through my lips as I sat up. "Probably not."

"Maybe there's other issues, too, I don't know. Like I said, think and pray. Mostly pray."

Everything she said made sense. More sense than I wanted to admit. "Thanks for calling."

"I know how this feels—it's tough. Call or text me later, 'k?"

"I will."

My shirt already over my head, I brushed by Patrick on the way to my room to change.

"Heard I missed a certain visitor over the weekend."

I pointed to my room.

He followed me in, closed the door, and plopped down on my unmade bed. "Mom went on and on about the baby—how cute she was and how she looked just like Alyssa." His eyes narrowed. "At least she didn't look exactly like you."

I tossed my pants at his feet and rummaged in the closet for my new jeans and a shirt. Hopefully one Maggie really liked.

"She's not yours, is she?"

"Not sure."

"She might be? Are you kidding?"

"Yeah, like I'd joke about that." I swiped on deodorant.

"So, what's the story?"

"It's long and complicated."

"Then give me the Cliff's Notes version." He scooted back to lean against the wall.

I buttoned the striped blue shirt Maggie said matched my eyes. "It's either me or this guy she was with right after she moved. But—" My blood boiled just thinking about it. "Unless I want to get back with her, she says she's not interested in a paternity test."

Patrick's eyebrows shot up. "Dude."

"I know, crazy, right?"

"Mom obviously knows nothing about any of this, huh?"

I shook my head no.

"Maggie?"

"She knows. Says she needs time to think about us. I'm headed over there now."

Patrick stood and thrust his hands in his pockets. "Don't push her. You've hit her with some major stuff."

"I'm not pushing. I just want to see her." I yanked my wallet from the back pocket of my work pants and shoved it in my jeans.

"What are you gonna do about Alyssa and the baby?"

"I have no idea."

Maggie

aggie! Preston's here." Michael's yell jolted me awake.
Preston? Rubbing my eyes, I grabbed my phone. 9:45
p.m. No missed calls or texts. He must've just gotten off work.

My phone vibrated in my hand. Preston. "talk on the porch?"

"Be down in a minute."

I grabbed one of his hoodies from the foot of the bed and ran
my fingers through my sleep tangled hair. Pulling the
sweatshirt over my head surrounded me with Preston's scent. I
held the soft fabric against my face as I slid my feet into fuzzy
purple slippers.

Preston shot from the swing and, with three long strides,
caught the front door before it swung shut. "Guess I should've
called. I just wanted to see you." The doorknob clicked and in
the next second his hand molded around my elbow. "I know it's
late—"

"It's okay." I hugged the extra folds of his sweatshirt close to
my body.

His eyes swept back and forth across my face as if one more
sweep would gain him access to my mind. No need to wonder
what he was thinking or feeling. His emotions were written all
over his face. Worry, fear, desperation even.

He guided me to the swing where a throw from the family
room couch—my favorite because it was the warmest, softest
one—waited, spread across the swing's seat and back cushion. I
sat, folding my legs underneath me.

Preston immediately wrapped the throw around me, carefully tucking the edges in between my back and the swing then sat beside me. Close but not too close.

How sweet of him. "Thanks."

He leaned forward, his hands clasped between his knees. "I know you said you needed time, and it's only been a couple of hours, but you gotta know I don't want to be with Alyssa."

I stared at the porch ceiling, torn between studying his serious-as-ever, yet somehow hot-as-ever profile or acting like I wanted nothing to do with him. "But what if Ryleigh *is* your baby? What then?"

"It won't matter. I love *you* and want to be with *you*." He wrapped his fingers around my arm. His warmth penetrated the layers of fabric. His profile won.

"You might not want to be with her *now*, but if you're Ryleigh's dad—"

"There's a good chance I'm not."

"But if you *are*, can you promise me you won't want to be with your daughter's mom?"

He turned me to face him. "If that's the case, I can be a dad to Ryleigh without being with Alyssa."

"You bonded with her, Preston. A part of you belongs to Alyssa, and it always will."

His mouth opened, then closed. Air puffed through his pursed lips. "I . . ." He grasped my arms as he shook his head. "I want you, Maggie. Not her."

"Ow." I wiggled against his grip.

"Sorry." He rubbed his hands up and down my arms and inched closer. "I don't want to be with anyone but you. If Ryleigh's mine, we'll deal with it."

His hand brushed along the side of my face and threaded into my hair.

My defenses melted, and I leaned into him.

He settled us back in the swing, my head against his chest, his arms around me. Pushing off with his foot, he set the swing in motion.

Little by little, I relaxed against his warm body. "How will you find out if she's yours?"

His lips pressed against my hair. "I have no idea yet, but I'll figure it out." His arms tightened. "Let's keep the lid on this. Especially, don't tell your parents."

"Oh, you don't have to worry about that. But if she *is* your baby—"

"Yeah. I don't even wanna think about that."

Maggie

S o, you've finished the amazing volunteer tracking system you promised to work on over the weekend, right?" Tyler beamed a quirky smile and slid into the chair beside me at the NHS volunteer table on Tuesday.

"Um, well, not exactly."

"Close though, right?"

I sighed and pointed to my laptop screen where the spreadsheet columns—all blank except for dates at the top— had been untouched since Sunday.

His gaze darted from the screen to my face that I hoped displayed adequate remorse, then back to the screen. "Hmm, not even close." He leaned in to get a better look at the unfinished project.

"I'm really sorry. The weekend was crazy. Last night was not much better, but I promise before I go to bed tonight, it will be done." Translation: I can barely function because my boyfriend broke my heart.

His hazel eyes, all full of concern, scanned my face. "You okay?"

I jerked my gaze to the computer screen. "Yeah, yeah, I'm good. Things are just crazy, like I said." I stole a glance at him. "If you want to fire me, I'll understand."

He nudged my arm. "Not on your life. You give this entire project depth. Without you, we'd probably be cataloging new library books with challenging titles like *STDs of the New Millennium* and *Why Today's High School Grads Can't Find a Job.*"

"Stop." I swatted his arm.

He raised not-so-innocent eyebrows, then turned the laptop to face him. "From what little you have done here this looks like a great setup." He winked. "Mind if I fill in some of the blanks?"

"Please do. My focus is so scattered with all the unpleasant scenarios racing through my mind—"

Again, his concerned eyes met mine. "Oh?"

Way to go, Maggie! "I mean, you know how annoying little brothers can be. And parents—let me tell you." I made a production of shrugging.

"Sorry—only child who gets along famously with his parents." Tyler typed away, a grin tugging at his mouth.

Bet you aren't concerned about paternity tests either. "Lucky you," I murmured, searching the crowded cafeteria for a glimpse of Preston. My gaze fell on Zach and Brittany, alone at a corner table. Brittany, who seemed frailer every day except for her sarcastic tone and lousy attitude, had skipped all things NHS related since the meeting with the reporter. Her hand was wrapped around a bottle of juice, but the table was empty in front of her. I hadn't checked in on her since before Preston's big confession. Shame on me.

"What's the sticky note about?" Tyler peeled a yellow sticky note from the edge of the laptop screen.

"Hmm?"

He waved the paper in front of me. "Mentors. What's up with that?"

"Oh, yeah, that's what the last column is for. The clinic is starting a mentoring program for teenage parents, single parents, and people struggling with life issues. They're hoping some of the teachers will volunteer." Alyssa's face filled my mind again.

"Great idea." Tyler's fingers flew over the keys. "I'll write something up for the announcements and get a memo together that we can put in the teacher's mailboxes."

I nodded as I continued to scan for Preston. Good thing he already had a mentor.

Preston

I leaned forward and draped my arm over the computer monitor to cover the screen each time someone walked by. The last thing I needed was gossipy mouths broadcasting that Preston Jacoby was reading up on Indiana paternity laws. I'd assumed few people sacrificed any part of their lunch half-hour to be in the library. I was wrong.

Ignoring my growling stomach, I reread the fine print.

> *Either parent may file an action in an appropriate Indiana court seeking determination of paternity... After the action is filed, the court will set a hearing date and notice will be provided to both parties. At the hearing, the parties may agree to paternity without the benefit of genetic testing, request genetic testing to determine paternity, or the court may hear evidence and make a decision about whether or not paternity should be established.*

Man, this sounded complicated, probably expensive, too. Could I pull this off without involving my parents? My heart hammered as the reality of the situation closed in. If Coach could point me in the right direction, maybe I'd never have to tell Mom and Dad. As long as she wasn't mine, that is.

I hit print then bolted toward the central printer to grab it before anyone else could. My sweaty palm stuck to the paper as I folded it and stuffed it in my pocket. I pressed a hand against the rumbling in my stomach. If I hurried, I could probably snag a little something from Maggie's brown-bag lunch to get me through the afternoon.

She'd be better at wading through all this legal jargon than me. Except I wasn't sure how much more she could take. At the mention of either Alyssa or Ryleigh, her teeth clamped down on her bottom lip and fear erased the golden spark in her eyes. And then came the tears.

Nah, I'd better figure it out on my own.

Maggie

If Preston had made progress on figuring out what to do next, he was keeping the plan to himself. He hadn't heard a peep from Alyssa—I did know that much. Honestly, how could she not want to know who Ryleigh's dad was?

My nerves were shredded, and my face hurt from all the fake smiling at home where it was getting more difficult by the minute to put on a happy face. At least I could be myself at tonight's "prize dinner" with Tucker and Claire because they knew every detail of this nightmare. I wouldn't have to pretend to be a normal, carefree teenager dating a sweet, hot guy. But that's exactly what I intended to do. To bury the entire mess and immerse myself in what I hoped would be a really special evening.

Preston insisted on picking me up which I didn't protest about too loudly. While a part of me wanted to keep him at arm's length, the rest of me missed the connectedness we shared B.B.C., *Before the Big Confession.* Not to mention the snuggling and making out, limited as it had been lately, and the amazing way I felt protected nestled against his solid body. Except now, being near him reminded me of all the other girls he'd held close.

The doorbell chimed, and with stubborn determination, I shut the door on all the uncertainty.

"These are for you." Preston plucked one long-stemmed red rose from a bouquet and caressed my face with the petals.

I accepted the beautiful flowers, passing them in front of my nose. "Thank you."

His button-up black shirt pulled snug across his chest, then hung loose over light, boot cut jeans that grazed the top of new, black sneakers. Sleeves rolled to his elbows, a little higher on the left arm, the one that reached to curl around my waist. He nudged me closer, obviously giving me the chance to protest if I wanted to.

I didn't.

His spearmint breath washed over my face when his lips brushed mine in the first "real" kiss since the big confession. The barely-there kiss deepened briefly. I'd missed this so much.

"Love you," he whispered against my cheek.

I nodded, soaking up his warmth, his scent, his presence.

"Beautiful roses," Mom whispered as she passed through the living room.

"Will you put them in water for me?"

She nodded, winked at Preston, and took the bouquet.

He hadn't pulled away from me even a little like he usually did when Mom or Dad appeared on the scene. And that made me happy.

His lips grazed my temple. "Ready for your prize dinner, ma'am?"

I nodded, barely, not wanting to separate myself from him.

Careful to keep me tucked against him, he led me to the car where, I swear, he considered crawling in from the passenger side so he didn't have to break contact. Instead, he sprinted around the car and hopped in, sweeping my hand from my lap and lacing our fingers together, all in less than thirty seconds.

Tucker and Claire pulled into Preston's drive right in front of us. A sharply dressed Tucker ushered Claire through the front door, and we followed.

Whisked to the couch in the living room and ordered not to move a muscle, Claire and I strained to hear the guys' muffled conversation in the kitchen. I pointed toward the far end of the room where the dining table was set with Jacki's china, delicate glassware, more red roses, several lit candles, and enough silverware for a five-course meal. Soft music floated through the air.

"I'm impressed." Claire spoke in a hushed voice. "But not that surprised. Tucker said Preston really wanted to—" Her fingers pressed against her lips.

"To what?"

"Dinner is served," Tucker announced, all maître d' like, as he strode toward us.

Claire stood as he extended his arm to her.

Preston appeared beside me, reached for my hand, and helped me up. "This way, ma'am." He tucked my hand in the crook of his arm.

The guys literally put the food on our plates but only after first slipping a napkin across our laps. Once he filled his own plate and cut his steak, Preston laced the fingers of his right hand through my left hand and placed our hands on his leg. Without the least bit of awkwardness, he ate with his left hand—something I could never do. As I enjoyed the delicious steak and baked potato, the crisp salad, grilled vegetables, and scrumptious hot rolls, the tension of the last few days melted away.

Tucker raised his glass of sparkling white grape juice. "To Claire and Maggie, whose golfing, bowling, and—most of all— spelling skills captured a stunning victory in our friendly guy-girl competition. An event we *will* repeat in the very near future."

Preston lifted his glass. "To Maggie and Claire."

Claire and I shared a giggly glance, and then my gaze shifted to Preston.

His eyes met mine in a deep, soul-searching way that silenced my giggle.

He tapped his glass against mine. Our eyes stayed connected as we tipped our glasses for a sip of the bubbly. I rested the smooth glass against my lips, far more interested in memorizing the silvery flecks that had finally returned to his eyes.

"Time for dessert." Tucker jumped to his feet, ending our private moment.

Preston set his glass down with a nod and followed Tucker to the kitchen.

They returned with four plates of this amazing layered, chocolatey dessert topped with whipped cream and chocolate drizzle.

"You must love chocolate as much as I do, Maggie." Claire scooped a huge bite of the brownie pudding yumminess into her mouth. "This stuff is incredible," she murmured, covering her mouth with her hand. She pointed at Tucker's very small portion and shook her head.

"Too much chocolate for me. It's my mom's version of death by chocolate. I'm not taking any chances."

"There's no such thing as too much chocolate." My eyes drifted shut as the rich, decadent taste relaxed my frayed senses another notch.

"I knew you'd like it." Preston squeezed my hand.

No one mentioned Alyssa or Ryleigh. Not a word about pregnancy, paternity, or babies. Only fun and lots of laughing, a stolen kiss or two, and pampering like crazy. Even a little serenading when our song played from the CD of our favorites that Preston had given me for Christmas.

"'Bout time you ate more than a few bites at a meal," Preston murmured when he whisked my empty plate away.

If only the night never had to end.

Preston

The dinner went off without a hitch. The food tasted
surprisingly good, but more importantly, I loved how
relaxed Maggie was. More than she'd been in weeks. Tomorrow
the whole Alyssa/Ryleigh nightmare needed my full attention,
but tonight it was all about us.

Back at her house, she snuggled close on the couch and
rested her head on my shoulder. All on her own, without any
nudging from me.

I kissed her hair.

She leaned into me, all soft and warm.

I let my lips brush across her cheek. "Where is everyone?"

"Michael's out, and Mom and Dad are probably in bed."

Another longer kiss on her cheek.

Her eyes fluttered shut. "They've been working crazy hours,
and they're both exhausted." Her breathy whispering tickled
my cheek. Then her mouth found mine with no hesitation. She
reached around my neck, pulling me closer. Her slow caresses
across my neck and shoulders sent shivers down my back.

Desire surged through me, followed by the familiar *don't get
carried away* warning that I so wanted to ignore. Now that she
was back in my arms, I couldn't push her away.

I can handle this.

I traced the hem of her shirt. My fingers itched to push it up.
But I moved my hand to the middle of her back instead.

The kisses deepened more, and her body molded to mine.

It was past time to end it, and I knew it. I eased my mouth away from hers and slipped the hair framing her face behind her ear. "You know I love you."

"And I love you, too."

That was all that mattered. We'd figure the rest out.

Preston

Alyssa had left the ball in my court, and I was going to run with it. A direct, to the point text should do the trick. "we need to talk name the time and place"

I hit send then headed for my mid-day shift. By the time I got off at five, a meeting should be set. Hopefully for tomorrow.

I didn't mind that there was lots of extra food to prepare for a big anniversary dinner. But the burn on my arm, even though covered with a band-aid, still stung when I reached across the grill. So, I volunteered for salad prep to give my arm a break and because filling one hundred twelve salad bowls would give me time to think about what to say to Alyssa.

For starters, I deserved to know if Ryleigh was mine. She couldn't keep me from finding out. Not to mention that she should want to know, too.

Every day that Alyssa didn't demand to know who fathered her baby added credibility to Maggie's theory that Alyssa already knew.

"What'd that lettuce do to you?" My supervisor glared across the prep table at me, his splayed hands jutting toward the ceiling.

"What?"

"You're slinging that lettuce like it's your mortal enemy, and it's going everywhere." He shook his head. "Stop wasting it and clean up the mess."

Lettuce covered the tray between the salad bowls and littered the table. "Sorry. I'll fix it."

If only all my problems were that easy to fix.

~ ~ ~

Only one missed text and it wasn't from Alyssa.

Mom. "Grab a gallon of milk please."

I checked to be sure the message to Alyssa had actually sent. Six hours was more than enough time to reply. I hit resend.

By ten, when she still hadn't answered, my blood ran hot. I shot her another message. "we really need to talk get back with me tonight please"

No response overnight. A lot of good it did to add the "please".

Sunday morning: "r u at grandparents? I can come there"

Sunday afternoon: "you rather come here? that's fine" Although not at home. Maybe Coach's office.

Sunday night: "meet you anywhere"

Monday: "WE HAVE TO TALK"

Tuesday: "don't ignore me Alyssa"

Wednesday morning: "stop ignoring me"

Thursday: "WHY U DOING THIS???"

Did she drop off the planet?

~ ~ ~

"I've texted her a dozen times this week and not one response. I'm about to lose my mind." I paced the worn carpet in Coach's office at the guys' Thursday meeting.

Coach scratched his head. "Have you called her?"

"If she won't respond to a text, why would she pick up my call?"

"She may not but it will show her you're serious."

Connor slouched on the old couch, fiddling with his IU hat. "Why not just leave her alone? If she's content to let it ride, maybe you should be, too."

I stopped in front of him. "A huge part of me wants to forget I know Ryleigh even exists, but I can't." My gaze slid to Tucker at the other end of the couch.

"The Tucker of a couple of years ago would have walked away and fast, no questions asked. But now—" He shook his head firmly. "No way I'd let up until I knew for sure."

"Preston."

I turned to find Coach's narrowed eyes focused on me.

"Why do you want to know if she's your baby?"

"Huh?"

He stood. "Why do you want to know?"

I flung my hands out. "Why *wouldn't* I wanna know?"

He pressed his palms against the desk and leaned forward. "What will you do if she *is* yours?"

I slumped down on the lumpy center cushion between Tucker and Connor. "Not a clue."

"I know why." Tucker's elbow jabbed my side. "You're anxious to clear yourself—to find out she *isn't* your baby—so you can get on with your life. With Maggie."

Coach walked around his desk and perched on the corner. "Do you think the baby's being taken care of? Are either of them in any danger?"

"Alyssa's grandparents are really good people. She said they're helping her, so I'm not worried about that."

Coach tapped his knuckles against his chin. "Okay, then, if I were you, I'd put the search for an answer on hold for a couple of weeks or so. In the meantime, think about *why* you want to know who Ryleigh's father is because once you figure that out, I bet you'll know what to do next."

Coach's gaze cut to the clock. "Sorry, I have to cut things short, but you guys can stay as long as you like." He grabbed a chair and straddled it right in front of me. "Whatever's going on, you need to be open to God's leading. He'll show you what you need to do, and I'm confident you'll do it." He removed his hat. "Let's pray before I go."

I pulled off my Colt's hat, the one Maggie gave me for Christmas, and rubbed the bill between my fingers.

Tuck and Connor grabbed their hats and slid to the edge of the couch.

"God, I come to you today, blessed to be sharing this journey with these young men. Men you are molding to be more like You. Continue to direct and guide their relationships with Claire and Maggie and Chelsea. Empower them to be the godly men You want them to be. Continue to use them to influence their friends to seek You and Your plan for their lives. Bring clarity about Alyssa and Ryleigh. Preston wants to do Your will, Father. Show him what that is. I thank you for the life-transforming power You pour out upon us every day. May we honor You with our lives. Amen."

Coach replaced his hat and stood. "Next week, gentlemen. Uh, no, let's get together sometime this weekend. Give me a call, okay?" He directed the question at me.

"Yeah, sure. And thanks, Coach."

He extended his fist to me. "Hang in there."

With a firm nod, I jabbed his fist.

Tucker and Connor did the same.

As the door closed behind Coach, I hopped up and sauntered over to his desk chair. "Maybe if I sit here long enough, some of Coach's wisdom will rub off on me." I sank into the huge chair, a birthday gift from Mrs. Coach, and stretched back.

"Good excuse. Doubt if it will work." Connor hopped up and flipped his hat around. "Need to head out, too. If you hear from her . . ."

"Yep."

With a scout's salute, he was gone.

I focused on the paint peeling around the water stain on the ceiling. "What do you think Coach is getting at with all this 'why do you wanna know' stuff?"

Tucker stretched out on the couch and scrunched a pillow under this head. "Do you have any feelings for Alyssa?"

"Annoyance, frustration. She's driving me crazy."

"Not what I'm talking about. How close were you two? The sex wasn't a one-time thing, was it?"

I sat forward and met his serious gaze. "No, but—"

"Did you love her?"

I swiveled left then right. "Maybe. Nothing at all like what I feel for Maggie, though. So probably not."

"Sex connects people in ways that aren't so easily forgotten."

Unfortunately, yeah, it did. "You been talking to Maggie? 'Cause that's exactly what she said."

"What's Coach getting at? My guess is he wants you to figure out exactly what, if anything, you feel for Alyssa."

I gripped the arms of the chair. "But I'm with Maggie now. Doesn't he get that? Don't you?"

"We do get that." He sat up and sighed. "Listen, at one time, you had strong feelings for Alyssa. Not saying you're in love with her now. But you care about what happens to her, don't you?"

I shrugged.

"I'll always care about Cami. I can't help it. The other two girls not as much, but I'll never forget them."

I planted my elbows on the desk. "Do you and Cami ever talk?"

"A couple of times a year or so."

"Really? You call her or what?"

"I call, or she call, kind of to check in. I haven't seen her for a long time, and then we just sort of ran into each other, nothing planned." He returned my intent look. "You think that's strange or something?"

"I don't know, maybe. I'm not sure what's proper when it comes to former sex partners." And what I wouldn't give to not have to worry about that now.

Tucker grunted. "Proper? All I know is we shared a pretty intense experience. I'm not in love with her anymore, but I still care about her. She's doing really well, and I'm glad." His expression sharpened. "We usually talk sometime around July 16, the day our baby was due."

My chest tightened. *I don't want to share any baby experiences with Alyssa.*

Tucker shot to his feet. "Coach is right. Give her some time. Maybe she'll come around."

My phone vibrated in my pocket. Probably Maggie.

It wasn't. "It's Alyssa."

"Yeah?" Tucker crossed his arms.

"Listen to this. "why are YOU doing this? have you changed UR mind? because unless U want both of us leave us alone!!!"

"Dude." Tucker shook his head. "Wow."

My fingers flew across the keys. "I have a right to know if she's my daughter!!"

I punched send, then flung my phone toward the couch. It bounced before landing in the crack between the cushions.

"What'd you write back?"

"That I have a right to know if she's my daughter." My fist slammed onto the desktop.

"You do, but this approach obviously isn't working. Hold off—"

I clenched my jaw and shook my head.

"Listen, it's not like a little time will change who the father is, right? Give her a chance to come around."

"And if she never does? What then?"

Tucker tugged his hat down on his forehead. "Cross that bridge only if you have to. But pray like crazy, Dude, 'cause this is way too big to tackle on your own."

Maggie

Just one quick peek.

I pulled Ryleigh Anderson's file from where I'd hidden it in the middle of today's files. My gaze darted through the waiting room window then down the exam room hall. No one watching. I flipped the cover open and scanned the patient information.

Mother: Alyssa Anderson

Father:

DOB: December 20

Address: 2023 W. Sycamore St., Cedar Hills

Home Phone:

Cell Phone: 555-2121

I didn't really expect a name to appear in the father blank, and we already knew she lived in Cedar Hills. But a home phone number would have been nice because Preston was thinking about going to Alyssa's parents.

I rolled the first page back, revealing the medical care/health issues section—the part of the patient files I wasn't supposed to see. "For the healthcare staff only," Mom had instructed, repeatedly, when she trained me. There'd never been a reason to go against the policy until now.

Skimming the small print, I discovered Ryleigh was super fussy, somewhat small for her age, and had digestive issues, resulting in several formula changes. But otherwise no serious health problems. My eyes returned to the top of the page, to the very first line under her birthdate.

Gestational age at birth: unknown

What did that mean?

The door on exam room one opened.

I slammed the file closed and promptly knocked it and several others to the floor. Footsteps squeaked against the linoleum, going away from me down the hall.

With shaking hands, I shuffled the files into a lopsided pile and placed them back on the desk. When a glance over each shoulder assured me the coast was clear, I gripped Ryleigh's file with both hands, wheeled my chair back to the wall of files and stuffed it in.

A quick Google search told me what I needed to know.

Gestational age is the common term used during pregnancy to describe how far along the pregnancy is.

If Ryleigh's gestational age at birth was unknown, then Alyssa really didn't know when she got pregnant or who got her pregnant.

Then why in the world was she refusing a paternity test?

~ ~ ~

Waiting to see if Alyssa would agree to testing was killing Preston. Every day, he sank deeper into himself. He spent extra time with Coach and Tucker over the weekend, which helped a little, but I hated how anxious and moody he was.

Hoping to cheer him up, I greeted him with hot-from-the-oven Ultimate Peanut Butter Chocolate Chip cookies on Monday morning. He wolfed down four in less than two minutes on the drive to school.

As I wiped a smudge of chocolate from his mouth, his lips puckered against my finger. "Awesome way to start the day. Thanks." A dazzling, signature Preston Jacoby smile lit up his face. Complete with eye crinkles and that adorable dimple.

But by lunch time, the creases across his forehead had returned. According to Connor, Alyssa had been seen around town with Ryleigh. Minor whispering would no doubt explode into major gossip at any second.

"Coach wants me to tell my parents." He pushed chips around his tray. "What do you think?"

I looked into his eyes that once again were too dark for the flecks of silvery gray to show. "Maybe . . . I don't know."

He shoved his tray aside. "If I can get her to agree to the test and find out Ryleigh's not mine, then my parents would never have to know. That's one conversation I do *not* want to have."

"I can imagine."

His eyes searched my face. "Do I tell them or wait and hope it's a non-issue?"

I chewed on my bottom lip and shrugged. "I don't know what to tell you." A sense that I was failing him washed over me. "Sorry."

He pulled my hand across the table and laced our fingers together. "I'm the one who should be sorry for dumping all this on you."

I squeezed his hand. "I'd probably wait a little bit. But if the rumors start to fly, you'd better tell them before someone else does. The same for my parents, too, I guess."

He groaned. "An even *worse* conversation."

The mere mention knotted my stomach. "Yeah, well—" I shook the thought away. "You're giving her until this weekend, and then you're going to her parents, right?"

He nodded. "It's killing me not to blitz her with texts, but since that did nothing last week, I'm praying the silent treatment will get to her. I don't wanna go to her parents, but if I have to, I will."

~ ~ ~

I couldn't get the whole unknown gestational age thing that I should have known *nothing* about out of my head. Guilt about snooping through the file made me so nervous. What if someone found out? But now that I knew, what was I supposed to do?

The longer I thought about it, the more I didn't like the red flag doing cartwheels through my brain. Alyssa really *didn't know* the identity of Ryleigh's father, but she knew who she wanted her baby's daddy to be. *Preston.* And, if she rekindled their relationship before any test, she could cling to the hope he wouldn't leave her later even if Ryleigh wasn't his.

If a paternity test proved Ryleigh wasn't Preston's, she'd never get him back. But as long as he *might* be Ryleigh's dad, there was hope—*in her mind*—that they could be together again. A cute couple raising their adorable baby girl.

Anger surged through me. He belonged to me, not her. Unless he chose her.

Maggie

The doorbell chimed at Preston's late Saturday afternoon.

"Great timing. Fifty-eight seconds left in the game." He teetered on the edge of the family room couch, super engrossed in a tournament basketball game on TV.

"You watch the game, I'll get it."

The bell chimed a second time as I pulled open the front door to the tear-streaked faces of Alyssa and Ryleigh.

Alyssa's blue eyes dripped big fat tears. She adjusted the crying baby clinging to her shoulder, and a stained pink diaper bag slipped down her arm. "Is Preston here?" she whimpered, sniffing.

Preston shuffled up behind me. "Who is it?"

I gripped the knob and opened the door wider.

His sharp intake of breath whistled through the air. He pressed close to my side, and his hand gripped my waist. "It's about time." The icy words hissed through his clenched teeth.

"I can't do this anymore." Alyssa thrust Ryleigh at Preston and tossed the diaper bag at his feet.

"Whoa, whoa." He fumbled to get a grip on the now howling baby.

She wrapped her arms around herself and swayed back and forth. "I can't . . . take care of her . . . by myself." Her voice combined whining, crying, and moaning into a desperate plea.

Panic poured from Preston's huge eyes.

Ryleigh's crying lessened to whimpering.

"What's going on in there?" Jacki's voice drifted from down the hall.

As if in slow motion, Preston and I looked at each other before we turned toward the doorway leading to the hall.

He pressed Ryleigh against me and sent the diaper bag skittering across the tile floor as he bolted across the living room, arriving at the doorway as Jacki appeared. His hands came down on her shoulders. "Mom—"

"Is that Alyssa and her baby?"

"Your room now, please." With a gruff voice and firm grip, he propelled her backward, out of sight.

A whiff of spit-up wafted by me as Alyssa brushed past and sank onto the living room couch all familiar like. She shrugged out of a wrinkled black coat, revealing a baggy blue sweatshirt with white blotches on the shoulder and ratty, gray sweats. A bad case of bedhead flattened her blond hair. Bloodshot eyes peered out above deep purple smudges.

Ryleigh rubbed her eyes and whined. Her thumb found her mouth, and she relaxed against my shoulder, her eyes heavy.

"So, who are you?" Alyssa sniffed and looked around the room.

I commanded my frozen legs to move and eased down into the rocking chair across from her. "I'm Maggie, Preston's girlfriend."

Her light brown brows jerked up once. "You must have the magic touch. She's been crying so much, I'm about to lose my mind."

I looked down at the sleepy baby. I shifted her to the crook of my arm and unzipped her pink coat. She snuggled in closer and released a baby-sized sigh.

Loud muttering from the hallway pulled my attention from the baby. A very grim-faced Preston strode through the doorway, followed by a tiptoeing, wide-eyed Jacki, her fingers pressed firmly across her clenched lips. Drew, his forehead creased the exact same way Preston's had been all week, trailed behind them.

Preston

The surreal scene jolted me and ground my feet into the floor. My girlfriend, my ex-girlfriend, and the baby that might or might not be mine all within ten feet of each other in my living room.

Mom's fingers poked into my back. "Preston."

Dad cleared his throat.

I picked up feet that suddenly weighed a hundred pounds each and trudged to where a now composed Alyssa sat on the couch, like she belonged there or something. I faced her, unable to even look at Maggie or the sleeping baby on her lap.

Alyssa twisted the edge of her shirt. Her eyes flitted to Mom then Dad then to me. "I . . . I need you, Preston. I can't do it alone anymore."

"So, you're agreeing to the paternity test. Well, good."

Her head dropped as her hands clenched together in her lap. "I didn't say that."

"Now, wait a minute."

"I can't believe you don't care enough to help me." Her composure dissolved in a flash as teary eyes pierced through me. "I really think she's yours."

With a gasp, Mom sank into the chair beside Maggie.

"Caring has nothing to do with it. What did you do, sleep with the first guy you saw in Cedar Hills?" I raked a shaky hand through my hair.

"Preston." Dad's hand clamped down on my shoulder.

I shrugged away from his grip. "This is insane. Agree to the test, Alyssa." My voice rose with each word. "Or you get nothing from me. Absolutely nothing."

Ryleigh squirmed and let out a loud cry.

"Preston. Lower your voice," Dad hissed.

Maggie stood and grabbed the diaper bag. "I'll take her into the other room." She hesitated beside me, her brown eyes wide.

I grasped her arm and pulled her against me.

Her lips trembled as she shrugged away and left with the baby.

I paced the length of the room twice then flipped a dining chair around in front of Alyssa and straddled it. She looked nothing like the hot blonde I'd dated forever ago. What had happened to her?

"When was she born, Alyssa?" Mom's shaky voice reminded me of her presence.

"December 20." She pressed her sleeve against her cheek to soak up new tears.

Mom should know about that kind of stuff. "Mom?"

"Don't look at me. I had no idea you and Alyssa—" She shook her head.

Dad sat down beside Alyssa. "Who's helping you care for the baby?"

"Mostly my grandparents." She sniffled and blinked.

"What about your parents?" I couldn't help the aggravation dripping from my tone.

Dad shot me a warning glare.

"They're having huge issues. They dumped us all at our grandparents this weekend so they can supposedly get their act together. Like that will ever happen." She leaned forward, closing the gap between me and her. Tears streamed in continuous paths down her cheeks. "I need someone I can count on, and Ryleigh needs a dad." Her voice weakened with each word. "Can't we give it a try?"

I shot from my chair and stumbled back. "No, we can't."

"Listen, this isn't getting us anywhere." Dad pulled his fingers slowly down either side of his face. "Alyssa, why don't you go check on the baby."

She nodded, and with a pleading look my way, left the room.

Mom buried her face in her hands.

I lowered myself onto the chair, closed my eyes, and dropped my chin to my chest.

Dad paced, his breathing loud and fast. On his third pass, he stopped in front of my chair.

I raised my head. "What now?"

His disappointed expression tore at my gut. "Yeah, what now?"

Maggie

Y ou're hungry, aren't you?" I laid Ryleigh on the couch
beside me and dug through the diaper bag in search of a
bottle. She whined, a high-pitched annoying sound, and rubbed
her eyes.

"She probably is hungry." Alyssa suddenly stood by the
coffee table.

I pulled a sticky bottle from the bag along with an almost
empty can of powdered formula.

"She needs changed, too." I handed Alyssa the only diaper in
the bag. Like a programmed robot, I went to the kitchen, took
the bottle apart, and washed it with hot, soapy water then
rinsed it.

Please don't let her be Preston's baby. I measured three
scoops of powder into the bottle.

She can't be Preston's baby. I filled the bottle with warm
water and shook it.

What will we do if she's Preston's baby?

I peeked back into the family room at Alyssa. What had
happened to the pretty, vibrant girl whose picture I'd studied in
the yearbook? Apparently, she'd been replaced by a tired,
desperate, and alone single mother.

Ryleigh let out a screeching wail and threw herself against
Alyssa.

I hurried in with the bottle. "Here you go."

Alyssa popped the bottle into the baby's eager mouth and
settled back on the couch.

I sat in Drew's recliner, keeping my distance.

"So much for saving my parent's marriage and keeping our family together." Alyssa's hand stroked Ryleigh's arm.

What was she talking about?

"Relocating to Cedar Hills didn't solve anything."

Now I understood.

Her eyes barely open, Ryleigh sucked on the bottle. Her tiny fist gripped Alyssa's finger.

Alyssa's gaze pulled from Ryleigh to me. Her lips pressed into a tight line, and her tired eyes tried to stare a hole right through me. "I'm sure an ex-girlfriend dropping back into Preston's life is the last thing you expected, but he was with me before he was with you."

My mouth gaped open. I wanted to scream, "He's mine now!" But I met her determined gaze and swallowed the urge. "He has a right to know if Ryleigh is his baby. Do the right thing and agree to the test."

Her eyes narrowed, but she didn't look away.

Neither did I. The stare down continued without so much as a blink from either of us.

Finally, she yanked the bottle from Ryleigh's mouth, set it on the floor, and sat her up to burp. The heavy silence exaggerated the baby's loud burp. As she continued feeding Ryleigh, her eyes connected again with mine. "He needs to do the right thing and take care of us."

I was done being nice. "I can't believe you expect him to jump in as Ryleigh's dad without proof." What didn't she get about that? But I'd already figured it out. She wanted Preston—baby daddy or not. I straightened my back and ordered myself not to become hysterical. "He's not going to back down. He'll go to your parents, take it to court—"

Her expression wilted from determination to desperation. "This is between me and Preston. Leave my parents out of it."

Preston

Alyssa's now dry eyes locked on Maggie in a way that made me more than uncomfortable.

Maggie had on that intense, don't mess with me expression I'd only seen a couple of times.

At least no one was crying or yelling.

I cleared my throat. "We're not done talking, Alyssa."

Her gaze cut away from Maggie and focused on me. "Well, I am. At least for today. I'm exhausted."

Relief zinged through me, though nothing had been resolved.

She stood and adjusted the baby against her shoulder. She walked toward me and stopped, really close, with only Ryleigh's body between us.

I dropped my gaze to the baby's sleeping face. Did she look like me?

Alyssa's hand moved from Ryleigh's back to my chest. "I need you, Preston. We need you."

I backed away, my body stiffening, and plunged my hands into my pockets.

She stared at me with an expression that promised she wasn't ready to give in. "I'll be in touch." With a momentary glance over her shoulder at Maggie, she slipped by me.

Mom and Dad's muffled voices mixed with Alyssa's as she passed through the living room.

I held my breath and waited for the thud of the front door. Then silence.

Until Maggie's sniffing interrupted the quiet.

In three strides, I reached her chair and knelt beside it. "I'm so sorry."

Her tears turned into gasping sobs.

I took her into my arms and pressed a kiss to the top of her head. I squeezed her tightly as if holding her could erase the past hour.

She clutched my shoulder. Her nails dug into my skin. "Ryleigh needs a dad." She gulped in a breath. "And Alyssa wants it to be you."

"That's not going to happen." I grasped her arms and held her away from me. "What did she say to you?"

She shook her head like a ragdoll. "Isn't it obvious? She doesn't really care who the father is. She wants you." Her finger jabbed my chest.

My mind raced for anything that would prove her theory wrong.

Her eyes fluttered in a long blink. "Please just take me home. I want to go home."

"Of course, sweetheart." I shoved down the panic that tried to engulf me. My fingers inched up the side of her face.

Her head tipped into my hand.

"I'm sorry, Maggie."

"I know you are."

~ ~ ~

A firm knock rapped on my bedroom door before it creaked open. Dad peered through the small space. "Preston. Take a drive with me."

I peeled my gaze from the ceiling.

He pushed the door wide, then, keys jingling in his hand, walked back down the hall.

Let's get this over with. I followed and was soon settled next to him in the front seat of his Ford Edge.

"So." His dark eyes burned into me for several seconds. "Do you think Ryleigh's yours?"

I shrugged. "No."

"What are you basing that on?" He backed onto the street. "Because when it comes to fathering children, there's only one way you can be absolutely certain you aren't that baby's father." The light at the end of our street turned green. "You hungry?"

"Not really."

"Well, I am. And since Mom never finished dinner, let's grab something."

Minutes later, Dad studied me across the table at Pizza Hut.

I fiddled with my straw.

He took a long, slow drink. "So, you don't *think* she's your baby, but she could be?" He leaned toward me, his arms crossed on the table.

"Yeah, I guess."

"You guess."

This conversation was as awful as I'd imagined.

He shifted his attention to the TV hanging in the corner opposite our table and said nothing more. He'd perfected the old "let'em sweat" approach years ago. Why not? It worked.

Finally, the smiling waitress delivered our pizza and dished up a slice for each of us.

Dad nodded her way and forced a smile. "Thank you." His shoulders slumped as he eased back in the booth. His folded hands rested on the edge of the table next to his untouched pizza. "You know, your mom assumed when Alyssa stopped in a couple of weeks ago that you had no connection with her baby—that it wasn't even a possibility."

"I hoped you guys would never have to find out." I shoved my plate away.

Dad leveled his gaze at me. "Are you sleeping with Maggie?"

I shook my head. "I don't ever wanna make that mistake again, and I'd never hurt Maggie that way. She's very committed to waiting. We both are."

The deep creases in his forehead relaxed a little. He grabbed his fork. "Did Maggie know about any of this before today?"

I nodded.

"Has she known all along about you and Alyssa?"

"Nope. She assumed I was a virgin, too, until a week ago."

"And you let her think that."

"I didn't want to scare her off." My throat tightened with defensiveness.

"I can understand that." He cleared his throat, then sighed like he'd been up for twenty-four hours straight. "Okay, tell me what you know about Alyssa's situation." He forked a large hunk of pizza and took a bite.

"Not much. She says she doesn't know if it's me or this other guy she was with right after moving to Cedar Hills." I downed half my glass of Mountain Dew, hoping to ease my dry throat.

"Terrific."

"Maggie's convinced Alyssa wants me back even if I'm not Ryleigh's dad."

His eyes widened. "Any interest on your part?"

"None. She's part of my past and nothing more."

"That's what I would have guessed." He took another bite and chewed slowly.

"She told Maggie her dad didn't actually get transferred. They moved, hoping for a new start, to try to save their marriage. I feel for her, but—"

"If you're Ryleigh's father, you'd better plan to do more than *feel* for her."

I shoved my drink aside. "What about her parents? Why aren't they helping her more? What's they're deal?"

He shrugged. "You don't have all the facts."

"Unless she agrees to a paternity test, I never *will* have the facts."

"Yelling at her won't help, Preston."

"I have a right to know." I knocked my fist against the table.

"Yes, you do, but you need to watch your tone."

I rolled my eyes.

"You will treat her with respect." Dad tossed his napkin beside his plate. "Her situation is tough. I think she'll agree to the test sooner rather than later because she needs help. Yours or someone else's."

She'd better, or I wouldn't hesitate to go to her parents.

Maggie

<hr>

The reality of Ryleigh and, therefore, *Alyssa* in Preston's life surrounded every moment of my day and haunted my nights. If Ryleigh was his baby, everything would change. Oh, he kept saying nothing would be different, regardless of her paternity, but I wasn't convinced.

I mean, come on. A positive outcome—or a *negative one*, depending on how you looked at it—would unleash a whole new reality. He'd have to pay child support. Spend weekends with Ryleigh. Learn about formula and diapers and sleepless nights. Take a crash course in diaper rash and burping and teething. And get over the grossness of poopy diapers. She would take up so much of his time, would he have any time left for me?

Was I up to this? A boyfriend with a child whose mother was desperate to push me out of his life? Even if Alyssa stopped pursuing him—and I wasn't holding my breath on *that* one— raising a child was huge. Did I want any part of this?

Was I considering breaking up with Preston?

Preston

Mom sat in Dad's recliner, a bunch of books spread across her lap. She hadn't heard me come in through the garage. Her fingers slipped across the pages, almost stroking them. A sad smile pulled at her mouth as she brushed away a tear.

She lifted something away from the page and held it close to her face. A baby picture of me.

I backed from the doorway, closing my eyes. Did Ryleigh look like me as a baby?

My heart thundered in my ears. Weakness seeped through my body, making me grip the counter's edge.

I hadn't let myself dwell on the "what if she's mine?" question too much. Instead, I'd poured every ounce of energy into keeping my relationship with Maggie from becoming a casualty. *That* I could control. I would prove to her there was nothing between me and Alyssa. I would convince her she was the one I wanted to be with. I would promise nothing between us would change.

I'd do all that and more, whatever it took. Because there was no way this was going to come between me and Maggie. *No way.*

Preston

P "at test clinic 10 am Saturday"

I blinked, blinked again, and reread Alyssa's text. Who or what had changed her mind?

Finally, the truth, but what if— Sweat instantly dotted my neck as relief clashed with dread. I sucked in as much air as my lungs could hold.

I texted back, "ok how much?"

"my parents paying"

Wait a minute. Not Maggie's clinic. A growl rumbled from my chest. "good but somewhere else not the clinic"

"Y?"

"Maggie's parents work there" Should I have told her that?

"too bad see you Saturday"

Could this get any worse? Wrong question because, yeah, it probably could get a lot worse.

I speed dialed Maggie. "I have good news, and I have bad news."

"Good news first, please."

"Alyssa set up a paternity test for Saturday."

"What? Are you kidding? Of course, you're not kidding, but what changed her mind?"

"Beats me."

"That's good, right?"

"Mmm hmm."

Silence. "Okay, what's the bad news?"

"She set it up at the clinic."

"The clinic? What clinic?"

"The—"

"Oooohhhh nooo, not The Least of These. Not my *parents'* clinic. Preston, you absolutely cannot go there for a paternity test!"

"I told her to set it up somewhere else, but she said no."

Maggie's quickening breaths signaled a rising panic, but she said nothing.

"Maybe it's cheaper there? I don't know. Her parents are paying."

"She knows I work there."

"She remembered seeing you?"

"I don't know, but I bet that's why." Maggie let out a long, anguished moan.

"Where else could we do it?"

"Oh, yeah, like I know about this kind of thing."

A heavy sigh pushed through my lips. "It's not like I know any more than you."

"Well, I'm not ready for my parents to know about this. I'm still clinging to the hope that she's not yours, and then we'll all be spared *that* conversation."

So was I, but what choice did we have? "You'll be at the clinic then, right? Could you sneak me in the back or somethin'?"

"I don't know. I don't know." A super exasperated sigh—the kind she usually reserved for Michael—filled my ear. "Give me some time to think, okay? I'll call you later." And she hung up.

This was bad on every possible level.

Maggie

Honestly, could things get any worse?

A second after ending the conversation with Preston, I called Chelsea. "You got a minute?"

"Sure, what's up?"

I fell back across my bed. "You'll never believe this. Alyssa finally agrees to a paternity test, even sets it up, and her parents are paying."

"Isn't that what you've wanted all along?"

"Ohhhh, there's more. She made the appointment at The Least of These Clinic." I pinched my eyes shut during the long moments of silence that followed.

"But Preston can't go to your *parents' clinic* to see if his ex-girlfriend's kid is his. Your parents will freak out."

"This is so bad. But maybe your mom could help us somehow, without my parents being involved?"

"Maybe." A sound like Chelsea's finger tapping against the phone filled the next five seconds. "Yes, we'll talk to her. In fact, let's grab something to eat—Mom, me and you. She was giving me grief the other day about you not coming over enough. 'You're with Connor every waking moment, you never have time to spend with Maggie.' Yada yada." Chelsea mimicked her mom's dramatic, throaty voice. "And don't worry she won't freak. She's hears stories way worse than this like every day."

~ ~ ~

I fiddled with my nachos, not sure how much food my stomach could handle.

Sarah had listened, nodded, and as Chelsea predicted, not freaked out. "While I'm really excited someone is using the clinic for paternity testing, I'm sorry it has to be Preston." Her mouth turned down in a sympathetic frown.

"You and me both."

"I should hang out with you girls more often. Yum, yum." Sarah wiped her mouth with a napkin, pushed her tray aside, and planted her elbows on the table. "The back door at the clinic squeaks unbelievably."

What?

"Good one, Mom." Chelsea smirked.

"Maggie." Sarah took my hand in hers. "This test has to happen. Preston and Alyssa need to know the truth. And the clinic is the closest option." She bounced our hands on the table. "Your parents are terrific people. They can handle this."

"But I can't handle it!" I tugged against her grip. "They love him almost as much as I do, but once they find out—"

"What? What will they do?" Sarah leaned toward me.

"Flip out for one thing," Chelsea murmured. "Will they make you two break up?"

"I don't know. Probably not, but maybe. But this totally messes up the perfect couple thing we have going, even if Ryleigh isn't his."

"Oh?" Sarah quirked an eyebrow.

"Virgin bride wearing white wedding dress weds virgin groom wearing black tux with tails." Chelsea's eyes rolled dramatically as her finger twirled in a what's-the-big-deal motion.

Sarah delivered the zip-it-young-lady look Chelsea got a lot. "Abstinence is a great goal, Maggie, for so many, many reasons. But everyone makes a bad decision somewhere along the way. Preston's was a biggie, in your mind, but your parents can deal with it. The question is, can you?" With a gentle squeeze, she released my hand. "I'll be there on Saturday to coach him and Alyssa through the paperwork, answer their questions, and help in any way I can."

"Is it okay for me to be there?"

"That's between you and Preston, but I bet he'd appreciate your support."

Preston

"You are just the cutest, most precious little thing." Mom's crooning floated through the whole house. "Yes, you are." Who was she talking to?

I dropped my stuff by the front door and followed her voice to the kitchen. Sitting in a baby seat on the counter, Ryleigh swatted at toys suspended above her. Mom stood by the sink, measuring powder into a baby bottle.

"Why is Ryleigh here?" I blurted, startling both of them.

"Preston." Mom shook the bottle. "Keep your voice down."

I bolted to Mom's side. "Is Alyssa here, too?"

"She needed a break, so I'm babysitting for a couple of hours."

"*What?* Why are you doing this?"

Mom nudged me aside, then scooped Ryleigh from her seat. "She's exhausted, Preston. It's the least I can do considering she might be my grand—"

"Mom. There's only a very slim chance that she's your—" I pressed my palm against my forehead, unable to finish the sentence.

"Alyssa showed up here looking like she hadn't slept in days. This little one doesn't understand that nights are for sleeping, do you, sweet pea?" She circled around me and made her way to Dad's recliner with Ryleigh. "Her grandma's almost as tired as she is. They both needed a break today. And she had to go to Madison to enroll for the final term."

"Madison? Are you kidding me?"

"She'll be staying with her grandparents, Sam and Mary, for the rest of the school year."

This couldn't be happening. I sank onto the couch.

"What was I supposed to do, Preston? She needs help." Mom cooed and made faces at Ryleigh.

Not our help. "Mom, *please*." A frustrated sigh sputtered through my lips. "Do not. Get attached. To her. The baby or Alyssa."

Mom's face morphed from ooey-gooey faces to the stern, thin-lipped expression that I'd grown extremely familiar with over the years. "I'm simply helping her out a little."

"I know you, Mom. You get attached to people like this." I snapped my fingers.

Ryleigh jumped and whimpered.

"Shhh," Mom hissed, her eyebrows scrunched in disapproval.

I ditched the angry tone in favor of begging. "Please, Mom, no more. And don't encourage Alyssa to come over here. If she's mine, we'll deal with it then. But keep your distance until we find out, *please.*"

Maggie

My stomach twisted in knots as I drove aimlessly around town after school on Friday. Desperate to get out of the house, I'd compiled a list of somewhat legitimate errands—library, drug store, grocery—and begged Dad to let me use the van. Anything to occupy my mind until six o'clock when we'd break the news to my parents. How do you tell your parents, who think your boyfriend is the greatest guy ever, that this awesome guy may have a baby with someone else?

When I left the grocery, I didn't even try to talk myself out of driving by Preston's. At least three times this week, Alyssa had turned up at his place, in full help-me, we-need-you mode. And Jacki, who treated everyone with the same enthusiasm, had welcomed her. According to some info Chelsea had coaxed from Connor, Jacki had gotten sort of attached to Alyssa while she and Preston were together. Great. Not what I wanted to hear.

"She's just being nice—that's all. She's that way to everyone." Preston's insistence didn't make me feel any better. At least he was anything but thrilled to see Alyssa. That was good, right? At this point, my objectivity had disintegrated.

No old green car in the drive. Thank goodness.

At the last second, I pulled in. A little last-minute strategizing couldn't hurt.

I slipped through the front door, listening. No crying baby. Even better.

I breathed a sigh of relief that lasted only until Preston's anxiety-filled eyes met mine. Jacki looked like she'd been crying, and Drew's stone-like expression made what we were about to do seem a hundred times worse.

Preston pulled me close, planted a kiss on my temple, and sighed. One of those sighs that told a long, sad story without any words. "Let's go and get it over with."

Preston

With our hands clenched in a show of unity or desperation—I wasn't sure which—we sat down across from Tom and Cheryl in the family room.

"There's something we need to tell you." Maggie's carefully rehearsed speech fell apart by the end of the first sentence, as tears trickled down her face.

Tom and Cheryl looked at each other with wide, panicked eyes, then shifted their gaze to to me.

I wrapped my arm around her shoulders. "Don't worry, Maggie's okay. I'm the one with the . . . problem."

Tom's face relaxed from panic to concern. "What's going on?"

Maggie trembled next to me. She lowered her head and let the tears drip on her lap.

"I . . . tomorrow—" I squeezed my eyes shut for several seconds and then focused on a picture hanging on the wall behind them. "My ex-girlfriend had, uh, *has* a baby. There's a chance the baby's mine."

Tom's arms jerked tight across his chest.

Cheryl pressed her fingers over her mouth.

"Getting a paternity test tomorrow at the clinic. Your clinic."

Maggie's hair brushed across my arm as she raised her head, no doubt to catch their reaction.

I pushed on. "I have no interest in getting back with Alyssa, my ex, but if the baby's mine, I'll do the right thing by her."

Tom cleared his throat. His grim face quickened my pulse.

"We thought you guys should know before you found out tomorrow."

Tom glanced at Cheryl. "We appreciate that, Preston."

"Yes, thank you for telling us." Tears threatened to spill over Cheryl's lashes as she sought Maggie's gaze.

"Mom, it's Ryleigh. Preston's ex is Alyssa Anderson."

"Oh, my." Cheryl's hand clapped over her mouth.

"You know her?" Tom quizzed.

"She's been my patient a few times. The baby, I mean. She's a cute little thing with a very tired, very young mother." Cheryl reached for Tom's arm.

"Has she said anything to you about the father?" The words flew from my mouth.

Cheryl shook her head. "I felt so bad for her. Little support from her family except for her grand—" Cheryl's lips pressed together. "I've said too much already." She swiped at a tear on her cheek.

Tom planted his elbows on his thighs. "Do your parents know, Preston?"

"Yeah, Alyssa showed up at our house."

"And she keeps showing up, saying how much she needs them." Maggie's irritation at Alyssa seeped into her tone. "At first, she refused a paternity test. She wants Preston to *be* Ryleigh's dad whether or not he really *is* her dad. Why she suddenly agreed to the test, we have no idea."

Tom shook his head. "Oh, boy."

"How long does the test take to come back?" *Please don't say weeks.*

"Seven to ten days. You'll get the results in the mail." Cheryl reached out to Maggie who rushed into her mom's arms.

Tom's gaze cut from me to Cheryl and Maggie.

The clock ticked loudly over the muffled sounds of crying.

Cheryl tucked strands of Maggie's hair behind her ear. "So, this is what's been bothering you."

Maggie sniffled and nodded. She glanced back at me. "In case you're wondering, we committed to no sex long before Alyssa showed up."

Tom's eyes met mine. "That's good to know." His shoulders lifted, then dropped with a deep sigh. "This could get messy. You'll keep us posted." It wasn't a question.

"Of course, I—I mean, we will."

Maggie returned to my side and rested her head on my shoulder.

I grazed her hair with my cheek.

"Anything else?" Tom held his hands up in front of him.

"That's enough, isn't it?" Maggie's tone aimed for humor but fell short.

"It is." Tom stood, reached for Cheryl's arm, and helped her up. His intense expression softened as it rested on Maggie.

I eased Maggie from my shoulder, and we stood, too.

Tom stepped toward me and stuck out his hand.

Without hesitation, I thrust mine into his firm grip.

"We've trusted you all along with Maggie." He glanced at Cheryl whose head tipped in a brief nod. "That won't change unless you give us reason to think otherwise."

"I appreciate that. Thank you. I love Maggie. I'd never do anything to hurt her."

Except I already had.

Maggie

H ey."

I looked up to find a stone-faced Preston leaning into the clinic's receptionist window. "Hi. How are you?"

"Been better. What about you?"

"I'm okay." I forced a smile—probably weak and pathetic—but at least I tried.

Dad wandered out of his office for the seventh time since eight o'clock. "Preston." His voice was as strong and confident as ever.

"Tom."

Dad opened the waiting room door. "Come on back. Sarah's got everything set up in her office."

My knotted stomach lurched as he trudged down the hall behind Dad.

Mom's hand pressed against my shoulder. "This is Preston's situation. Let him and Alyssa do this by themselves."

"But I want to be there—"

"Maggie. Being in the room when Sarah swabs his cheek isn't how you show Preston your support."

"But Alyssa—"

"She knows he's with you."

I covered my face with my hands.

"Here she comes. Be nice, please." Mom squeezed my shoulder. "Alyssa. How are you and little Ryleigh today?"

I pulled a mask over my oozing emotions and faced Preston's ex and the bright-eyed baby in her arms.

"We're good." Alyssa's gaze focused first on Mom, then flitted to me. Her eyes narrowed as she inched toward us.

"Yep. She's my daughter. We couldn't pretend otherwise if we wanted to." Mom walked around my desk and opened the door. "I'll take you back. Preston's already here."

Preston

This is quick and painless. I promise. Now open wide."
Chelsea's mom, Sarah, stretched up on her tiptoes. "Wow,
you're tall." She twirled this swab thing with tiny bristles
against the inside of my cheek for what seemed like forever.
Her head bounced back and forth, like she was counting to
herself. "Five, four, three, two, one. All done." She slipped the
swab inside a long tube and sealed it.

Nothing about this was quick or painless. I propped myself
against the wall, anxious to get out of there.

"Okay, Alyssa. At least I don't have to wrench my shoulder to
reach you." She pointed at me, grimaced, and rotated her
shoulder. With a wink, she lowered her arm and faced Alyssa.
"You ready?"

Alyssa looked like she could burst into tears at any second
and hadn't uttered a word. She simply nodded for like the tenth
time. Her eyes bore right through me the entire time Sarah
brushed the swab against her cheek.

What I wouldn't give to know what the heck was going
through her head right now. And three months ago, when
Ryleigh was born. And last year, when she found out she was
pregnant.

Alyssa averted her eyes, finally, and closed her mouth.

"Now it's your turn, little one." Sarah carefully pried
Ryleigh's pacifier from her mouth, squeezed her cheeks gently,
and swooped in with the swab.

Ryleigh squirmed against the intrusion. Her face puckered like she was about to start wailing, but only whimpers came out.

"Now that wasn't so bad, was it?" Sarah popped the pacifier back in the baby's mouth.

She dropped the three sealed tubes in a Ziploc-type bag. "Okay, guys, look over your paperwork to make sure it's complete—especially the address where you want the results sent. Then I think we're finished here."

I re-checked the address on my forms and handed her my clipboard.

Alyssa gripped her board with both hands, her head down like she was going over the information.

"Need some help with yours, Alyssa?" Sarah stepped toward her.

Alyssa pressed the clipboard to her chest and shook her head.

Sarah placed her hand on Alyssa's arm. "Are you finished?"

Alyssa thrust the clipboard at Sarah.

Unfazed, Sarah continued in social-worker mode. "Only the two of you will receive the results. But if you need help going forward after that, I'd welcome the opportunity to assist you any way I can." She handed each of us her business card. "I mean it. I hope to hear from you—separately or together. Got it?"

"Thanks, Sarah." While I'd kind of always known Chelsea's mom, and thought today would be awkward, it wasn't so bad. She mixed professional courtesy with an easy going, laid back vibe that actually made the situation a little more bearable.

"Thanks," Alyssa mumbled and wrapped her arms around herself.

Sarah carried our paperwork back to her desk, stopping to tweak Ryleigh's sock covered foot along the way. "You're a cutie. No question about that."

I grabbed my jacket.

"Can you help me?" Alyssa's voice sounded as if a huge lump had lodged in her throat.

"Uh, yeah, sure." I picked up the diaper bag.

She slipped a fuzzy cover over Ryleigh's car seat and pulled up on the handle until it clicked. "This thing weighs a ton. I'll trade you." She pulled the diaper bag from my grasp and stepped back.

"Um, okay. Thanks, again, Sarah."

"You bet. I'll see you later. You, too, Alyssa."

I swung my arm through the handle of the car seat and lifted it. It did weigh a lot.

I followed Alyssa, keeping my head low as we plodded down the long hall.

Ryleigh peeked at me through the zippered opening in the car seat cover. A huge smile spilled out around her pink pacifier. Her bright blue eyes sparkled right at me.

Something clenched in my chest like the wind had been knocked out of me. I tapped Alyssa's back with the seat. "Can't you walk any faster?" I sputtered.

She glanced over her shoulder. "Huh?"

I shook my head, motioning toward the exit.

Cheryl stood beside Maggie's desk, her hand on the back of Maggie's chair. "So, are we all finished?"

Maggie

He's carrying the baby. Panic pushed up my throat until I could barely catch my breath. I blinked, willing the sick image in front of me to change. But it didn't.

The blood pounding in my ears muffled Mom and Alyssa's conversation. " . . . a weight check . . . exam room one."

Mom took the car seat from Preston and led Alyssa back down the hall.

"I have to go." Preston stood beside my desk, his hands stuffed in his jeans' pockets.

"But—"

"Working a double today. Have to be there at eleven."

"A double?"

He zipped his coat. "They're short on help. I'm off at ten. I'll call you." And he strode out the door.

No love you. No kiss on the cheek. He didn't even touch me. Just a ten second conversation and poof, he was gone.

I stumbled toward the bathroom, ignoring the ringing phone and the waiting room full of patients. Tears stung my eyes as I pressed a wad of wet paper towels to my flushed cheeks and burning neck.

Was he choosing her—even before the test results?

~ ~ ~

"Maggie, hey." Preston's voice, even scratchy and tired, had never sounded so good.

"Hi." My heart pounded with relief as I propped myself up in bed. Boy, did we need to catch up. "How are you?"

"Tired. Long day."

"I know. That's a bummer you had to work a double."

A long yawn muffled a "Yeah."

An awkward silence stretched between us.

Preston moaned or sighed, like he was falling asleep.

"You still there?"

"Uh huh."

"So, how was it, the test I mean?"

Another muffled yawn. "Was okay."

That's it, "okay"? "The results will come in the mail, right?"

"Yep."

"In a week or so, I guess."

"Mm hmm."

This was ridiculous. I pushed down the swelling waves of panic along with my quilt as heat prickled across my skin. *Keep him talking.*

"Too wiped out to talk—sorry." Another yawn waffled through the phone.

No, don't hang up. Panic clamped a vise on my throat. "Oh, sure," I croaked. "I . . . understand." *That I'm losing you to the mother of your maybe baby.*

"Call you tomorrow?" He murmured.

"Yes, *please* call tomorrow. I love you."

"You, too. 'Night." The line went dead.

And a chunk of my heart died with it.

Preston

I jolted wide awake, heart pounding, and jerked to a sitting position. 2:37 a.m.

I raked my hands through sweat drenched hair and across my sticky neck.

What a nightmare. The vivid, too-real image burned like a white-hot poker across my mind. Me, standing beside the mailbox, pulling out a massive envelope, ripping it open to find a message scrawled in huge block letters:

YOU ARE RYLEIGH'S FATHER

In the dream, I crumpled the paper, but it flattened out on its own and floated from my grasp to hover in front of my face. A second line of writing appeared below the first, the letters even bigger:

ALYSSA NEEDS YOU

Pressing the heel of each hand against my eyes, I rubbed hard as if I could erase the image. The hammering of my heart slowed a little.

I crashed back onto my pillow. *Eww.* It was wet. I flipped it over, desperate for the escape of sleep. But my mind swam with one horrific scenario after another, and the rapid pulse pounding in my ears made sleep impossible.

I'd thought of nothing but Ryleigh since carrying her from Sarah's office. Since staring into her perfect face, I couldn't focus on anything but a possible future as her dad.

Seventeen-year-olds shouldn't be fathers.

Fifteen and sixteen-year-olds shouldn't have sex.

Waiting for the results just might kill me. Mom's eyes had become permanently red and teary. Dad's line-creased forehead might never smooth out. And Maggie—

Man, she deserved better than this. Better than me.

Her support so far had been pretty obvious, but could I expect her to stick around if Ryleigh was mine?

I may have dozed a time or two the rest of the night, but when my alarm went off at eight, I stared at the ceiling, wide awake. Church was out. No way could I sit there like my whole world wasn't caving in. If I psyched myself up enough, maybe I'd make it through lunch with my family and Maggie.

Maybe.

~ ~ ~

By the time Maggie's parents dropped her off after church, I was as pumped as I was gonna get, which was basically just a fraction above the barely functioning mark.

Tom waved as their van pulled away. At least he was still letting me see her.

I waved back as Patrick and Emily pulled up behind Dad's Ford Edge where Mom and Dad waited. I drank in the sight of Maggie. Sweet, innocent, and beautiful, but walking too slowly up the sidewalk. Something wasn't right.

I hopped over the bottom step to meet her. "Hey, there."

The breeze blew waves of her dark hair across her face.

I smoothed the loose strands behind her ear. "You okay?"

She nodded, but her eyes—sad, worried, confused—told a different story.

Not her too. One of us close to the edge was enough. I tipped her chin up. "Hey."

She forced a half-smile.

"How you doin'?" I wrapped my arm around her waist and stepped toward her.

She shrugged and dropped her gaze to the ground.

"That good, huh?" I pulled her against me.

She resisted for like two seconds, then practically melted into my chest.

Closing my eyes, I kissed her hair, letting her scent wash over me. If only I could hold her like this forever.

A car sputtering to a stop between our house and the neighbor's tugged at my attention. An old green Ford.

My hold on Maggie tightened. Not Alyssa. Not now.

I stroked Maggie's back, encouraging her to stay molded to me.

The doors on the Edge opened at the same moment Patrick hopped out of his car. He shot a questioning look my way as Mom wasted no time getting to Alyssa's car. Dad trailed behind her.

I heard whispers and then realized it was me murmuring something to Maggie.

She snuggled into me more.

What had I said to her? It didn't matter. As long as she stayed pressed to my chest.

My eyes drifted shut. Maybe Alyssa wasn't here again for the umpteenth time. *One, two, three.* I held my breath and opened my eyes. She *was* here. Toting Ryleigh in that heavy car seat.

"Hey, I asked where we're having lunch." Maggie's fingers tapped against my shoulder.

"Hmm? Oh, I don't know." My eyes roamed her face. "Where would you like to go?"

"Food and I have a rather iffy relationship lately." She glanced over her shoulder. "Did someone pull up?"

I caught her chin and turned her back to face me. "You should eat something. What sounds good?" I stroked her cheek.

"Chocolate and Diet Coke."

"Not very nutritious, but I'll see what we can do."

Ryleigh let out a loud wail.

Maggie whipped around. "She's here *again*?"

I gripped her shoulders.

"Why, Preston? Why is she here again?"

"Stay here, and I'll find out." I strode to where Mom and Dad stood next to Alyssa whose foot rocked Ryleigh's car seat on the driveway.

"Why are you here?"

Mom cringed at my harsh tone.

Dad's glare cut through me.

I ignored them both.

"I need a sitter, just for a couple of hours." Alyssa's eyes darted from me to Mom. "Ryleigh just loves Jacki."

An exasperated sigh sputtered from me. "Oh, come on—"

"It's okay, Preston." Mom's tone was unusually firm. "I don't mind, we can take her with us."

"Mom."

Dad stepped toward me. "This is Mom's call, not yours."

I stalked back to Maggie, who sat on the front steps beside Emily, her head on her knees.

Patrick paced the sidewalk, hands stuffed in his pockets. "What's with her anyway?"

"I wish I knew."

"You've got to be kidding me." Maggie's voice rose with each word. She elbowed Emily. "You know what she's doing, don't you?" She jumped to her feet, not waiting for an answer. "She wants you all to get attached to Ryleigh, so it won't matter what the paternity test says. You'll want the two of them around. You know, kind of like they're part of the family even if they aren't."

"Maggie . . ." I reached for her, but she jerked away.

"I can't believe you don't see it, Preston." She snapped her arms into a tight fold across her chest.

Patrick reached a hand out to Emily. She hopped up, and they walked toward his car.

I brushed a finger along Maggie's arm. "Let's go eat."

"I'm not hungry. You go ahead."

"I'm not going without you."

"Well, I'm not going at all." Her foot tapped a frantic rhythm against the step.

"Fine, we'll stay here. Let me go tell Mom and Dad."

"No, you go." She pulled her phone from her pocket. "My parents can come get me."

"No." My harsh tone returned.

Maggie's face wilted.

"I'm sorry. I'm sorry." Cupping her chin, I peered into her eyes. "If you don't want to go with the family for lunch, no big deal, okay?"

"Mm hmm."

I motioned to Dad that they should go without us.

By now Ryleigh was tucked in their backseat. Alyssa's car sputtered to life, then crept by the front of the house.

I turned Maggie away but trained my eyes on the car as it disappeared around the corner.

I shifted my attention back to Maggie. "So, you still need to eat."

She stiffened. "I said I'm not hungry."

"Takeout from Guido's then?"

"What don't you understand about *not hungry*?" She snapped.

My jaw tensed. "So, I can't eat either?"

She whirled out of my arms. "I'm going home. Do whatever you want."

"Maggie, stop it."

"I can't do this anymore." Her anguished voice fit the way her head and upper body swayed back and forth. "I thought I could deal with it, but I can't."

"Don't say that."

"She'll never stop trying to be with you." She gasped through a wave of fresh tears. "Why can't you see that?"

I cradled the sides of her face. She resisted, still swaying in slow motion. "It doesn't matter. I love you." The gruff tension was gone from my voice. "I don't want to be with Alyssa."

Her watery eyes glazed over. She stared right at me. No, right through me.

Fear knotted my stomach. "Maggie, please."

Her shoulders rose in an exaggerated shrug. "I understand exactly where Alyssa is coming from."

What?

She leaned closer. "I know why she wants you back."

I shook my head.

"Oh, yes. You're a far better catch than whoever the other guy is. And she probably only slept with him once. But she *bonded* with you, and that still means something to her."

Not the bonding thing again.

"Whether you'll admit it or not, you bonded with her, too. That's what sex does, Preston. And when the results come back that she's your baby," her fingernail jabbed into my chest, "that connection will rekindle. You'll want to be with her."

"How can you even think that?" My hands dropped from her face. "Unless you don't trust me. Is that what you're saying?" I didn't even try to hide my irritation now.

Her lips pressed together in a thin line. "I don't want to talk about this anymore."

"Do you trust me or not?"

Her entire body pushed out a heavy sigh. "I want to go home."

"No. We need to talk about this."

She shook her head decisively. "I can't—not anymore."

Panic shot through me. "Don't go, please. I want you to stay—"

She shook her head again. "No."

"Then I'll take you home."

Maggie

Let's sit on the porch." Preston brushed some twigs from the swing's cushion before sitting down.

I wanted more than anything to escape inside to the privacy of my room. But I sat, not too close, bent my knees, and pulled them to my chest. The warm breeze blowing through the budding trees ruffled my hair. I let the strands flap against my face.

"I thought you wanted us to be together." Preston pushed off from the porch floor to make the swing rock. He surely knew it would take a lot more than a swaying swing to calm me today.

"I thought that's what I wanted, but this is too hard. The worrying, the wondering, the uncertainty, it's too much."

His finger swiped across my cheek to catch the wayward hair and tuck the strands behind my ear. "In a week, we'll know about Ryleigh. Surely you can hang on that long."

I faced him. "And then what?"

"We'll figure it out."

"That's all you keep saying. 'We'll figure it out.'"

He thrust his hands into the air. "What do you want me to do? Just tell me."

"The only thing I want is the one thing you can't give me."

His hands dropped to his lap. "No Alyssa in my past, present, or future. Well, that's what I want, too, but it's not gonna happen. You have any idea how much I want to guarantee you everything will be fine, that nothing from my past will ever be an issue again? But I can't." He inched closer. "All I can guarantee you is how much I love you."

I didn't doubt he loved me.

His fingers stroked my hand. "Isn't it enough that I adore you? Can't we figure this out together?"

Was it enough?

"Can't who I am right now be enough for you?" His finger traced my jaw and lifted my chin until our eyes connected. "My heart is yours. Isn't that enough?" His voice, so soft and soothing and gentle, begged me to believe in him.

The hardest question I'd ever faced. "I love you, too," I whispered. "But I . . . I don't know if it's enough."

His hand dropped from my face, and his expression hardened.

I put my hand on his arm, but he shrugged away from me.

His jaw clenched. And his eyes—now the darkest I'd ever seen them—swam with hurt and anguish. I'd just broken his heart.

A deep, sharp, very physical pain pierced my chest.

He stood, hooked his thumbs in his pockets, and stared toward the street. "Then there's nothing more I can do." He strode across the porch, down the sidewalk, got in his car, and drove away.

I simply watched him go. I didn't say anything. Didn't go after him. I did nothing.

Preston

I hadn't spoken to Maggie in days. By rerouting my path to avoid her, the exact opposite of how I'd plotted to be with her every possible minute at the beginning of the year.

When Mom found out we'd broken up, if that's what you called it, she cried more than she did about the Ryleigh situation. "Whatever you do, do not mention this to Alyssa," I begged. I could only imagine how Alyssa would use the breakup to her advantage.

On Monday, Coach had me round up some guys to paint the dugouts at the ball park. Tuesday night, I mowed the outfield before my shift at Guido's. Wednesday, I tackled a mile-long list of stuff he wanted done before try-outs next week. "You're praying, right?" he asked every day—usually more than once. "Even if you can't see Him, God is in all this."

Really, Coach? I felt abandoned by God. Why wasn't He fixing this mess? Why wasn't He helping Maggie cope or finding someone else besides my family to help Alyssa? I'd done everything He asked me to do. He wasn't keeping His end of the bargain.

"He's not finished yet. Trust Him." How could Coach be so sure?

Anyway, trust was the last thing I wanted to talk or think about.

Maggie

Had I spied a tiny bit of relief in both Mom's and Dad's expressions when I sobbed out the news that we'd broken up? Did Mom's eyes maybe say, "It's for the best," as she pulled me in for a mega hug? Dad's silence, and the tear he swiped away when he thought I wasn't looking could have meant any number of things.

My emotions swung like a pendulum. From a burning, aching desire to see Preston to an absolute, heart-pounding dread of bumping into him. But I'd barely seen him. A glance or two in Psychology and the same in AP English because now he sat on the opposite side of the room in the first row. He *hated* the first row. He once bribed a teacher for a back-row seat. He was avoiding me at all costs.

If I loved him, if I didn't want Alyssa to have him, then *why* had I let him walk away? Was I ready to move on? Maybe I really didn't trust him. Could it be we didn't belong together anymore?

Chelsea's undisguised rooting for him and us came as no surprise. "Get him back, whatever it takes." But Brittany backed up her new guys-are-jerks attitude by announcing, "You're better off without him." I apologized for spending every waking minute on my own issues when I'd promised to be there for her. She waved it off with, "I'm making it, and so will you." But if 'making it' looked that bad, *wow.*

I limped through the week, without a word from him. Not a call, a text, or a word in passing. *Nothing.* Of course, he didn't hear a peep from me either. Maybe there was nothing left to say.

Preston

Mom met me in the kitchen after school on Tuesday, an envelope boasting the Genetics Laboratory, Inc. logo clenched in her hand.

"It's about time." I pried the long-awaited results from her grip and sank onto a chair at the breakfast table.

Mom busied herself at the sink.

I fingered the smooth envelope.

"Oh, I can't stand it. Will you open it already?" She hovered over my shoulder.

I pulled on a loose corner of the back flap, ripping it off before the opening enlarged. The other end reacted the same way.

"Here." She handed me a butter knife.

With shaking hands, I slit the envelope's crease and shook the contents onto the table. Three folded pieces of white paper.

Mom's breathing quickened to almost panting.

I held my breath as I unfolded the pages with stiff fingers.

A line in the middle of page one grabbed my attention. "*The probability for paternity is 0%.*"

Breath whooshed up my throat. "It's negative. She's not mine."

"She's not yours? Ryleigh's not your baby?" Mom's hand clamped down on my shoulder.

"No." A thousand emotions raced behind a massive adrenaline rush. *She isn't my baby.*

"Maggie will be so relieved."

Would it even matter to her? "You think she'll even care?"

"Of course, she cares. She's hurt and confused, but she loves you."

Did she? Who knew? I glanced over my shoulder at Mom. "Are you relieved?"

Mom dabbed at her eyes with one hand and squeezed my shoulder with surprising strength with the other. "My goodness, what a question! You're far too young to take on the responsibilities of fatherhood." Her grip morphed to a light pat. "She really was a sweet little thing, though."

Maggie

Today was the tenth day since the paternity test. What if days or weeks went by and Preston never let me know the results?

"No, nothing." I headed off Mom's questioning gaze with the same answer for the third day in a row. My teeth sank into my sore, quivering lip that couldn't take much more waiting.

Her warm hand stroked my back.

"Don't," I gasped, desperate not to cry.

"It's more often ten days than seven days. I checked." She turned me around and enveloped me in a hug.

I buried myself in her embrace and let the tears pour out.

"I bet you hear from him tonight."

Hope flickered like a match about to go out. My hemorrhaging heart wanted—even more than knowing the test results—to hear from him. I longed to know he cared enough to call or text or something. Missing him had swelled into a deep, non-stop ache.

As much as I longed to hear his voice, I wasn't sure about anything else. Especially about fighting what might be a losing battle against Alyssa's determination to win him back *and* his denial of her intentions. How could I handle always being freaked out that the bond they'd shared would eventually win?

Did I want to be with him enough to live with *that*?

Of course, Maggie deserved to know. But why the heck was it so hard to decide between a call or a text?

I'd texted the guys—Coach, Tucker, Connor, Zach—as soon as my fingers stopped shaking enough to tap out a message. Dad and Patrick, too. Dad called me back with a more emotional response than I'd ever remembered from him. "What about Maggie?" he asked.

"No letter in the mail about that."

"Give her time, son."

Maybe I needed time, too. It still stung like crazy that she didn't trust me. I know I'd been less than honest in the beginning. But as open as I'd been with her since then, how could she not trust me now?

I'd get a feel for where her head *and* heart were if I could hear her voice. Stretching out on my bed, phone in hand, reminded me of so many other conversations. Would this be our last one?

I jabbed speed dial one. Three rings. Four. Then five. Finally, she answered with a hoarse, "Hello?"

"Maggie, it's me." Breathe. "I have news. Good news."

"The test results?"

"Negative. Ryleigh's not mine."

Maggie's sharp intake of breath oomphed through the phone. And then silence.

"Maggie?"

"That's good. You're relieved, right?"

"Absolutely."

"I'm so happy for you."

"I thought you'd want to know."

"Yeah, I've been waiting, hoping to hear from you."

"Me too. Waiting and hoping."

This was like no other conversation we'd ever had. Even with the uncertainty gone, had nothing changed? A bitter taste filled my mouth. "Listen, I don't want to bother you anymore." *Say I'm not a bother.*

"Thanks for calling."

"You bet."

"I'll see ya."

"Yeah, see ya."

~ ~ ~

Alyssa called Mom, who dabbed at teary eyes while Alyssa sobbed on and on about the test results.

"Don't promise her anything," I scrawled on a piece of paper and slid it across the table to her.

"I won't," she mouthed, pushing the note aside.

Then I hit the park. Six laps left my lungs burning, my legs as wobbly as a limp noodle but did nothing for the fog in my brain. I trudged home to find Mom still on the phone with Alyssa.

When she finally hung up, she blew her nose and rested her forehead on her palm.

"Well?" I refilled my glass with water. Did I really want to know? No, but I needed to know.

Mom twisted a crumpled tissue around her finger. "The other guy's a jerk, and Alyssa wants nothing to do with him. But her parents are pushing her to go after him to make him take responsibility."

"Took her that long to say that?"

She tossed the tissue aside. "No . . ." Her gaze darted from the tabletop to me, then back down.

"What?"

Mom sighed. "She wanted it to be you. She went on about how disappointed she was and how she didn't think she could do it without—" She took a deep breath. "Without you."

"Well, she better figure it out 'cause it's not my problem." My glass clinked hard against the bottom of the sink.

Mom jumped, her face wrinkling in a grimace. "I know, but—"

"*No*, Mom. Taking care of Ryleigh is that other guy's problem. Not mine."

~ ~ ~

Midnight found me lying in bed clutching my phone again. The rush of knowing I wasn't Ryleigh's dad should have psyched me like nothing else, but all I could think about was Maggie. Did I want to pick up where we'd left off before this nightmare? Yeah, I did. But only if she got over the trust issues. I couldn't wonder every day whether or not she trusted me. She had to be all in or nothing.

I had to know where we stood.

If Maggie was half as miserable as me, she'd still be up. I flipped off the overhead light, stuffed an extra pillow behind my head and sent her a text. "R U awake?"

"Yes." Super quick response.

"can I ask U something?"

"Sure."

"is there hope for me and U?"

Seconds turned into a minute, then two. Heat prickled up my neck. I tossed the blanket off.

"What about Alyssa?"

"what about her?"

"She won't give up on you."

"doesn't matter"

"But it matters to me."

This is crazy. I swung my legs over the side of the bed and punched one. "So, you still don't trust me," I started in, trampling over her weak hello. "My feelings for you don't come with an Alyssa factor."

"Don't yell," she whimpered.

"Sorry." I huffed out my frustration. "I'm not with you *because* I'm not with her. I'm with you because I love you."

Nothing but soft breathing.

"You're making this too hard when it's really simple. Do you want us to be together or not?"

"Yes, but . . ."

My exasperated sigh echoed in the phone. "But what?"

"I need a chance to catch my breath. Don't you, too? The past couple of weeks have been awful."

"It's been rough, yeah, but it's over. We can finally move on." I swallowed my impatience to give her a second. Or twenty.

"I never said I didn't trust you."

"Well, that's what it felt like."

"I'm sorry." Pause. "There's hope."

"Huh?"

"You asked if there's hope for us. The answer is yes, but I need time to sort stuff out."

"What kind of stuff?"

"Like—"

"You're waiting to see what Alyssa does, right? So, I guess it's *your* feelings for *me* that have an Alyssa factor. Wow." Anger surged through me.

"She's determined, Preston. You don't get that—"

"What I get is that you're basing *our* future on her. You're obviously not willing to fight for what we had. Un-be-lieve-able."

"I did not say that." She bit off each syllable.

"The ball's in your court, Maggie, not Alyssa's. It's your call." Each second of her silence fueled my anger. "I want you. I want us. When you figure out what *you* want, give me a call."

Maggie

Tears rolled down my cheeks into my hair and dripped into my ears. I want you, too, Preston. Exactly the way it was before anyone knew Ryleigh existed.

I wanted the Preston who never got mad at me or raised his voice or gave me ultimatums. The Preston I thought was a virgin. Who didn't drink or party or make out with half the girls in his class.

That's who I wanted. That's who I wanted to take me to the prom next month. But that Preston didn't exist.

My phone vibrated. Claire—who'd probably heard the paternity results. "So HAPPY for U guys! Now you can get on with UR lives! Let's get together soon. ☺"

Yeah, get on with our lives.

Her advice a couple of weeks ago flashed through my mind. "You'll either get over it, or you won't." Then, it seemed harsh and unfair and overly simple. And it kind of made me mad. But was she right? Was it that simple?

Preston

Why was I so reluctant to give Maggie time? Everyone—Coach, Tucker, Patrick, Dad, Connor, and even Zach—had told me to give her some space.

"You dumped a lot on her." *Yep.*

"This is a big deal to her." *True.*

"Don't push her." *Then, why did I?*

Why couldn't I back off and let her catch her breath like she asked?

Because I was so desperate to get back to the amazing, uncomplicated way things had been before, and this raging fear that we'd never find that again kept messing with my mind. How many times had I told Zach to be patient with Brittany? Yet I was being anything but patient with Maggie. Fear had been pushing me, so I pushed her.

What would it hurt to give her some time?

What other option did I have?

"Miss Jennison." Tyler reached around me to open the door to the school. "You can thank me later." He handed me a sheet of notebook paper.

Dollar amounts lined up across the page. "Did I miss—oh, no." I slapped the paper to my forehead.

"The NHS meeting yesterday. Yep, you missed it. But I covered for you." A confident smile matched the tone in his voice. "I whipped out a piece of paper and jotted down the donation amounts so quick, Mr. Martin assumed we'd arranged it ahead of time." He tapped his notebook. "And I had last week's numbers, so in like ninety-four seconds, I announced the awesome new total of eight hundred twelve dollars and thirty-six cents."

I'd blown it big time. "I'll have to apologize to Mr. Martin."

Tyler shook his head. "I wouldn't. Really, he totally thought I was covering for you." A dimple pressed into his cheek. "A batch of those cookies you're famous for will just about cover it."

"Hmm?"

Tyler's arm bounced against mine. "You can thank me with some of those cookies Preston's always raving about. Or is he the only one you bake them for? Hey, bring enough cookies to the next meeting for everyone, to celebrate going over eight hundred dollars. Just as long as I get my own personal stash." His eyebrows jerked high.

Would I ever bake cookies for Preston again? A painful longing squeezed my shredded heart.

Now his eyebrows scrunched together. "Or not."

Every second of last night's phone call played through my mind. Tears sprang to my eyes.

"Hey, hey. Forget the cookies. Are you okay?" His arm pressed into mine.

I blinked a bunch, and averting my gaze to the floor, murmured, "Yeah."

Tyler's warm hand on my elbow guided me away from the mass of students to a bench by the office. His gaze swept across my face.

Mine flitted everywhere, avoiding his sweet but too-concerned expression. "I can't believe I completely spaced the meeting. Thank you so much for covering for me." I gripped the meeting notes, squinting to see the numbers that blurred and slid around the page.

"No problem. What's wrong?" His hand continued to hover near my elbow.

I straightened the books in my lap, sniffling as quietly as possible. *Everything.*

"Maggie?"

I jerked to my feet. "I'm fine. And thanks again. I gotta go."

Preston

If only I hadn't been mad when I spewed my feelings to Maggie. Instead of calmly explaining what I wanted for us, I'd lashed out. And probably made her cry, *again.*

"I want you. I want us. When you figure out what you want, give me a call." What an idiot.

Now, after three days, every hour that passed without hearing from her drove the knife deeper in my gut. I was convinced that calling or texting her, even to apologize, would seem like more pushing. But doing nothing was torture.

I begged God for the chance to tell her she could have all the time she needed.

I'd give it one more day. If I didn't hear from her in the next twenty-four hours, I'd call her or maybe even show up at her door. I'd risk pushing her further away on the off chance that she wanted to hear from me as much as I was dying to hear from her.

Maggie

Yeah?" Preston's voice, even groggy and scratchy from sleep, was like a shot of painkiller to my wounded heart.

"I know what I want."

"Maggie, is that you?"

"Sorry I woke you, but I need to tell you I know what I want." Before I lost my nerve.

"It's okay." His muffled yawn rumbled through the phone. "I've been hoping for a chance to apologize for pushing you. And for losing my temper."

"You've been under a lot of pressure. We both have. That's why I need to tell you—" Panic tried to crawl up my throat, but I swallowed it back. "I still love you, but—"

Preston inhaled, sending a whiz through the phone.

"No buts, really. I *do* love you. And I loved everything about us. But things are different now. Not bad, not wrong, just different. We need time to work through what that means—for you, for me, for *us*. And I promise, this is not about Alyssa. Really, it's not. I mean, there's no way to know if or what she might do. And you're right. It's crazy to make any decisions based on her. This is about you and me and God's direction for us. And that will take some time to figure out." I gulped in a breath. And waited.

"I'm okay with that."

"Really, I'm not mad— Wait. You're okay with us taking some time?"

"I am."

I slumped against my headboard. "Oh, good. This just feels right to me." The cold needles of nervousness prickling my body began to warm. He wanted the same thing. Time.

"I get that you need time, and I can wait. I want us to be together, but as long as there's hope it'll work out, I'll wait. However long it takes."

"Thank you, thank you." Warmth continued to trickle through me. "That means so much to me."

"You deserve as much time as you need." Preston muffled a yawn.

"Sorry again about waking you. I should let you get back to sleep."

"It was worth it."

A comfortable silence surrounded us like a hundred other late night calls when neither of us wanted to say good-bye.

"Maggie?"

"Mmm hmm?"

"I love you, too."

About the Author

Beth immerses herself in the YA world via substitute teaching, connecting with the teenage staff at the fast food joint where she claims the back booth as her office, and reading YA fiction.

She's a cheerleader for saving sex for marriage. Her "Waiting Matters … Because YOU Matter" blog helps people of all ages navigate the choppy waters of saving sex for marriage and "renewed waiting."

Beth is also a genetic genealogy enthusiast who used DNA to find her birth parents. Her journey to find and connect with her biological family is chronicled in "A Doorstep Baby's Search for Answers". Her "Slices of Real Life" posts find GOD in the day-to-day moments of real life.

All of Beth's writing endeavors can be found on her website. Connect with her on Facebook, Goodreads, Pinterest, Instagram, and Twitter. Check out her books available on Amazon in both print and ebooks.